IMMORTAL SORCERESS

BOOK 2

FEAR OF THE SORCERESS

KRISTA WALSH

RAVEN'S QUILL PRESS

OTTAWA, ON

For those of us who strive to put

love before fear

1

Katerina

"Aim for the eyes!" I shouted, leaping out of the way as fire burst from the wyvern's maw.

"I am!" Rhys yelled back. "They're too damned small!"

Size, of course, had nothing to do with it, but I didn't begrudge Rhys the excuse. The eyelids were as scaled as the rest of the creature, and every time it blinked, the potions splashing from the shattered glass vials he threw were rendered useless. Unfortunately, the eyes were the only accessible weak point on the beast. The other option would be to get it to roll onto its back, and I didn't think Rhys was quite at that level yet.

The wyvern swung out its tail and slammed it against Rhys's middle. The potion he'd been about to throw hit the ground with a flash of green flame as he flew over the muddy snow. He landed on the edge of the water, his red hair bright against the white, but I had no time to panic before he jumped up and fled the wyvern's snapping teeth.

I summoned fire into my palms but held it in check. This fight wasn't mine, but neither would the wyvern catch me unprepared. The only one not walking out of these woods today was the creature that had eaten more than one hiker and tried to devour my friend.

Another fireball shot out, and the tree next to me burst into flames. I dove into the melting snowbank to escape the worst of the heat and stayed in a crouch as I rushed to Rhys's side.

"You've got to time it better. The moment you notice the eyes starting to open, you throw."

Rhys scowled. "I'm sorry, it seems I haven't yet developed my magnified vision or ability to slow freaking time."

"Now!"

He threw another vial, and the glass shattered against the side of the wyvern's face. The liquid splashed against its dark pupil, and its scream rattled my eardrums as the spell took hold. Blood dripped from eyes that were no longer golden but grey as stone. The greyness spread over its scales, locking each of them in place, down its legs, over its back, and along its tail, until the raging monster was nothing more than a stone statue decorating the walking path along Mindemoya Lake. Something for tourists to gawk at and wonder about for centuries to come.

I wondered where the creature had come from. Wyverns weren't common fare on Manitoulin Island, though it wasn't unheard of for them to make their way across the Atlantic.

Once I sensed the magic from the potion sink into the stone and become inert—removing the risk of any interested hiker making contact with the statue and becoming part of the installation—I rested my hand on Rhys's shoulder.

"That was good work."

Rhys's throat bobbed with a hard swallow. "That—I didn't think the potion would do that. It's…"

"Incredible?" I suggested, staring at the monster in admiration.

"I was going to say sad."

Sure enough, his green eyes were downturned in grief as he stepped towards the wyvern's remains.

"Sad?"

He shot me a look over his shoulder. "You don't think so? A moment ago, this was a living, breathing creature. Just trying to survive, the way we all are. And now it's… this. Do you think it suffered?"

My heart both warmed and ached at the empathy pouring off this eighteen-year-old man. Rhys had seen more than his share of suffering, not only with his physical eyes but also thanks to the psychic visions that had started when he was fourteen. The events of recent months had pushed him out of the safety of the mundane world into the chaos of the magical, but he clung to his humanity like a shield. I both admired him for it and worried what it would mean for his mental health if he continued on the path he'd started down. As I'd learned often in my almost nine hundred years, my world didn't always leave room for compassion.

"What of the people the wyvern killed?" I pointed out gently. "What of the destruction it caused in the days since it arrived? Unfortunately, as with much of the magical world, it came down to us versus it."

He nodded slowly. "I get that, I just…" He frowned at the satchel at his side. "I'm going to need to label these potions and take the time to learn what each of them does. I think with something like this wyvern, I would have preferred something quicker. Less… horrifying."

I threw my arm around his shoulders and pulled him close. "That's fair. I'll make sure you get a thorough rundown on everything we buy. You only need to carry the ones you're comfortable using, okay? I need you to stay safe—your mother will have my head if you're not—but that doesn't mean it can't be safe on your terms."

He nodded and gave me a faint smile. "Do you ever get used to it?"

Automatic assurances balanced on the edge of my tongue. Centuries of dealing with rogue beasts like this had made them commonplace, to the point that I'd fallen into a rut with the repetitive nature of clearing them away.

But that wasn't what Rhys was looking for. Not the worn indifference of a powerful immortal, but the empathy of a human being whose conscience was undented by so much death and destruction.

"I think it's okay if you don't," I said. "Not the taking life part, anyway. Experience helps with the fights, satisfaction comes with the challenge, but I don't think it's the worst thing to hang on to your respect and remorse for the deaths of others."

When his expression didn't change, his glumness a weight on his shoulders, I nudged him with my hip. "You saved a lot of people today, Rhys. They'll never know it, but you made a difference."

That earned me a faint smile. Although it seemed to take an effort, Rhys shook off his blues, and his smile broadened into a grin. "That fight, though, that was pretty awesome. I really thought it was going to get me once or twice."

I laughed and shoved him away. "Once or twice? That thing had you pinned at least a dozen times. Adrian would have been disappointed you didn't use his trick to trigger a vision to help you."

He rolled his eyes. "Yeah, because zoning out in the middle of a fight would have been really helpful."

"You're lucky I was here, or you'd have been dinner."

"What? No way."

"Totally way. But don't worry," I winked at him, "I won't tell your mother."

Rhys laughed. "No way in hell are we telling mum *any* of this."

2

Katerina

"You did what?" Maera asked once Rhys finished telling her what he'd done.

"A real live wyvern! And they're not like dragons like I always thought. They don't have arms, for one thing. But they're big and scaly, and this one was white, so it blended in with the snow, which is why we had so much trouble tracking it. Its tail was longer than I am—and huge. I had to jump over it once, and it nearly caught me from underneath, but I thought of that time we were up at Uncle Finn's place, and he was playing lake monster and—"

"Rhys," I cut in, suspecting my housekeeper didn't need to know all the ins and outs of how her son might have died today.

Not that I would have stood by and let the wyvern kill him,

which I hoped Maera remembered as she processed her son's wild tale.

"Oh, right. Yeah. Sorry." A deep red flush spread over his cheeks, and I might have pitied his embarrassment if I weren't tempted to throttle him.

His mother wasn't thrilled with the steps her son had taken to move more deeply into the magical world. She'd stated her desire not to be left out of the loop, wanting to make sure I didn't lapse back into the apathy that had dominated my life for decades, but that didn't mean she relished the idea of Rhys putting himself in danger.

"Don't worry, mum, Kat kept a close eye on me the whole time."

"Mmhmm."

Her mouth had become the thinnest of white lines, but she said nothing as she turned back to the kitchen counter and resumed folding dumplings for tonight's dinner.

Cooking was Maera's way of coping with stress, and I wasn't so self-involved that I'd missed the overstocked pantry, fridge, and chest freezer of late.

I slid into a seat at the kitchen table and tried to put my companion of fifty-five years at ease. "We just received a new set of potion vials, and Rhys wanted to try them out. With that wyvern terrorizing the hiking trails, I figured we might as well tackle two problems at once. I had everything in hand, but Rhys did all the work. Your son is a hero."

He beamed at me, but Meara didn't turn around, her tense shoulders rolling with every new dumpling. "I wish you could be satisfied with working on your second sight."

"Mum…"

"I know, I know, we talked about this. I agreed. You're doing what you have to do." Her shoulders slumped, and she turned away from her dinner prep. "I'm proud of you, Rhys. My boy is literally slaying dragons. I guess all those years playing video games are paying off."

She attempted a smile. Rhys took pity on her and threw his arms around her neck. His six-two frame towered over her five-three, but she looked snug enough with her ear pressed against her child's heartbeat.

A pang of grief that I would never experience such a moment again made grabby hands at my chest, but I mentally swatted it away.

"And for the record, I have been working on my second sight," Rhys said as he released his mother and made a stealthy attempt to snatch some shredded pork from the metal bowl on the counter.

Maera smacked his hand. "And? How is that going?"

He shrugged, dragged his feet back to the table, and dropped into the seat beside mine. "Well enough, I guess. I've triggered a few but haven't Seen much."

"Maybe that means there isn't much to See?" Maera suggested. "That would be a nice change."

"I guess," Rhys said. "I just wish I had something useful to offer. Like tracking down your witch, Kat."

For the past four years, he'd been struggling to find his place in the world—too magical to fit in with his non-magical peers, not magical enough to fit in with super-magical me. All this training was his attempt to find purpose. I didn't blame him for feeling discouraged that it was slow-going.

I kicked him gently under the table. "None of that. There's no failure here." I scowled. "Just increasing frustration at this woman's knack for staying off everyone's radar."

The only information we'd dug up over the past month of poking around was that the stooped figure who'd fled during my fight with the blood witch Mikhail No-Last-Name had likely been his patron, a witch who went by the name of Abigail No-Last-Name, probably no relation.

I would have forgotten all about her if it weren't for the magic she'd used to ward Mikhail and the intensity of the spell circle she'd thrown at me. Not to mention Mikhail's hint right before I'd accidentally killed him that this mystery woman had given him the immortality ritual he'd tried to cast.

The ritual that wasn't supposed to exist, no trace of it having been found after all my and Emrick's years of hunting.

Anyone who had voluntarily worked with Mikhail was in

my bad books. A powerful witch working with Mikhail was doubly so.

A powerful witch with access to the spell that had slaughtered my entire community and inadvertently left me immortal?

There was no way in the infernal realms I would let her stir up more trouble. At the same time, the thought of finding her terrified me almost as much as the thought of not finding her in time. How had she learned that spell? What had been her goal in giving it to Mikhail? And now that he'd failed to cast it, what would her next move be?

Unfortunately, until I had something more to go on than "she exists," I was stuck cooling my heels, refreshing my emails, coaching Rhys, and attempting to get myself back into shape.

After decades of not caring whether or not I woke up in the morning, I had a goal. One that extended beyond a stale promise I'd made to the dead almost nine hundred years ago. In finding Abigail and ensuring—hopefully for the final time— that the immortality spell never rose again, I could put my past to rest.

I thought I had. Centuries ago. But over the past few months, I'd begun to appreciate how well I'd lied to myself. Mikhail's venture had been my wake-up call to the fact that I hadn't so much put my history behind me as allowed it to become a cracked, tarnished shell on my back—a safe space that prevented me from doing anything more with my life.

That burden was why I still heard my parents' voices in my head whenever I made a big decision. Why my breast still ached whenever I heard a baby cry. Why I'd latched on to Emrick so fiercely that his absence was like a missing organ.

Sure. That was why. I didn't miss the spirit-herder because one of the shedding fragments of his soul had embedded itself in my heart, keeping us intertwined in a way that left me bleeding without him.

Nope.

Unable to sit still any longer, I left Rhys and Maera to chat and headed to my room.

At this time of day, the sunlight reflecting off Lake Huron seeped through my south-facing windows and bounced against my muted sage-green walls. The lap of water where it brushed against our private beach soothed me with its gentle symphony, and I fell into its rhythm as I stripped off my mud-caked leather pants and black T-shirt—my usual hunting uniform.

Next, I pulled off my elbow-length leather gloves and set them in the wooden box on a shelf in my closet. Home was the only place I didn't wear them, giving my hands and arms a chance to air out. The magic infused in the leather and in the runes etched across them helped me channel my magic, but by the same measure they were a leash. A reminder of the promise I'd made to my fallen people to stand between the magical and mundane, a bastion of defence against any magical.

I didn't want to be that woman at home.

Here, I was just Kat—lover of ramen, hot baths, and lilac-scented candles.

Goosebumps pebbled my skin, but I drew my magic closer to the surface to chase away the chill. Spring was taking its sweet time getting here, and I looked forward to wearing clothes that served the same purpose in the morning as they did in the afternoon.

Settling for a summer storm aesthetic, I grabbed a pair of dove-grey leggings, a light-blue boyfriend sweater, and a pair of fuzzy green socks, wrapping myself in cozy.

It was my favourite part about the current era. I had lived through corsets and petticoats, stiff shoulders and low waistbands, but the freedom I had these days to wear what were essentially pyjamas out in public made the cheap materials and cheaper quality worthwhile. If only they came with more pockets.

I drew in a deep breath and let it out in a whoosh, allowing the tensions of the day to go with it. Feeling far more myself, I returned to the common area—only to pull up short when I found Maera standing alone, stiff behind the couch that separated the kitchen from the living room. Her gaze was fixed on the television, where a flash of flame had just burst out of a manhole on a city street.

"Since when are you an action movie fan? Nice to see you

broadening your horizons."

"It's not a movie." Her words were as stiff as her posture.

I took a closer look at the screen and was confused by the words skimming along the bottom: *Suspected terrorist activity in Hamilton, Ontario, or infrastructure gone wild?*

I rounded the side of the couch and dropped onto the cushion to get a better idea of what the hell I was looking at.

A man stood in the middle of the street. Well, not stood so much as cowered, his arms over his head to fend off the embers raining over him. Another manhole cover flew upwards, followed by another flash of fire. Then another. The street had been closed off, with empty cars pulled to the sides and people standing at a distance watching in amazement.

What had the guy done? Poured gasoline into the sewers and lit a match?

"Rhys?" I called, and he darted up the stairs in a clean white T-shirt and unstained jeans. "What read do you get on this?"

He came farther into the room to look at the TV. "A guy with a serious death wish?"

"Not the kind of read I meant."

His mouth twisted with a wry smile, and I recognized his fear to try.

"No harm if nothing comes of it," I said.

Rhys dropped onto the couch beside me, and Maera rested her hand on his shoulder. He closed his eyes and drew in a deep breath, then another. The footage on the TV played on, but he remained silent, his body going still, his chest rising and falling with increasingly larger breaths.

While he attempted to tap into his second sight, I absorbed the news broadcast.

The crowd had become more agitated. They crushed against the barriers the police had put up, their arms reaching for the cowering man, fingers pointing. As though they weren't so much afraid of him as wanting to tear him apart.

A tendril of unease coiled in the pit of my stomach.

I took a closer look at the man, wondering what the bystanders saw that made them so afraid.

"Fire in his hands."

Rhys's empty, haunting voice made me jump, and I turned to find him staring at the television, his bright green eyes faded to a milky white.

"Uncontrolled. Wild. Destroying everything in his path. His face, but not him. A puppet-master behind his eyes. Directing. Playing."

Rhys slumped back, his vision ending and his brain falling into its usual post-Sight nap. I jerked my attention to the screen, trying to get a better look at the man's hands.

Sure enough, Rhys's vision was right. A hint of fire in the man's palm. Running over his skin. Coming from inside him.

"It's not possible," I said. "It can't be."

I pushed myself up from the couch and walked towards the screen, as though proximity would help me see beyond the limitations of the video footage.

"What is it?" Maera asked.

"This guy." I leaned in, scanning him over from his bare feet to his smouldering T-shirt. "He's a sorcerer. A living sorcerer."

I couldn't process it, but I also couldn't deny it.

I'd believed myself to be the last person who could create fire from within, but by chance or by fate, here I was, watching a magical being that had gone extinct almost five hundred years ago burn up on the national news.

3

Katerina

RHYS GROANED AND pressed his hand to his head. "Will that ever stop being uncomfortable, do you think?"

Maera patted his shoulder. "I'll get you a cookie."

While she went to fetch his snack, I dropped onto the couch beside him and waited until he shook himself the rest of the way awake. My thoughts were too scattered to pin down. I wanted to talk to Adrian and get his take on the situation and cursed that the sun was still up. Adrian was my mentor and my sounding board on all things magical, personal, and psychological, but even after being alive—or unalive, vampire that he was—for two thousand years, he was still governed by celestial cycles. And he got grumpy if he was woken up early.

Maera returned with a chocolate cookie from the batch

she'd baked earlier today, and Rhys bit into it with a moan.

Only after the cookie was gone did I shift on the couch to face him. "Anything else to tell us?"

"Not much," he said. "A lot of fire. Everything he touched burned. What looked like a whole city street burning."

I rubbed my brow. It wasn't a far-fetched visual. Given my experience with untrained sorcerers, I didn't need a psychic to tell me the danger Hamilton faced if this guy wasn't contained.

"Anything beyond the sorcerer?" I asked. "Some hunched-over figure lurking behind him?"

"You think Abigail is involved?" Maera asked as she leaned her crossed arms on the back of the couch.

I picked at a hangnail. "I don't know. I have no reason to think so except for the timing. Mikhail got so close to finishing that ritual, and some of the magic he performed trying to take me down… it was old magic. Powerful. The kind I haven't seen since the last of my people died out. He had to have learned it somewhere. Abigail fought right beside him, and I swear her ward was manipulated air, just like how the sorcerers used to do it. Now there's this guy. It's a wild coincidence otherwise."

"I don't get it," Rhys said. "What do you mean your people died out?"

"Clearly I've failed in your history lessons." I turned off the TV and stood up, needing to pace to offset the whirring in my head. "Sorcerers were never an overpopulated group. We stuck to our small communities, spread mostly across the Isles, Europe. As the world got bigger, we were forced to blend in with the mundane. Bloodlines thinned, the magic weakened. The communities that didn't merge disappeared. As the years passed, they lost their ability to draw power directly from the source—from the environment. Instead, they learned how to channel it through external sources. Potions, spells, blood. People born with even a hint of latent magic today tend to veer towards witchcraft. A fragment of what we were." I frowned at the TV. "Until this one."

My phone buzzed against my hip, and I pulled it from where I'd tucked it into my waistband to see Adrian's handsome face staring at me.

"I didn't expect you to be up for another hour," I greeted him as I put the call on speaker.

"James thought it best to wake me."

"Ah." I wrinkled my nose at the mention of his human thrall. No matter that James Barrett and I had come to some sort of understanding during the whole Mikhail debacle, the habit of showing my distaste remained strong. "I take it you've seen the news, then?"

"Is he what he appears to be?" Adrian's tone was split between confusion and curiosity, and I was impressed that something in this world had left my friend stumped. It happened so rarely these days.

"Based on the vision Rhys just triggered, yes, he is."

"Well done, Mr. Byrne."

"Thank you," Rhys said, almost glowing under that minimal praise. Adrian had that effect on people.

"Rhys also said this guy has someone behind him pulling his strings. My bet is on Abigail. I don't suppose we know anything new there?"

"Nothing, I'm afraid. James's connections within the witch hunters don't have a file on her. My contacts are equally in the dark, though a few of the covens in Toronto and surrounding areas have heard of her. She's reputed to be powerful, knowledgeable in the old magics, and an outright bitch. I'm quoting that last one."

"If she was dealing with Mikhail, I wouldn't expect her to be a ray of sunshine." The wrinkle in my nose grew deeper. "Considering her power, I'm amazed the hunters don't have anything on her. Do you think we could ask them to dig deeper?"

I didn't want to lean on them. The witch hunters had proved time and again that despite their mission statement their goal was not the safeguarding of magic but the oppression of it. Even the witches in their ranks tended to frown on everyone else. But they did have resources I lacked.

The hunters were split into three groups. There were the witch hunters, the vampire hunters, and the Hunter's Guild— the group that went after creatures such as the wyvern Rhys and

I had pursued this morning. They were worldwide organizations with varying levels of influence in every country. I recognized that such bodies were necessary—the global population growth had made it increasingly difficult for magicals to remain hidden and made threats by magicals that much greater—but I didn't trust the hunters to be the solution. Not as they were.

Still, they were what we had.

"James will see to it," Adrian said. "What about the sorcerer?"

I clenched my teeth and rolled my gaze skywards. Reluctantly, I said, "I need to know where to find him, but I don't want the hunters getting close. He looked terrified, and if he's afraid, his magic will be unpredictable. I'm going to guess his power is a recent revelation. Anyone who gets too close is likely to be killed."

"So what do you intend to do?"

I wanted to stick my tongue out at the line of smugness running under his words.

"Yes, yes, I'm going to Hamilton. Dammit, Adrian. I don't want to go to Hamilton."

He chuckled. "I'll have James meet you there."

Maera covered her mouth with her hand and turned away under the guise of returning to her kitchen. I scowled at her quivering shoulders as she laughed at my expense.

Rhys didn't bother to hide his grin, and I shoved him backwards into the couch.

"Are you sure that's a good idea? Barrett hates magic." In fact, hate was a kind word for Barrett's opinions about magic users. For someone who'd sworn his life to a vampire, the man was as mundane as they came. "Forcing him to join this hunt would be cruel. He might never forgive you, and you know I'd hate for there to be a rift between you."

"Much as I appreciate your lies, Katerina, James can help you with crowd control if nothing else. He can also be your point of contact with the hunters. Unless you want to deal with them yourself."

"Ugh. Fine. It'll take me a few hours to get down there. The Ancaster house?"

Adrian owned houses across the world, most of them centred in his regular urban haunts. While he preferred the isolation and privacy that Muskoka offered him—not to mention the incredible views and enormous property—he always made sure to have an escape plan in case his situation changed and he needed a quick identity shift. Every house was equipped for a hunt, which made them more convenient than lugging everything with me.

"I'll see that it's ready for you. And Katerina? Do be careful. I can't help but think there's more going on here than we know."

I hung up, groaned, and sagged into the cushions.

"So," Rhys said, still grinning at me from across the couch. "Hamilton, huh?"

4

Katerina

IT TOOK US seven hours to drive to Ancaster.

For the first few hours, I felt confident. The music was on, my hair was down, the roads were clear.

Then Adrian had to ruin it with a phone call. "We may have a problem, tesoro. James reached out to the witch hunters in Hamilton, and they've lost eyes on the sorcerer. Someone seems to have whisked him away without anyone noticing. Or remembering."

My thoughts went to Abigail. Was that her popping up again? I hated not knowing who she was.

Every second stuck in traffic amped up my impatience, and by the time we reached the house, I was practically vibrating.

It had been a while since I'd been to Hamilton. On my last

visit, the steel mills were at their peak. Back then, the grime of soot and smoke had become a near-permanent fixture, filling the cracks in both buildings and people.

Since then, however, it had shifted away from its post-manufacturing depression by remodelling itself as an arts town, and I had to say, the view was brighter. The new life and colour offset its previous dreariness, and the youthful faces loping down the sidewalks as they hit up the nightlife offered hope for its future.

Ancaster was on the west side of Hamilton—a more upscale community populated with older detached homes on large, beautiful properties. Exactly what one might look for if one were, say, a blood-drinking immortal who never saw daylight. Or even a ramen-eating immortal who preferred not to see people.

The lights were on when we reached the house, giving me the heads up that Barrett was inside, so I took my time pulling up the long driveway. Rhys got out of the car to open the garage, and sure enough there was Barrett's red SUV. Parked right in the middle of it, leaving no space for me.

I ground my teeth. It was exactly the kind of petty move I would have made if I'd arrived first.

Rhys looked back at me, his eyes wide, no doubt ready for me to firebomb the SUV. Instead, I calmly, maturely, pulled to the side of the driveway and put my car in park.

"You're taking this well," Rhys said around a poorly hidden smile.

"Of course I am. I'm an adult."

I grabbed my backpack from the trunk, and while Rhys hauled his duffel bag over his shoulder, I sauntered into the garage and set my hand on Barrett's car. Reversing the flow of my magic, I absorbed the heat in the air. Frost spread from my fingers and crawled over the red paint. It clouded the windows and thickened over the windshield until the entire left side of the vehicle was caked in ice. Temperatures weren't due to rise overnight, so Barrett would have a lovely surprise waiting for him in the morning.

With a bounce in my step, I closed the garage and followed Rhys up the cobblestone path to the front door.

Before I had a chance to hit the doorbell once or thrice to drive my unfriend inside batty, Rhys opened the unlocked door and stepped into the large, well-lit foyer. Dark hardwood floors stretched down the hallway towards the kitchen, into the living room to my right and a home office to my left.

There was no sign of Barrett, but voices reached me from up ahead, so I guessed he was in the kitchen. I kicked my boots into the hall closet, dropped my bag on the floor, and headed down the hall.

A crystal chandelier lit our way, leading us to where Barrett sat on a barstool at the white island, bent over a laptop as he watched a video. From what I could make out from the sideways angle, the same video played on the tablet to his left and on his phone to his right.

Barrett had cut his dark hair even shorter since I'd seen him a few weeks ago, but whatever weight he'd lost in his curls, he seemed to have gained in muscle. His torso filled out his black T-shirt, and his bicep flexed every time he moved the mouse. How he didn't burst the seams of his clothes every morning was nothing short of miraculous.

If he were anyone other than who he was, I might have found him attractive, but he held the allure of a battle axe. Impressive, lethal, useful, but not anything you wanted to take to bed except as a defensive weapon. Adrian obviously saw something else in him, but it eluded me.

Barrett didn't acknowledge us as we came in, too wrapped up in what he was doing or making a point.

I wasn't about to let either reason hold me back as I settled my elbows on the counter beside him and leaned over his screen to block his view. "You know there are easier ways to get the stereo effect, right?"

Barrett grunted in response—always so eloquent—and hit a button on the laptop to play his video from the beginning. Rhys came up on his other side to take in the different screens, his expression scrunched into a deep frown.

Undaunted by Barrett's lack of response and knowing how

to bide my time, I turned my attention to the videos.

And all desire to mess with the battle axe vanished.

On every screen was footage from the news. The manhole covers popping, the spurts of flame. The terrified man cowering under his arms as his magic flared in all directions, wild and furious.

"I got Adrian's message," I said as I straightened. "Any updates? Break it to me gently."

Barrett didn't take his eyes off the screen. "We have no idea where he is."

"That was not gently. That was more of a kick to the crotch."

"At least it was over quickly."

I looked more closely at the different screens. It wasn't the same footage playing three times over—each one came from a slightly different angle. I picked up the phone and watched the video play through again. This angle showed the man running up the street, looking over his shoulder at a manhole cover before it flew into the air. The man appeared to be East Asian, mid-twenties, dark hair. Handsome if not for the abject horror twisting his features. "Witness footage?"

Barrett nodded. "Tony sent it over an hour ago. The hunters in the police force confiscated everyone's phones to wipe the videos and gather what they could. These were the best three angles." He finally looked at me over his shoulder.

"I've been going through them to see if I could spot this witch you're looking for. Or anything else that might give us an idea of how to track the sorcerer down."

"Anything yet?"

"Nothing. No one else is on the street with him, no sign of any hunched hooded figures."

"Of course not," I huffed. "I never have that kind of luck."

He started the video on his laptop from the beginning. "Witnesses say the man emerged from this side street over here and made his way up. They think he was limping, but he's so covered in soot I can't see any injuries. Most people started recording right after the first fire started."

I watched the man run down the street, watched the heavy metal discs fly into the air, the fire surge, the man cower. Nothing new.

A large part of me wished all these angles would disprove my suspicions about what he was. That the source of the fire might be something mundane.

But no. On every screen, the evidence was clear. As he ran, his surging power caused the air around him to shimmer. He had no control, and it was pure chance he hadn't burned to cinders in his flight.

"What is he looking at?" Rhys asked.

"What do you mean?" I watched the repeating footage and saw only the same steps as the last dozen times.

"There." He pointed at the screen as it played through. "Just before he ducks under his arms, he looks back."

Barrett scrolled backwards. He let it play, then hit pause as soon as the man turned his head.

"You're right," I said. "He's staring too far to the right to be looking at the fire. Someone in the crowd? And immediately after—look at his face. He's terrified. I thought he was running from his magic, but what if it's something else? What if the fire bursts were defensive, not accidental?"

The thought made me feel better. A sorcerer using magic to protect himself was far less dangerous than someone who had no control over it. The former would be able to limit his power to fight the threat; the other was the threat.

On the next few replays, I paid attention to the crowd instead of the sorcerer, hoping to find something that stood out. Even the knowing look of a fellow magical so we could follow up with them.

Barrett was right—no hunched hooded figure.

For the most part, all I saw was fear. A deep, soul-crushing fear that didn't make sense in the context of the scene. It wasn't like the guy was attacking anyone. Yet everyone along the street looked ready to piss themselves.

"They're *all* terrified," I said.

A whisper of dread crept up from the soles of my feet, raising goosebumps as it went. My brain automatically went into denial mode, refusing to let me consider any possibilities about why that might be.

"The street is on fire," Barrett pointed out, dry as a tinderbox.

"That's not the-street-is-on-fire fear. That's Godzilla-is-crushing-skyscrapers fear. That's my-death-is-imminent fear."

What was I missing?

"Can you play it one more time?"

Barrett backtracked the video, and I leaned close to take everything in while Rhys and Barrett set to work on the phone and tablet to check if any other footage showed the side street. It took a few play-throughs for Rhys to squint at something.

Barrett loaded the video on the larger laptop screen, and I sank onto the stool beside his to watch the section of the crowd where the man seemed to be looking. Dozens of people had gathered on the sidewalk, no doubt having rushed outside at the first explosion. Because it was always a great idea to run *towards* a spontaneous street fire.

After three more replays, I realized our sorcerer wasn't looking at the crowd itself, but at something beyond them.

A figure only half-visible from where it stood between two buildings.

From what little I could see, it was a man dressed in a three-piece suit. His arms were unusually straight at his sides, his black hair carefully styled, his jaw clean-shaven. His eyes glowed red.

My mouth went dry, and I pointed to the figure. "Tell me what you see."

Rhys leaned closer. "Al Pacino from *The Devil's Advocate.*"

Barrett rolled his eyes and did his best to zoom in on the image, as though any kind of manipulation on our end would make the pixels clearer. "I hate to say it, but the kid has a point."

"Can you play the video one more time?" I hated the tremor in my voice. Despite what my subconscious brain had added up, my conscious brain was stubbornly in the sand.

Barrett did as I asked, and my attention never moved from the figure. I watched the man's cold calculation as he watched the growing crowd. I caught the faint upturn of his lips as they slid into a smile so cold it chilled me to my marrow. The smile coincided with the rise in the crowd's terror, which turned my whisper of dread into a full, blaring siren.

Then the human mask he wore slipped. Just for a moment. Just long enough for me to recognize the features hidden underneath.

"Kat?" Rhys asked. "Are you all right?"

I barely heard him as I rose from the stool and backed away from the screen.

The reek of burning flesh filled my nose. The memory of nerve endings screaming, of wool melting into my skin, my fingers lost to the flames.

"That man," I said, my voice sounding far, far away, "is a

demon."

My legs gave out, and the floor rose to meet me. Before I hit the ground, the temperature dropped and a pair of strong arms caught me. I looked up and found myself staring into a familiar silver gaze.

5

Emrick

IT TOOK EVERYTHING in me not to gather Kat to my chest and bring her into the afterlife. At least there she would be safe from the fear that haunted her.

Instead, I summoned my strength, helped her to her feet, and let her go.

My arms felt empty without her, so I shoved my gloved hands in my pockets to give them something to do.

Kat pushed her hair out of her face and turned her back on the room, taking a second to compose herself. She hid her efforts—poorly—by going to the fridge and pulling out a pitcher of orange juice.

"Anyone need a hit of Vit C?" she asked, her tone so falsely cheerful, I was surprised no one laughed.

Rhys slid onto the stool next to Barrett's. "I feel like I'm missing… a lot."

His gaze jumped to me, but I said nothing. It wasn't my story to tell.

Barrett, as usual, remained silent, but his furrowed stare followed Kat as she filled a glass and chugged the contents. I pressed my lips together to hold my tongue. In the state she was in, she risked revisiting that juice if she wasn't careful, but my warning wouldn't do anything but make her drink faster.

When the glass was empty, she washed it by hand and took her time drying every last drop.

The silence drew out, and I used the opportunity to watch her. The way her long black hair slid over her shoulders and down her back, drawing the eye to her slim waist and rounded hips. From where I stood, I made out the angle of her jaw, watched how it flexed and her chin wobbled as she worked through her thoughts. I imagined the flutter of her long eyelashes over her ocean-blue eyes as she fought back tears.

If she didn't start talking soon, I wouldn't be able to stop myself from going to her.

Adrian had warned me he felt change in the air. That Kat would need me soon. Was this what he meant? Had he known somehow that the next threat Kat faced would be one that shook the foundations of the life she'd built for herself?

She put the dry glass away and turned towards the room,

her hands braced behind her on the edge of the counter. Her gaze landed on my chest. "If you're here, I can only guess it's because my eyes weren't playing tricks on me. It's really him?"

I wished she'd look at me so she could see how much I hated bringing her this news. "I only just found out myself, or I would have warned you. You didn't deserve to be blindsided."

She jerked her head up, and her expression when she looked me in the eye was one of concern. "Did you come for the sorcerer?"

My fingers itched to brush away the strand of hair clinging to the corner of her mouth. "No. There were some magicals in the crowd. They got too close to the first fires before the streets were blocked off." Their souls hadn't been too pleased when I'd appeared to escort them to the afterlife. Lives interrupted were my least favourite charges, even after fifteen hundred years.

Barrett huffed and spun on his stool to put his back to the island. He crossed his arms and glared at me. "Anyone want to fill the rest of us in, or are we free to go?"

I looked to Kat, whose gaze had dropped back to the floor. Her face was pale, and she'd wrapped her arms around herself. I knew what memories she battled, but I wasn't about to invite Rhys and Barrett to intrude while she processed them.

Her nostrils pinched as she drew in a sharp breath, but when she raised her head, her eyes were steely. "His name is Shogaur, and he's a fear demon. He feeds on terror and despair, and he's not satisfied with your standard fears and phobias. No, he prefers to climb into the social psyche and stir it into hysteria so he can gorge on the horror. If he's here, whatever happened on that street is small beans compared to what's coming."

Barrett showed no reaction beyond a tightening of his mouth, but the blood drained from Rhys's face. "If you're scared of this guy, he must be really bad news."

"Since I was turned immortal, he's the only one who's come close to killing me for good."

I clenched my teeth and fought off my own memories of that day. I'd spent almost seventy-five years with Kat by the time Shogaur caught her, but that was the moment I'd realized my eternity would be empty without her. Not even she knew how far I'd gone or how much I'd sacrificed to ensure she remained among the living.

Behind my eyelids, the scene played out. A large stone church behind a raised wooden platform. The churchyard around the platform crowded with demon-influenced Crusaders holding innocent Cathars hostage to keep Katerina in place. My beautiful sorceress tied to the stake as the flames swept over her body.

At the last, I'd stolen her away, but not before she'd come so close to Death's door I'd felt the tug on the tether that bound us.

Her frown deepened. "But Shogaur doesn't show up out of the blue. I cast him back to hell on his last visit. Someone summoned him."

I turned away to hide my reaction to her statement. For eight hundred years, Kat had believed she was the one who'd banished him, and I'd never found it in me to tell her the truth—that she'd blacked out before she'd finished the incantation, and I'd stepped in to do the rest. It hadn't struck me as relevant at the time, and to a point, it still didn't. She would have succeeded without me if not for the smoke clogging her lungs.

"Could the sorcerer have done it?" Barrett asked.

I was as curious about this sorcerer as they were. As far as I was aware, they'd all died out. I certainly hadn't escorted any into the afterlife for over five centuries.

Kat tilted her head, considering. "It's possible, I guess. Anyone with a book and a smidge of magic could pull off something as stupid as a demon summoning. If he did, it certainly wasn't a controlled effort." A shiver ran through her, and she rubbed her arms. "We need to find him. Shogaur has to know what the man is, which means the demon will try to possess him."

I didn't think it was possible for her to turn any paler, but even her lips turned white as she looked to Rhys. "The puppet-master. I thought it was Abigail, but it's Shogaur. Shit. Shit, shit, shit."

She pushed away from the counter and paced the length of the kitchen. I didn't blame her for her rising concern. Demons and sorcerers were not a good combination. Not for the rest of the world, anyway.

"Why is this worse news?" Rhys asked, his eyes wide.

"Demons need a host," Kat explained. "They can function just fine without one in theory, but they can't manoeuvre around the world as easily. It's hard to get inside people's heads if everyone is running away from you. Behind a human face? There's no limit to their evil. But mundane hosts decay too quickly. Magical is better because the demon can use the host's power as well as their own. The stronger the magical, the longer the host lasts. If the demon possesses the sorcerer, he could unleash hell."

Rhys gulped. "Please tell me there's a silver lining in here somewhere?"

"Somehow I doubt it," Barrett grumbled.

I shifted my weight on my feet. "The soldier gets it."

Kat stopped at the island across from Barrett. "If we don't find the sorcerer before Shogaur does—if we don't find Shogaur before he gets under people's skin—we're looking at the deaths of millions."

Rhys paled, and even Barrett turned ashen. I wished she were exaggerating, but, unfortunately, history told us exactly what we faced. And how difficult it would be to stop it.

6

Katerina

EMRICK'S SILVER GAZE locked on mine, swirling with so many emotions my breath caught in my chest.

Fear for me, anger at Shogaur… and beneath it all, a driving need to protect me.

I felt everything, heard everything as though I'd climbed into his head.

Why did the bastard have to look so good? His short blond hair was stylishly messy, and a light stubble lined his jaw. A dark blue long-sleeved tee hugged his wide shoulders and muscular arms and made his silver eyes pop, and his jeans hugged everything they were supposed to. The only part of his attire that didn't look like he'd pulled it out of *Vogue* were the thick leather gloves that climbed halfway up his forearms. The style of the gloves was similar to mine—though his were centuries older and lacked the magical runes—and served a similar purpose. My fingers remained bare to allow me to channel my magic. His skin was covered to prevent him from whisking away souls not yet meant to be whisked.

My people would have called him *gàst-ladman*. Spirit-herder. A servant of Death that escorted magical souls to the afterlife. One touch of his skin, and you wouldn't have time to wave goodbye to the land of the living.

Longing for him to sweep me away overpowered me. I didn't want to deal with Shogaur any more than I'd wanted to deal with the ritual that had killed my family. My past was dogging my heels, and I wanted to be anywhere but here.

If I asked, he would take me away. I had no doubt about that. But where would I go? The afterlife with Emrick until someone else found a way to send a powerful fear demon back to hell?

Despite knowing it was a non-plan, the temptation remained.

All because Emrick had shown up and saved me from a cracked skull and any lingering denial I might have hidden behind.

My heart ached, my body trembled, but I forced myself to stay rooted where I was.

He shouldn't have come. Every word out of his mouth

risked being judged involvement in the mortal world. How many fragments of his soul had he given up since he arrived? What had he sacrificed? Another pigment of his blond hair? The memory of when we first kissed?

We never knew what his deal with Death would steal from him for interfering, and I never stopped fearing the next part of him to fade would be his feelings for me.

"So… what do we do next?" Rhys asked, looking between me and Emrick as though prepared for one of us to pop. I admired his restraint in not asking the questions that had to be burning through his teenage mind. I also appreciated his attempt to keep us on track.

"We find the sorcerer," I said. "He's flesh and blood, so he can't have just disappeared, and I don't believe he was quick enough to outrace a demon, which means Shogaur has him. The clock is ticking on this."

"I'll reach out to Tony, see if he's managed to scrounge up any more footage from the area," Barrett said.

He grabbed his phone and headed into the living room. Rhys swung around to face the laptop, looking for all the world like he wished he were anywhere else. "And I'll go through the footage we have again, I guess? Maybe someone caught what happened after the sewers stopped exploding."

"Great idea, Rhys," I said through numb lips. "Thanks. I need some air."

I pulled open the French doors and stepped onto the patio. The pool was still covered for the winter, the patio furniture stored away, but the cool breeze and privacy were exactly what I needed to try to get my head on straight.

Overhead, the moon caressed the patio stones with its near-full glow, and the stars sparkled, their brightness muted thanks to the closeness of the city centre.

"It's not the same, is it?" Emrick said as he stepped outside behind me.

I tightened my arms around my middle and refused to look at him. "What's not?"

"The night sky. Do you remember the way it used to be? How many nights we stayed up counting the stars?"

"At least you haven't lost that memory. Yet." I hated the bitterness in my voice, but it coated my tongue and the back of my throat, impossible to swallow.

"No," he said softly. "Not yet."

For a while we stood there, staring upwards, not talking, not touching. As distant from each other as if he really were dead.

"Kate—"

"Kat," I corrected him.

He shoved his hands in his pockets. "How are you going to stop Shogaur?"

"The same way I stopped him before. You taught me what needs to be done. I haven't forgotten."

Separate him from his host, spill his blood, recite the words to cast him back to the infernal realms. Easy as pie. As long as he didn't stir up a mob and burn me at the stake again.

I squeezed my eyes shut and blocked out the memory of fire closing in around me. The empty eyes of the manipulated Crusaders charging me with swords to speed up the slow process of my immolation.

Tens of thousands of people were dead thanks to Shogaur using fear against the Cathars to glut himself on their terror and hatred.

A tear slipped down my cheek, and I tried to brush it away before Emrick noticed.

Of course I failed.

He moved to stand in front of me, blocking my view of the moon, warming me with his body. His gloved fingers rose to caress my cheek, but he dropped his hand to his side before he made contact. "You know I have every faith you can do this, but you need to be sure you're ready before you take any action against him."

Anger prickled under my skin that he saw my weakness enough to know the warning was necessary. At least he'd waited to voice his concerns until the others were out of earshot.

"I know."

"He'll only have grown more powerful over the past few centuries."

"I know." My response came out more clipped this time. He could have saved his breath—I knew how much trouble we were in.

I raised my gaze to his, and my legs nearly gave out at the desperation staring back at me. He said he had faith, but his fear for me was apparent in every flex of his jaw and twitch of his hand.

"Even at the top of your game, you'd be hard-pressed to match him," he pushed.

"I *know*, Emrick. What more do you want me to say?" I stormed to the other end of the patio, trapped in a deluge of self-doubt. I didn't need him to tell me how unprepared I was for this.

"I want you to ask for help," he snapped.

I whipped around to face him. His moonlight eyes flashed with restrained frustration, and his shoulders were so stiff they'd crawled close to his ears. The tension between us sparked as though the electricity contained in my hands had been set loose, and images of him slamming me backwards into the wall and claiming my lips left me breathless.

"I can't," I said, though it pained me to say it. "I won't. Not from you."

"Katerina—"

"No!" I tore at my hair and struggled to keep my magic buried. It screamed to be released—anything to extinguish the all-consuming frenzy of my emotions. Seventy-five years ago, I'd ordered him to stay away for exactly this reason. Because he couldn't help himself when I stepped too close to the fire, and every time, he slipped further away from me. I loved him with every breath in my body, and the agony of watching him fade was too much to bear. "Emrick, please. Stop making this so much harder than it is. Go. Go away and let me deal with this."

He huffed and glared at me, but in another breath, his shoulders dropped and a swirl of mist surrounded him. "I'm not going anywhere. As soon as you need me, I'll be here."

My vision blurred as he stepped out of this life and into the next. I took a moment to catch my breath and cool my blood. Finally, I returned to the kitchen, where Rhys was trying to pretend he hadn't heard any of our conversation.

I pulled a stool up beside him and dropped onto it, ignoring the shake in my hands as I reached for the tablet. "All right, let's go from the beginning. There has to be something here that tells us what happened to the sorcerer."

7

Katerina

AFTER ANOTHER TWO hours of watching videos with nothing to show for it, I called it for the night and ordered everyone to bed. "Whether Tony finds something for us or not, at dawn, we hit the streets."

I didn't sleep well. Shogaur's face haunted my dreams. At every turn, I woke up gasping. My bare skin prickled with the memory of charred flesh, and my ears echoed with demonic laughter.

Beneath the horrors were gentler memories that were no less painful. Emrick's encouraging words as I lay in barely conscious agony, his light touch on my healing skin. His silver eyes full of torment that he couldn't do more to help.

I also couldn't shake the thoughts of the unknown sorcerer's terror. Whatever it took, I would find him. If the crime scene didn't give me what I needed, I would find another way.

On a whim, I sent a message to Poppy Lister. The Toronto witch hadn't replied to any of my texts after she'd sent the sleeping potion recipe that had helped with Rhys's rush of visions during the Mikhail hunt, but I prayed she'd break her radio silence. I didn't trust witches at the best of times, but Poppy knew her stuff—and owed me her life.

While I waited for her to reply, I finally fell asleep until just before dawn.

During non-crisis times, this would have been my time to sit on the patio with a coffee to enjoy the silence. Barrett, of course, deprived me of my small joy. I found him in the kitchen dressed and ready to go. A cup of coffee and a plate of bacon and eggs sat in front of him, with more food warming in the oven.

We didn't exchange pleasantries as I downed my breakfast, but Rhys got a nod from him and a smile from me when he shuffled in a few minutes later, bleary-eyed and scraggly-tailed.

"For the record, I hate this part," he mumbled as he poured himself a coffee.

I nudged him with my shoulder. "You could always head home to Manitoulin, to your nice, safe, cozy bed."

"Nice try."

He took a few gulps of scalding caffeine, then looked at

Barrett. "What are you still doing here? Don't we have to leave soon?"

Barrett frowned. "What do you mean?"

Rhys raised an eyebrow at me, and I pressed my lips together. I'd forgotten about the present I'd left on Barrett's SUV last night. It would take at least half an hour for him to scrape the ice off, and we didn't have the time.

Huffing at my failed vengeance, I put my dishes in the dishwasher and headed to the foyer to pull on my boots. "If anyone needs me, I'll be in the garage taking care of something."

Half an hour later, Barrett pulled up outside the cordoned-off area. A mix of detached and semi-detached homes lined both sides of the street, but there were no signs of life within the curtained windows. Everyone had been evacuated until the scene was cleared, and I wondered how long it would take for the city to come up with a story about what had happened.

"Great," Rhys grumbled from the back seat as he took in the police tape. "How are we supposed to take a look around?"

"I don't suppose you have any second-sight revelations to offer before we go in?" I asked.

"I tried on our way here and nothing, but maybe now that I'm closer? Do we have time for me to try?"

Impatience barked at me to say no, but in truth, we couldn't afford to rush. If Rhys did manage to See anything, it would save us time in the end.

"Go for it," I said.

While he worked to regulate his breathing, I scanned the area. Aside from a single cop car parked halfway down the blocked-off street, no one patrolled the scene. The investigators had likely taken a quick walk-through, found nothing, and called it a day. It made sense—there would be nothing to find. No accelerant in the sewers, no lighters, no matches. Nothing to explain why a series of raging fires had burst from underground and drawn such a crowd.

"I bet they blame it on a gas leak," I said.

Barrett shook his head. "Electrical fire."

I raised an eyebrow. "Put a twenty on it?"

"Done."

I glanced behind me. Rhys's eyes were closed, with no empty voice or ominous message to show for his efforts, so I pulled out my phone. Still nothing from Poppy.

Not sure whether I should be worried or annoyed that she was avoiding me, I slid my phone back into the pocket along my thigh and tapped my fingers on the windowsill.

Beside me, Barrett remained an immovable object. I might have wondered if he'd fused to the vehicle if it weren't for the way his eyes moved every few seconds to assess the street.

"I'm sorry, Kat," Rhys said dejectedly after another few minutes had passed. "I got nothing."

I threw a smile over my shoulder. "There's nothing to be sorry for. It just means we do this the old-fashioned way." I looked at Barrett. "Ready?"

He dropped his chin in a nod and pushed his door open. I followed him onto the sidewalk and wrinkled my nose at the stench.

"What's that smell?" Rhys asked, covering the lower half of his face with the crook of his elbow.

"Burning sewage, charred trees, and sulphur," I said as I scanned the sidewalk slabs. I didn't know what I was looking for yet, but I didn't want to miss anything by not being thorough.

"Sulphur?" Rhys asked. "From the fires?"

Barrett followed the gutter. "From the demon."

"Is it… is he close, then?"

At the note of panic in Rhys's question, I looked his way. His green eyes were wide as they searched the shadows between houses.

"Unlikely," I reassured him. "The smell lingers long after they're gone." I scowled. "The stronger the demon, the stronger the odor. Shogaur didn't smell nearly this bad the last time we met. He's been busy climbing the demon ranks."

Which meant my odds of taking him down might be as slim as Emrick feared. He was right—I would need help, and while Barrett was handy with a wide range of mundane weaponry, I needed magic on my side. Where the hell was Poppy?

I pulled out my phone and handed it to Rhys. "Can you call the number labelled 3rd Strike? If she doesn't answer, call back and keep calling. If she picks up, keep her on the line."

"On it."

I looked towards the cop car. "And keep your eye on that. If anyone gets out of the car, shout."

Rhys stood to the side as Barrett and I slipped under the police tape and followed the path in the direction the sorcerer had run. Trails of magic crept over my skin, faint but undeniably strong.

While Barrett wandered into the road, I continued down the sidewalk towards where Shogaur had stood. The hair danced on the back of my neck, and I found myself looking around to make sure no one was watching me. The street was clear aside from the police car, but that didn't mean anything. For all I knew, Shogaur had possessed the cop and was waiting to see what I'd do.

To be safe, I reached for my magic, keeping it at the ready as I left the sidewalk and headed towards Barrett.

"No sign of Shogaur," I said. "Any luck here?"

He kicked his chin towards a spot a few metres from where we stood. "There's blood."

I approached the dark stain on the ground and crouched

beside it. "Not a small amount, either." I stood up as Barrett joined me. "There's no evidence the sorcerer injured himself while running, so he must have been in a bad way already." I chewed on the side of my thumb as I thought it through. "It supports my idea that there's someone else involved. Someone who must have hurt him. Shogaur devours fear, not pain. If he wanted to possess him, he'd want the host in good shape."

"Unless they struggled?"

"If they struggled, the guy would have lost. But somehow Shogaur knew where to find him, which tells me someone did their homework. Everything points to a magical. They tracked down the sorcerer, hurt him—probably to keep him down until Shogaur could possess him—but he slipped his leash and ran. Shogaur chased him, and now they're both missing."

Barrett watched me with his usual blank face, and I found myself wishing Emrick were here. He would have bounced ideas around with me instead of leaving me to piece everything together by myself.

My shoulders slumped as I looked around, feeling more than a little overwhelmed. Halfway through my scan, I spotted another dark patch on the road up ahead. "Shogaur might not have left us any handy breadcrumbs, but maybe the blood will lead us where we need to go."

Barrett and I spread out, tagging spatter when we found it and working together to move up the street until the trail stopped. I pulled a handkerchief out of my pocket and used it to scoop up some of the crumbling, bloodstained asphalt. If this was the most the sorcerer had left for us, maybe we could use it.

"Um, guys?" Rhys said, keeping his voice low as he jogged towards us. "I'm shouting."

I looked over my shoulder and cursed as the cop got out of the car, his tall, bulky frame unfolding as though he'd been tied up in a box inside.

"Hey, you! What are you doing over there?" he called. "You're not supposed to be here." His voice lowered as he approached, barely above a growl, and I readied my magic just in case.

I slid the handkerchief to Barrett, reclaimed my phone from Rhys, and gestured for them to leave before turning to the officer. His movements were stiff, each step a little jerky. Sign of a demon lurking behind that human face, or simply discomfort from being crammed in a car all morning?

"I don't suppose you'd care to give me a statement about what happened here?" I asked.

He closed the distance between us, flexing his muscles in an attempt to look intimidating. "You a reporter?"

I laughed. "Heaven forbid. I run a local occult blog. Is it true the guy's hands were on *fire*?"

Confusion lit his dark eyes. I watched them closely but saw

no sign of red and no recognition. He also didn't stink of rot. Sweat and too much cologne, but no sulphur. Not the demon, then. I was almost disappointed—having him here would have made my life easier.

"What? No. Ma'am, no one's hands were on fire. It was a gas leak."

Ha—Barrett owed me a twenty.

I hid my amusement at the clichéd response behind a disapproving frown. "I don't know what you saw, but that man was certainly on fire. He might have been some kind of demon. Are you doing anything about that? Do we have demon hunters on the police force?"

He huffed and pointed at the line of yellow tape. "We have it under control, ma'am. Please leave."

I returned his huff and stomped towards the sidewalk. "I didn't think you'd give me the details, but I will get to the bottom of this. My readers will know the truth. Hamilton is under demonic threat, and we won't stand for it! I'll take it to the mayor if I have to!"

The officer mumbled something under his breath as he returned to his car, and I strode back to the SUV. Barrett had the engine idling, and I threw myself into the passenger seat.

"I didn't expect you to lead with the truth," Rhys said.

I chuckled dryly. "When in doubt, always go with the truth. Not many people will believe it." I rubbed my forehead and stared out the window.

"Where do we go from here?" Barrett asked, handing me the gross, red-stained handkerchief.

I shifted in my seat to alleviate the pressure of dread weighing down my gut. "Emrick says the sorcerer's not dead, and he would have popped up to tell us if that had changed. We work on the assumption that he's still alive, that the demon has him, and that we have increasingly less time to track them down before shit gets bad."

"How will we do it?" Rhys asked. "We can't exactly go street by street across Hamilton sniffing for sulphur."

I looked around the empty street, at the police tape and the melted asphalt. The sorcerer had caused a lot of damage. If something had set his power loose, it was unlikely he would know how to contain it by himself. And in the hands of a demon? There was no end to the hell they could rain down.

Once more, I pulled out my phone. "No luck with the witch?"

"Sorry," Rhys said. "I let it ring all the way to voicemail three times before the cop noticed you."

The side of my thumb found its way between my teeth. I could reach out to another witch to help us, but that would involve a lot of explanations and trust I didn't have. From a pragmatic perspective, I didn't want to make the mistake of confiding in Shogaur's summoner by accident. The only person

I knew wouldn't be involved was my missing necromancer.

Did we have time to track her down?

I didn't want to look too closely at the fact that my worry over her disappearance was pushing me into irrational decisions.

Cursing Poppy under my breath, I buckled up. "Barrett, can you call Tony? I want witch hunter eyes on every neighbourhood in this city. Any hint of the demon or the sorcerer, I want to know immediately. Once that's done, take us to Toronto. There's a shop owner I need to have a word with."

8

Katerina

To say Barrett was not thrilled with my plan was the understatement of the week. He grumbled most of the way to the 403-ON, but at no point did he suggest another approach.

"Who is this witch exactly?" Rhys asked. "Is this the necromancer you're blackmailing?"

"It's not blackmail," I argued. "If anything, it's extortion. But it's not even that. It's a deal."

"For her life," Barrett said.

"To save lots of other people's lives."

"Dead lives," Rhys pointed out. "She's a necromancer."

"If you think necromancers stop at messing with the dead, then we need to expand your magical curriculum. They don't use the corpses they raise to peel grapes. They use their undead armies—which are both difficult and disgusting to put down—to gain more power."

Poppy had never come close to that level of dark magic, which was why I'd allowed her to live when I'd shut down the rest of her coven.

"Is she really our best option?" Barrett asked.

"She knows the stakes if this demon possesses someone like me. She hates dabbling in demons, so she wouldn't have summoned him, but she has enough contacts that maybe she knows who did. And she'll know the tracking spell I want to try."

Barrett's eyes narrowed. "Blood magic?"

"Magic using blood," I corrected.

"Is there a difference?" Rhys asked.

"Blood is as much a medium as herbs or crystals. It's how you use it that determines how dark a witch you are." I shot a look at Barrett. "Which is something your witch hunter buddies like to forget."

The witch hunters' tendency to come down on anything magical and ask questions later was one of the big reasons I preferred leaving them out of my affairs. There was no room for black-or-white thinking in our world.

"To answer your question," I continued, "yes, I believe she's our best option. Though I reserve the right to change my mind depending on what the situation is when we find her."

"But what about—" Rhys began, and I held up my hand to stop him.

"Worry not, my friend. All your questions will be answered soon."

The drive to Toronto was blessedly short compared to my last trip, and it was midmorning when we arrived outside Poppy's storefront.

Or what had been Poppy's storefront.

Instead of the happy little sign in the window declaring the shop to be Moon in Venus, there was a bright pink placard on a table that read *Tea Room Boutique*. Gone were the tarot cards and cases of crystals in the window, replaced by cheerful little teacups, saucers, and English-style tea tins.

"All right, what the hell?" I said to no one as I gawked at the transformation.

"You were wrong," Rhys said. "I have more questions."

Barrett eyed the scene, his face blank. "A shift in business pursuits, perhaps?"

"Sure," I said, "and you can call me Aunt Paulene. Poppy would never be caught dead in a place so… so…"

"Full of ribbons?" Rhys suggested. "Pink? Flowery? Something my grandma would have liked?"

"Your grandmother would have hated every inch of this," I corrected. I would know, as Lily had been my housekeeper before Maera, and the woman had hated tea almost as much as she'd hated pink. "But yes, all those things are accurate. Except the pink. Poppy is fond of a good bright colour." I heaved a sigh and set my hand on the door handle. "I guess the only way to find out is to go in. Stay strong, everyone."

The interior was as gaudy and awful as the front window advertised, but it was also warm and smelled deliciously of strawberries and cream.

"Good morning!" a woman trilled from behind the counter. "Welcome to the Tea Room Boutique! I'm Cyn. If there's anything I can help you with, please let me know, but feel free to browse."

I nodded for Barrett and Rhys to do just that, and although both men gave me a look like they wouldn't know how to even pretend to browse in this beribboned and gilded house of horrors, I ignored them and navigated around delicate China displays on my way to the counter.

With every step, my worry for Poppy's fate rose.

Despite knowing they wouldn't be here, I couldn't help looking around for the occult paraphernalia that should have lined the walls. Proserpine Lister had built her store from scratch. It was her baby. She'd curated her inventory to service the covens of Toronto and had made quite a name for herself over the years. While I had reason to mistrust she'd kept her nose entirely clean, nothing had raised any red flags about what she got up to outside work hours.

Until now.

Setting aside my concerns for the moment, I peered over the counter at the rows of baked goods behind the woman who was as beribboned, pink, and gilded as the rest of the shop. Cyn must have been about fifty years old, with bleach-blonde hair pulled back in a relaxed bun, a soft, dimpled face over a soft, dimpled neck over a soft, dimpled chest. Her apron was white with pink roses, her blouse pink with white roses, and her skirt teal with white and pink roses. Her bright brown eyes sparkled with genuine joy, and I realized I was in the presence of a woman who loved her job.

Unusual. Unnerving.

"What smells so amazing?" I asked.

Cyn's eyes widened with awareness. She dipped behind the counter and came back up with a plate covered in strawberry scones. "I just baked these this morning. Shall I set a few aside for you?"

"Please."

I didn't want to spend any extra time in this place, but I had no qualms about walking out with food.

"I wonder if you could help me, Cyn. I'm looking for a friend of mine. Poppy. She used to live upstairs?"

"Oh, she still does, dear."

My eyebrows hiked up on my forehead. "She does?"

"Oh yes. The lease is only for the store. About two months ago, the sign went up looking to sublet. Miss Lister told me she'd decided to retire. Lovely to see a woman as young as she is having done so well for herself. Or perhaps it was that business didn't do so well? I don't know how anyone could have stepped foot in here the way it was with all those bones and books and dark magic stuff."

She shivered, and I forced a smile. "It was quite a shop, it's true. Have you seen Poppy lately?"

Her brow creased into a frown, and some of the shine went out of her eyes, as though it suddenly occurred to her that if I was friends with Poppy, then I was exactly the sort of person who might have wandered into an occult shop. "No, dear, I can't say I have. I thought I heard someone moving around upstairs a week or so ago, but nothing since then."

She set to work packing up my scones but made no further conversation. I paid and left, and Barrett and Rhys rushed out behind me.

"What next?" Barrett asked. "We find another witch?"

"Stop sounding so hopeful. We'll leave—after we break into Poppy's apartment and have a look around."

I gestured to the private door half-hidden behind some falling ivy next to the shop, and Barrett crossed his arms.

"You check the door first," he said.

I smirked and peered closely at the door handle. No taste

of magic, no caustic powder, no axes. "You're clear."

Barrett shot me a suspicious side-eye as he knelt to pick the lock, checking for himself before he touched anything. His trust in me warmed my heart.

Seconds later, the door was open, and he, Rhys, and I headed into the claustrophobia-inducing, ugly-wallpapered stairwell. On Barrett's and my last visit, we'd triggered a shrieking spirit illusion that served as Poppy's alarm system. Today, no hand of death appeared, and we reached her apartment without a single unpleasant surprise.

The quiet worried me more than anything else. She must have left in a rush.

"Why do you have her in your phone as '3rd Strike'?" Rhys asked as we reached the top.

"Because she only has one strike left."

His eyes were wide as he looked back at me. "Before what?"

"Trust me, kid," said Barrett. "You don't want to know."

Rhys's mouth fell open, and I nudged him up the final steps before we poured into Poppy's apartment.

The heavy silence pressed down on me. It was the kind of quiet that made it clear no one was here or had been for a while nor would they return anytime soon. Yet the place was far from spotless, as though Poppy had been in the middle of everything before she left. Dishes in the sink, magazine open on the arm of her mint-green couch, an empty mug and a single cookie sitting on the coffee table.

My stomach twisted, and I breathed through it. Poppy was a big girl and a powerful witch. She could take care of herself. We had a missing untrained sorcerer and a fear demon on the loose. The wisest move would be for us to leave and deal with the demon. I could track Poppy down after.

Yet even as I lay out my rational arguments, I found myself needing to know where she'd gone. And what trouble she'd found herself in.

"Let's split up," I said. "See if we can find out where she went."

I'd only just reached the master bedroom when Rhys called out, "Guys? I might have found something."

My stomach tightened as I hurried down the hallway to the second bedroom and stood in the doorway. When I found the room clear of anyone other than Rhys, I blew out a sharp breath and realized I'd been braced to find Poppy dead. Instead, Rhys stood beside a suitcase lying open on the floor beside the closet. Inside were books, baggies, bones, and vials that contained potions similar to the one Rhys had used on the wyvern.

"Is that dirt?" He poked his toe into a small heap on the purple rug.

By the magic trickling off the mess, it couldn't be anything other than grave dirt, something that shouldn't have existed anywhere near this apartment. Anger warred with relief as I took in the scene. Either Poppy was in serious trouble, or she was going to be when I tracked her down.

"We have until sundown to find her," I said. "And when we do, I might need you guys to hold me back."

Katerina

ARE YOU SURE we have time for this?" Rhys asked as he settled on Poppy's couch.

I sat in the armchair across from him, while Barrett surprised me by sitting beside Rhys instead of on the wooden dining chair. Had it been Poppy that had sent him across the room on our last visit, or had the man discovered the benefits of soft surfaces?

"We do," I assured Rhys. "If I'm right that Poppy's gathered up everything she needs for a raising, we've got a timeline ahead of us. The process to raise a body isn't quick. It can take hours to days depending on the state of the body, the strength of the witch, and the stage of the lunar cycle. She may have raised one or two by now, but if she's planning something big, she'll make use of the full moon tonight."

"What about the demon?" Barrett asked. "Or have we decided he's no longer important?"

Red swam in my vision as my blood pressure spiked, but I did my best to talk myself down. "The timing of everything is too convenient. I thought Poppy was too smart to summon anything, but if she's back to raising the dead, all bets are off. If she's not involved, we need her help. The witch hunters have Hamilton covered for now, and unless they catch a glimpse of Shogaur or the sorcerer, we'd be driving around waiting for something to happen. At least this way we stand a chance of clearing up one mystery."

And letting me work out the frenetic energy building in my veins with every passing moment. If I didn't find a way to vent it, the entire street was at risk of going up in smoke.

Rhys wiped his palms on his jeans, then closed his eyes and breathed into his stomach. His shoulders relaxed and his face fell slack as he sank deeper into his relaxation.

Barrett's attention remained on the front door over my left shoulder, but I never took my eyes off Rhys. The last time he'd tried to trigger too many visions at once, his brain had gone into overdrive and it had taken a magical sleeping potion to help him reboot. The techniques Adrian had taught him would help prevent him from going that far again, but I still worried.

His eyes flew open, the bright green irises washed out with

filmy white. When he spoke, his words came without inflection. "Choking on darkness and dirt. Groans of the dead. Orange light all around. Life crawling out of an empty grave, craving orders. Serve. Defend. Destroy."

Rhys slumped back, and I pushed myself out of my chair to pace the length of the living room. Poppy had broken her promise—but why? She'd never been the sort for willful destruction, but the situation with Mikhail might have pushed her over the edge. Yet the second command—defend. Everything about her apartment suggested a woman who'd been in a hurry. If she was running scared, she would be looking for ways to protect herself.

Rhys stirred, and I forced myself to sit back down, although my legs screamed at me to keep moving. He blinked his eyes open and offered a tired smile. "Worked that time."

"I had every faith in you," I said. "You confirmed one of my fears, but what else did you See? Any hints about which cemetery it was?"

He frowned and rubbed his brow. "There was a mural on a wall across the street. Metal gates. I'm sorry, pretty much all I Saw were tombstones. Lots of crosses and cherubs."

Barrett sat up straighter and pulled out his phone. He searched for something, then showed the screen to Rhys. "Was this the mural?" When Rhys nodded, Barrett gave a satisfied nod. "I know where she'll be. It's not far, maybe a ten-minute drive."

If the cemetery was nearby, would Poppy already be there, lying in wait for the sun to set? Or would she keep moving, afraid to stay in one place for too long? It wasn't yet noon, which meant we had almost seven hours to wait until dark. More than enough time to head back to Hamilton to begin the hunt for Shogaur.

Frustration tore a groan from me. "Any word from the witch hunters yet?"

Barrett scrolled through his text messages. "They sent an update half an hour ago. No strange activity and no new sightings."

And no Emrick stopping by to say the sorcerer was dead.

Seven hours was too long to leave the sorcerer in Shogaur's hands. We needed to find Poppy now.

"Let's head over to the cemetery. If Poppy's trying to stay out of sight, it's possible she's holed up there as the safest place. If we don't find her within the hour, we'll head back to Hamilton and do what we can to find the sorcerer ourselves. We don't have the wiggle room to drag our feet."

I prayed I hadn't made a huge mistake already by bringing us all the way out here. My gut told me I hadn't, though, and that Poppy remained our best choice for finding our missing sorcerer. Hopefully with enough time to save him before Shogaur took over his mind and unleashed his power on the world.

10

Katerina

THE CEMETERY FROM Rhys's vision was a large one that stretched several blocks behind a row of storefronts. The graves were a mix of old and new, with a few mausoleums scattered throughout.

At this time of day, the gates were open, but by fate or luck, there didn't seem to be any funerals going on. There was only one car parked at the entrance, one visible farther in, and very little foot traffic. All the better for us to go unnoticed as we wandered the paths in search of our buried loved one.

Or not-quite-yet buried loved one.

It would depend on what I found when I reached Poppy.

I pointed to a copse of trees. "Let's start over there, and we'll work our way around."

I wished I felt more confident that we were putting our efforts to good use. Every minute spent in this empty cemetery was another minute we lost in preventing Shogaur from taking the sorcerer's body and powers for a test drive.

My gut said to follow the witch, but my gut had been wrong before.

As we approached the copse in the centre of the cemetery, the bare branches of the trees leaving little space to hide, a loud thump from inside the mausoleum tucked between the dark trunks caught my ear.

"What was that?" Rhys whispered.

It had sounded like a sack of potatoes falling onto a dirt road, a sound I hadn't heard in a very long time.

I gestured for him to step behind me. Barrett reached for the knife at his side, and I commended him for his choice of arsenal. Bullets would do nothing against the undead, but while a decapitated corpse could still come at you, they'd lack some essential advantages. Like eyes.

Another sound came from within the mausoleum, this one more of a low moan. Either someone was doing maintenance and had decided to mess with any visitors, or we'd stumbled upon something untoward.

I nodded my head for Barrett to check the door. He scowled at me but knelt in front of the handle without argument. Rhys and I kept watch as he went at the lock. It took longer than usual, and even after the bolt clicked, the latch wouldn't open. I frowned and reached for the handle. A thread of magic tingled against my skin—a simple ward to encourage non-magicals to turn around and leave.

I worked quickly to unravel the spell, and as soon as the power was gone, the door swung open.

Revealing Poppy Lister standing inside. Her tight curls, tipped in pink, dangled below her shoulders, and her heavy red knit sweater hugged her curves over a pair of jeans. Her hair, sweater, and jeans were caked in mud, and the dark hues of her skin weren't much cleaner.

She stood in the middle of a salt circle, and the light of five candles positioned around the edge of it flickered in the dim light.

Her eyes bulged in terror, her arms stretched wide as though she could block the sight of the man rising to his feet behind her. The sound of him rolling out of his coffin must have been my sack of potatoes. His ragged clothes were covered in more dirt than hers were—barely—and he had a decomposed hole where his right cheek should have been.

Rhys bolted backwards, but Barrett darted his hand out and grabbed him by the shoulder to hold him steady.

I crossed my arms. "Proserpine Hera Lister."

"Fuckety-fuck, fuck, fuck." Poppy's gaze jumped around as though she were searching for an escape route, but the only way out was through me.

While she debated her life choices, I kept my attention on the dead man. I had to admit, he looked scary—like a rotting sack of meat that stank as badly as he looked. But that was the most threatening thing about him. Unless Poppy ordered him to attack, he was harmless. Lucky for me, even if she gave the command, corpses didn't respond well to fire.

"This isn't what it looks like," she said at last. Her eyes remained wide, and a tremor ran beneath her words.

"No? Because it sure looks like someone broke her promise. Ix-nay on the orpse-raising-cay, remember?"

"No, it's—" The fear in the witch's eyes flashed to anger, and she dropped her hands to her hips. "You know what? You're right. It's exactly what it looks like. You know why? Because you came to me in the middle of the night asking questions about a big bad blood witch that you knew would get me in trouble, and then you went and battled him and left me undefended. A witch has to have some protection, you know what I mean? You left me hanging, so I had to make do with what I have. Which is this."

The corpse's jaw fell into the dirt, and I raised an eyebrow to hide a smirk. "Some help."

"Okay, well, it wouldn't have been just him," Poppy said, grabbing the jawbone and tossing it into the recently vacated tomb. "I would have summoned two or three more tonight to follow me around and attack anyone who came after me."

"Thank you for not sending him after us," Rhys said.

Poppy gave him a once-over. "Who's the runt?"

"Hey," he objected.

"This is Rhys, my housekeeper's son."

Rhys grimaced. "I'm also a psychic who helps you find people and avoid horrible situations. I'm also your battle apprentice, helping you take down the local supernatural wild-life. Couldn't you have led with either of those?"

I prayed for patience. "I was trying to keep a few secrets close to my vest, champ."

Poppy nodded. "Smart. I can think of a few people who'd love to get their hands on him. Nice to see you again, Barrett. As grumpy as ever, which is fantastic. Always great to know where I stand with a person."

He dropped his chin. "Poppy." His narrowed eyes remained firmly on the corpse.

"Now that we've all said our hellos," I cut in, "would it be possible to put your friend to bed so we can go somewhere less disturbing to talk?" I wrinkled my nose. "And less offensive-smelling?"

Poppy dropped her hands. "I'm still trying to dig myself out of a hole from the last time we talked. Did you know my business failed because of our little chat?"

I did not. "Why?"

"Let's see." She tapped her index finger against her bottom lip. The impressively tipped nails were covered in dirt, but the white-and-blue polish shone through. "How about because no one wants to deal with a witch they can't trust? I ratted out their secrets, and you barged in on their meeting and killed a bunch of witches."

"Dark witches," I pointed out.

"You think that matters to my customer base? To them, you're judge, jury, and executioner. They're afraid they'll get involved in something you disapprove of, and I'll direct you right to them."

"If they're involved in dark magic, I fail to see the issue. They should just say no to evil."

Poppy waved a hand in dismissal. "Sure, but let's not pretend all witches are saints. And the witches who are saints don't spend enough money at my shop to pay the bills."

I crossed my arms. "You're really selling yourself well here, Poppy."

She groaned. "The point is every time I help you, my life goes to shit in some new explosive way, all right? So no, I'm not talking to you. I'm taking my new friend, and we're going to hide somewhere no one can find me."

"Is someone after you?" I frowned. "Who?"

"If I knew that, they wouldn't stand a chance, would they? They'd be toast."

"Have you seen them?" Barrett asked.

Poppy shook her head. "I came home one night to see lights in my apartment. I hid across the street, and about twenty minutes later, two people left. They were dressed all in black, faces covered. More than once I've walked down the street and sworn someone was following me. It started after you killed Mikhail, so if it's not related, that's a big spanking coincidence."

The news of Poppy's supposed stalkers didn't sit well with me. Barrett and I hadn't discussed visiting Poppy with anyone. No one should have known unless she'd told them herself. So first, how did anyone know about her involvement? Second, why would they care enough to stalk her now that Mikhail was dead?

Unless she'd gotten herself involved in some new evil.

"Have you ever heard of a demon named Shogaur?" I asked.

She startled at the abrupt subject change. "I've seen him referenced in the old texts. A fear demon, right?"

Rhys shuffled behind me, edging farther away from the undead man who'd turned his milky eyes on him.

"I don't suppose you know anything about him currently wandering the streets of Hamilton?" I asked Poppy.

The terror that grew in her eyes reflected what existed in my soul.

"No fucking way," she said. "Someone summoned him?

Who the fuck would be so fucking stupid as to do a fucked-up thing like that?"

Poppy might be a good actress, but it would have taken the willpower of a minor god to cower against a walking corpse like she now was, which made me inclined to believe her.

"We don't know," Barrett said, crossing his arms. "But we think it has something to do with the sorcerer setting fire to the streets. Know anything about him?"

"No fucking way," she repeated in the exact same intonation as before. I worried we'd broken her. "That guy on the news? He's a *sorcerer?*"

"What'd you think he was?" I asked. "Some kind of illusionist?"

"I don't know. A witch whose spells went wrong? Someone with really bad gas and really bad luck? What do I know about your kind? I thought you'd all died out. Or is that what you tell us *lowly* witches to make yourself feel important?"

"I thought I was telling the truth. Turns out I was mistaken."

Poppy gasped. "Mistaken? You?"

Rhys snorted a laugh and hid it behind a cough.

"It happens," I said. "Once or twice a century. Point is, he disappeared, and we need to find him before Shogaur gets into his head. If you know about this demon, then you can imagine what interesting games he might choose to play."

Poppy breathed out a curse and pressed her fingers against

her forehead. "I do not want to imagine that, thanks very much. Fuck! All right. Fine. Let me clean up, and we can go to my apartment and get what we need for a tracking spell. If you guys are here, no one's likely to mess with me."

With a few quick words to unbind the dead man behind her, she sent him shuffling back to his tomb. He fell, face-first, into the open casket. Deed done, she stooped to gather the herbs and crystals she'd laid around her salt circle and tucked them into the pouches on her belt. As she turned away from the grave, a low yowl caught my ear, and I spun around to glare into the shadows of the mausoleum.

"Is that a cat?" Rhys asked, joining me in my search. "How did it get in here?"

I was about to tell him to let it be when I spotted the glimmer of fear in Poppy's eyes. I propped my fists on my hips. "Proserpine?"

"Yes?" It was a sad attempt at defiance. Her trembling fingers dropped one of her crystals in the dirt, and she scrambled to find it and brush it off.

"What did you do?"

"*Rowr.*"

Now that I heard it again, I caught the subtle wrongness of the meow. It lacked the demanding assholeishness of an adult cat or the mewling of a tiny kitten. This was a passive noise. Noise for the sake of it.

I spun around again and spotted the grey-furred mass sitting in the corner. Its yellow eyes stared pointedly at me, though without the disdain I'd come to expect from most felines.

"*Rowr*," it said, and I noted the way its jaw was slightly off angle.

From there, I noticed the missing patches of fur on its back and sides, the kink in its tail, the reek.

"*Proserpine*." Fire was in my hand before I realized I'd summoned it.

Poppy leapt between me and the undead cat, her hand raised to fend me off. "No, wait! He's harmless, all right? I needed to practice on something small before I raised my soldiers. He was buried on the edge of the cemetery and… well, isn't he just the cutest?"

The fondness in her gaze as she swept the stinking cat into her arms baffled me.

"It's a dead cat, Poppy."

"He is not. Okay, he was a dead cat, but now he's walking around just fine, aren't you, Cuddles?"

She stroked his head, and I dropped my hands by my sides, too stunned to move. I had to admit, he was pretty adorable. Or he would be if he were less… rotty. Maybe a bath would help?

"You can't seriously want to keep that creature around," Barrett said as another clump of fur from the creature's rump fell to the ground. Luckily for Cuddles, he was—had been—a long-haired cat, so the bald patches were mostly covered.

"Oh, I don't know," I said. "What harm can an undead cat do, really?"

I reached out to remove a lump of dirt from one of his ears, and he bared his remaining teeth with a low growl.

Barrett snorted. "You can't even get a dead cat to like you."

I scowled at him, then flashed Poppy a bright smile. "All right, you can keep him. But you have to pick up any body parts he drops."

She beamed and snuggled the cat to her chest. "I promise."

Barrett's expression turned murderous. "It's not getting in my car."

11

Katerina

TEN MINUTES LATER, Barrett parked on the street in front of Poppy's apartment. I climbed out of the front seat, while Rhys and Poppy, who carried a blasé-looking Cuddles, emerged from the back.

The moment we'd gotten into the car, Cuddles had padded over the console, dropped into Barrett's lap, and refused to move. I suspected Barrett would have been happier to steer the vehicle into a streetlight rather than spend a second with his snuggle buddy. He'd rolled down every window despite the temperature and kept his teeth clenched throughout the entire short trip.

Poppy frowned at the unlocked door to her apartment but didn't say anything as she led us up the confined stairwell. She set Cuddles on the dining chair Barrett usually claimed as his and disappeared into the room that housed her magical kit. While we waited for her to return, the rest of us made ourselves comfortable around the dining table.

Well, Rhys and I made ourselves comfortable. Barrett stood in the corner of the room with his arms crossed and his eyes narrowed, every bit the poster boy of disapproval.

I wasn't sure how much of his discontent was the need to have his car detailed, the spell Poppy was about to perform, or our delay in returning to Hamilton, but if his unease was anything like mine, the latter counted for a lot.

"Any word from Tony?" I hoped that by reminding him of the witch hunters' radio silence, he might relax enough that a single twitch wouldn't snap his rigid frame.

He shook his head. "He's sending updates, but there's been no movement."

"Is that a bad thing?" Rhys asked, looking between Barrett and me as though trying to read the unspoken conversation.

Unfortunately, there was no conversation to read. I had no idea. "Knowing Shogaur, he's biding his time for something big and unpleasant. Emitting energy, stirring up a latent state of dread in whatever area he's hiding in. But it bodes well for us that the sorcerer hasn't been seen. Maybe not for the sorcerer, but for the rest of the world. No movement has to mean Shogaur hasn't taken over his mind. If he does, we'll need to brace for the worst."

Barrett grumbled something about magic users I didn't need to hear to understand, then continued to bore a hole into the kitchen table with his dark stare.

A few minutes later, Poppy emerged from her room carrying a map and a wooden box about a foot long by half a foot wide. She sat at the head of the table and opened the box to reveal a selection of powders, herbs, crystals, and a sleek, black marble mortar and pestle. Before removing anything from the box, she spread the street map of Ontario across the table, arranging it so the Greater Toronto Area lay central in front of us.

"Do we have any reason to think he's left the city?" she asked as she pulled out her kit.

"Not that the hunters have told us," I said. We exchanged a look, sharing an unspoken "as much as that means," and Barrett huffed behind us.

"Well, we'll start here. If we need to, we can go wider." She bit her bottom lip, then added, "Though maybe not today. This spell takes a lot out of me."

Rhys watched with fascination as she readied the scene. She began by sliding a thick chain over her neck, leaving the attached chunk of obsidian sitting against her breastbone.

"For focus," I explained to Rhys so the witch didn't think he was staring at her boobs.

Next, she ground up some herbs and mixed them with a

bright purple powder. The herbs I was pretty sure I could name if pressed, but the powders were well beyond my knowledge of witchcraft. Poppy, however, was completely at ease with them, and despite the issues that existed between us, I knew this was why I'd come to her and no one else. If anyone stood a chance of magically tracking our sorcerer, it was this woman right here. She was a hoarder of knowledge. Any opportunity she had to learn, she took it, and the result was a powerhouse of ability.

Which was also why she wound up in trouble so often.

Her brow furrowed in concentration as she focused her intentions on the concoction. "It's a pretty basic spell on the surface, but the more specific you want the results, the more complicated it gets. I guess you don't have anything that belongs to the guy, do you? Blood? Hair?"

I pulled the handkerchief of bloodstained asphalt out of my pocket and handed it over, happy to be rid of it. After the stench of the rotting, walking corpse, I didn't relish being in close contact with any more oozing body matter.

Right on cue, Cuddles meowed. I reached out to pet him, wondering if I could wrangle him into the sink to get some of the grave dirt out of his fur, but he walked out of my reach, sat down, and started grooming his butthole. I levelled a stare at him. He stared right back, his leg hovering.

Poppy cleared her throat, drawing my attention back to the matter at hand. But Cuddles and I weren't finished. I'd broken eye contact first, and that couldn't stand. Next time, I would come out the winner.

"All right," Poppy said at the end of a deep exhale, "here goes nothing. Let's see what we can find."

She sprinkled some of the asphalt into her mortar along with another purple powder, then topped it up with a clear liquid from one of her many vials. The powder sizzled, and a pink steam rose from the bowl.

The words she mumbled under her breath were unknown to me, and I watched her expression, searching for any hint of betrayal. I'd been burned often enough to be prepared for it. But her eyes remained focused on the mortar as she grabbed the pestle and ground the asphalt and powder together.

As soon as the contents were a mess of pink-smoked, black-and-purple goo, she gestured for me and Rhys to hold the map down. I laid my hand along the edge, taking in the twists of streets and highways between Toronto and Hamilton. I prayed the sorcerer was close. The sooner I got to him and dealt with Shogaur, the sooner I could go home, eat my weight in homemade cookies, and question why my past had recently decided to challenge what was left of my sanity.

Once the map was flat, Poppy poured the goo onto the paper, still mumbling the unknown words. Rhys never took his eyes off the goo, and I had to admit to a deep curiosity about what this spell would do beyond make a mess. I glanced over my shoulder at Barrett to find his face had settled into its usual blank slate. Inside, I was sure, he was seething. He probably would have been happier if we'd knocked on every door in Hamilton instead of relying on Poppy's help. Sure, it might have taken six months and the world might have devolved into a fear-induced mania, but at least we wouldn't have used any of that pesky magic.

Not for the first time, I wondered how he and Adrian survived together. Did Barrett acknowledge the hypocrisy of loving a vampire and benefiting from the effects of Adrian's blood while hating the rest of the magical world? Did Adrian get frustrated with his thrall's close-mindedness, or did he find it amusing?

Knowing Adrian, he got a kick out of it. My old friend always did find humour in the infuriating.

I went back to ignoring Barrett and returned my attention to the map. My eyes widened as the goo shifted on the paper, first spreading out across the city, then evaporating into smoke until only a small circle ringed northeast Hamilton.

Poppy's murmuring fell silent, and she sagged into her chair. Her face was pasty, and her lips were chapped. Without saying anything, Barrett fetched a glass of water from the kitchen.

"Thanks," she said before downing the entire cup in a few loud gulps. "Damn I hate that spell. But there you go, kitty Kat. It's not pinpointed to the exact coordinates, but you have a general idea."

Rhys leaned closer. "It looks like it's narrowed down to within a few blocks. That's not so bad."

A few blocks would still be a lot of real estate to check out, but once we got close, I hoped to detect the sorcerer's magic. Or the demon's.

I swallowed hard and longed for a glass of water of my own but doubted Barrett would fetch it for me just because.

He stepped forward and pulled the map towards him, obviously less put off now that Poppy had finished the magic part of the spell. He tilted his head to get a better read of the area. "Barton Street? That's a rough neighbourhood."

"It fits," I said. "No doubt everyone within a ten-block radius is sharpening their knives and restocking their ammunition, braced for a fight they can't see coming. The longer we wait, the higher the odds that as soon as we step foot within range of Shogaur's power, we'll get blown away by people who otherwise wouldn't look at us twice."

Rhys licked his lips and fiddled with the edge of the map. "He's controlling them?"

"Fear, Rhys, remember? He doesn't have to control them. He doesn't have to do anything except stay in one place long enough and whisper a few words in the right ears. Entire civilizations have toppled because of this monster. Wars have started. Millions have died because he knows the perfect tipping points to put pressure on."

He shivered and dropped his gaze to the circle. "So what do we do?"

"I'm tempted to send you home." He raised his chin, eyes burning green fire, and I chuckled. "But I know better. Our first step will be teaching you some mind-protection techniques. Simple meditations to safeguard your head against this demon poking around in it." I frowned. "It's strange you haven't had any visions about him."

Rhys's brow furrowed as his expression mirrored mine. "I know, right? I Saw the sorcerer that one time, but nothing since. I've tried, but nothing's coming."

I patted his hand. "No worries. It'll happen. Until then, at least now we have something to go on. What do you think, Barrett? Do you want to head out now or go downstairs and see if we can sweet-talk Cyn into giving us a few chocolate cookies to go with the scones?"

He stared at me, and I shrugged. "All right, then. Arm up, everyone. We're going demon-hunting."

12

Katerina

WE STUCK AROUND long enough for Poppy to pack a bag and ensure Cuddles was comfortable in the trunk—after a long, drawn-out battle of wills that ended in Poppy swearing to personally ensure no stray cat hair or stench was left behind after the trip—then set off for Ancaster and arrived at Adrian's house around three o'clock. Early enough in the day to give us time to wander the four-block radius Poppy's spell had pinpointed before exhaustion kicked my ass.

Though considering how tired I felt, the cutoff would be close.

Especially since it took half an hour to decide who was coming along for the ride. Barrett and I were a given, but Rhys refused to stay home, and Poppy dragged her feet over pursuing a demon.

"Maybe I could help from a distance," she said. "By watching the news or reading something fluffy to improve the vibe of the group."

In the end, I persuaded her—gently—that her magical knowledge would help speed things along and potentially save the world. Failing that, her job would be keeping Rhys magically shielded. After much grumbling, she agreed.

Before we left, Poppy set Cuddles up in the bathroom with a blanket and the radio—"So he isn't lonely," she said—and joined us as we piled into Barrett's SUV. I'd almost offered to drive, feeling bad that he'd played chauffeur this whole time, but then I'd remembered where we were going. In that area of Hamilton, any vehicle was likely to be tagged, if not outright stolen, within minutes of arriving, and I didn't want to deal with the insurance claim.

Twenty minutes later, Barrett pulled onto a side street in the centre of Poppy's location spell and found a place to park. The streets were busy with car and foot traffic, and I assumed everyone had somewhere to be, but as I looked around, I had to wonder where. Many of the storefronts were shuttered, and the apartments stacked above them were boarded up. Graffiti marked almost every flat surface, confirming my fears for my car.

"What a place to hide," I said as I led the way towards Barton Street and the heart of the spell. "Certainly not a place anyone would look too closely at strange goings-on."

"I think it's charming," Poppy said. "So much potential—and can you feel that energy? I wonder what rent is like."

"Thinking of opening a new shop?"

She shrugged. "Why not? Might be easier to start somewhere new than kick Cyn out of her sublet."

I raised my eyebrow. "You'd reopen in Toronto? I thought your business failed."

She pressed her lips together. "I may have exaggerated a little. It's possible I subletted the shop so I could disappear."

My jaw dropped. "You tried to guilt-trip me? Well played."

"How do we want to do this?" Barrett interrupted. "Split up? Go door to door?"

I doubted the effort of going door to door would net us much success, and splitting up sounded like a horrible idea. To get rid of Shogaur, we needed to spill his blood, recite the incantation, and not get killed or possessed while doing it. For all Rhys's training, he wouldn't stand a chance. Or Barrett, for that matter. He could carry enough guns and knives for an entire action film and still not fend off a demon. Poppy stood the best chance, but given the strength of her power, she would be hard-pressed to keep Shogaur out of her mind.

More important, we needed to move fast. If the sorcerer had been in Shogaur's hands for the past twenty-four hours, we were dangerously close to catastrophe. A mortal's mind could only hold out for so long against a demon's tactics.

I stepped into the doorway of an empty building and closed my eyes, breathing deep to sink into the flow of the environment. I tuned out the noise and the movement, blocked out the smells, and focused on the invisible magical current in the air. I sensed the faint traces of water I could use to reverse the flow of my fire magic and the stillness I could manipulate to form lightning.

And there. Something darker. Headier.

"He's close," I said without opening my eyes. "I might be able to follow his trail, but everyone has to stay quiet and let me concentrate."

"Would this help?"

I opened one eye as Poppy held out a slim, polished amethyst wand she must have pulled from her bag.

"It reacts to negative energy," she said. "You hold it out, and it sort of vibrates in your hand when the energy gets strong enough. At that point, you're supposed to cast a spell to cleanse the area, but I don't think that'll help us here."

"Demons aren't the sort to apologize for mucking up one's aura, no." I took the wand and held it out in front of me. Immediately, the stone shivered in my palm. "I hope everyone's wearing their walking shoes."

Following the buzz of power, I started down the block, and before too long, I tasted magic on the air, ashy and rank.

Its bitterness coated the back of my throat, and nausea gurgled in my stomach.

After another block, it faded, and I stopped and turned back the way we'd come.

"What is this?" Barrett grumbled. "A game of hot or cold?"

"You're welcome to wait in the car." I was too focused on the pull of the wand to put much heat into the suggestion.

"We can?" Poppy sounded more than a little eager. "Because that sounds like a great idea. Come on, Rhys, why don't we go make sure no one steals our ride home?"

Rhys pulled his arm out of Poppy's reach. "I want to stay with Kat. What if she needs us?"

"I'm sure your visions would be very helpful," she said. "I still don't know why I'm here."

Barrett glowered. "I'm wondering the same, witch."

Poppy batted her long lashes at him. "You are such a charmer—you always know what to say. If my interests didn't lie elsewhere, I'd pucker up and give you a big smackeroo. Laced with poison."

"I'd expect nothing else from you."

"Will you two please be quiet?" I snapped, my concentration broken.

"Is their griping affecting your ability to do… whatever you're doing?" Rhys asked.

"No, it's just annoying. No one gets to gripe with Barrett

except me. It's one of my few vices. Now hush and let me focus."

Block by block, we followed the trail of magic. My terror over the idea of finding Shogaur lurked beneath the surface of my thoughts, but I kept it tightly restrained. He didn't deserve the meal.

The last time I hunted this demon, I'd come across him by accident, but we'd gotten up close and personal enough for me to familiarize myself with the stench of his power. That familiarity allowed me to recognize the particular demonic tang when we turned another corner, strong enough that it grated along my skin like sandpaper.

I wasn't the only one who felt it. Poppy's face turned ashen, and Rhys's hands trembled, his gaze darting around in search of trouble. Barrett was the only one who appeared unfazed, but I didn't believe for a second that he couldn't pick up on the wrongness in the air.

I drew to a stop on the street corner. Firelight danced in my vision, heat seared my skin, and my entire body tensed to escape the pain I knew was coming.

"Kat?" Rhys asked. "Are you all right?"

"I'm fine." I passed a hand over my face. "Memories, that's all. Bad ones." I shook out my arms and shrugged my shoulders to dispel the panic. "All right. Let's plan this out. Does everyone remember what we went over in the car to keep him out of your head? The words to send him back to hell if something happens to me and I can't do it?"

"Kitty Kat, if something happens to you, I'm not sticking around long enough to chant anything," Poppy said. "I'm high-tailing it out of there so quick, there'll be dust clouds."

I sniffed. "We should have left you in the mausoleum and brought your undead friend instead. What about you, Rhys?"

"I haven't stopped the protection exercises since we left the car. But I think I'm with Poppy. If you don't make it, there's no way in hell I'd win."

"Guess it comes down to you, Barrett."

He raised an eyebrow as if to ask what was new. "What about the blood you need? Think a bullet would do the trick?"

I eyed him, wondering where on his rippling body he'd tucked the weapon. From experience, I knew he carried a knife in the small of his back and another tucked into his boot, but in the brightness of the day I couldn't make out any lumps that might be a gun.

"If you're a quick enough shot, you might get lucky. If he doesn't possess you and force you to turn it on yourself. I've never had a chance to test it, though. Bullets weren't exactly a thing the last time we crossed paths. Feel free to be my guinea pig."

I edged towards a boarded-up commercial duplex tucked between a banquet hall rental and a tire centre. The single-storey building was short and squat, with no parking lot, no pathway, and no personality. It would have been easy for anyone to overlook the place, and I guessed that wasn't a coincidence. No ward or cloaking spell covered the door, but someone had used the natural environment to cover their steps. A far more practical approach than anything a demon would consider, but maybe he'd learned some things in hell over the past eight hundred years. Or maybe his summoner had chosen the venue.

A few metres away from the door, the amethyst wand snapped in my hand. The magic in the purple stone evaporated, leaving me with nothing but two sharp, moderately useful weapons.

Poppy stared at the pieces, her expression gutted. "I loved that wand. This damn demon owes me."

"Then you'd better stick around to make him pay," I said. "But maybe stand behind me. Far behind me. Go with her, Rhys."

Barrett crossed his arms. Was that a glimmer of amusement I saw dancing in his dark brown eyes? "What about me? Want me to hide behind you, too, or am I on the front lines for this one?"

I flashed him my biggest grin. "Front and centre, big guy. But only to start. Get the door open—the one on the left, the magic's leaking—then join the others. If you're fast enough. Once we're inside, our priority is the sorcerer. If he's possessed, we'll have to kill him to get Shogaur out. If he's not, we have to hope he'll come with us quietly. If he doesn't… Barrett, you have my permission to clobber him over the head with your meaty fist."

He grunted his understanding, but Rhys looked uncertain. "If he's possessed, is there no way to save him?"

I rolled my shoulders to release the tension hugging my spine. "Not easily. Certainly not before he tries to turn us into overdone Christmas turkey."

The blood drained from Rhys's face. "Gotcha."

As my team moved into position, my pulse raced with anticipation. The sort I hadn't felt in a long time—that of going up against someone whose magic rivalled mine. More than a little fear crept around the edges of my adrenaline rush, but I did my best to cage it off. Fear would only make Shogaur stronger. I was here to bring him to his knees before casting him back to the infernal realms.

I stood close behind Barrett to shield his actions from view, though I doubted anyone would try to stop us from breaking into what appeared to be a long-empty store.

The lock clicked, and I nodded for Barrett to move. He frowned, his hand already on the hilt of his blade, but I glared at him until he fell into place behind me. I didn't know what we would find inside, but whether it was an untrained sorcerer terrified for his life or a demon, I didn't want to have to explain to Adrian why his thrall was nothing more than a fine layer of dust in an abandoned shop.

I rested my fingers on the door handle, and the prickle of magic ran all the way up my arm to shake my teeth. With a deep breath, I pushed the door in. A wave of power swept over me as though I'd stepped into an Arizona heat wave in the middle of summer. The oven-like dryness buzzed along my skin and made breathing a challenge.

Behind me, Poppy gasped and Rhys let out a strangled, "What the hell?" Barrett remained quiet. Was he immune to the power levels in this room or just good at hiding his reaction? One day I'd ask him.

I pushed through the discomfort, my breaths growing shallower, as though the oxygen were growing sparse. The metallic prickle along my taste buds grew sharper, almost painful. I wanted to order the others to leave, but the fear I struggled to suppress kept me quiet. If Shogaur was here, I couldn't go against him by myself. Or at least, I didn't want to.

Fire. Screams. Searing agony as my flesh bubbled and burned.

I gave myself a shake and steeled my resolve. That wouldn't happen again. I was prepared this time. I knew what the monster was capable of. First, we had to save the sorcerer—if there was anything left to save—then I would cast the demon back to hell. I had the words; all I needed was to shed Shogaur's blood, which I would do happily.

I turned the corner towards a back room and summoned a small fireball to hover over my trembling palm. A red streak caught my eye. I dropped my gaze to the floor where a splash of blood, dark and dry, stained the peeling white linoleum.

I stepped around it and followed the blood trail to a door at the back of the shop. Barrett moved behind me, his back to mine, with his knife raised as he cleared the room. I grabbed the door handle. Unlike the front of the store, this one wasn't locked, though the rust on the hinges made it difficult to pull open. If we were aiming for stealth, we lost it with the ear-splitting creak.

The stench of blood, piss, and shit, layered over a hint of something floral, hit me with brute force, and I pressed the back of my hand over my nose as Poppy and Rhys gagged behind me.

"I'm going to be sick," Poppy gasped. She hurried towards the front of the store. Rhys lasted a moment longer, going white around the mouth, until he also broke and ran.

I didn't blame them. I'd experienced worse, but even I had to admit this was bad. There was no ventilation, so the odour had a stale quality that struck me as older than twenty-four hours. Whatever had happened in this room had been brutal.

With my hand on the door, I pulled it open the rest of the way and stepped into darkness.

13

Emrick

I STOOD NEXT to the body of a witch. The corpse lay on the floor of her apartment, her hand outstretched towards the cell phone on the table. Her heart had given out—a perfectly mundane death for a magical, and yet the energy in the room made me uncomfortable. It was murky. Not quite touched with dark magic, but not far off.

The woman's soul stood next to the body, a shimmering version of herself. Her body had been in her mid-sixties, heavy-set, dressed in jeans and a loud red sweater, but her soul was nothing but a muted white light, with the vague idea of facial features shining within it.

"What were you involved in?" I asked, curious despite myself.

I had no good reason to wonder, and the answer wouldn't affect me, but I had to know. For a while now, the rumours drifting through this slice of the universe had made me uneasy. Whispers of dark magic, of a spreading evil, of dark plans. Spirits I'd escorted to the river were afraid for the loved ones they left behind.

"Spells." Her voice came as though from a distance, wavering in and out as the sound passed from death to life. "Enchantments for a woman in need."

Her words sent a tingle down my spine. "In need of what?"

She didn't register my question, drifting closer to me, the lightness of her eyes shining brighter. "The immortal sorceress drags trouble behind her. So many are going to die before she's finished."

"What do you know?" I demanded.

A shudder ran through her, her light dimmed, and she remained silent. I wished I could grab her and give her a shake, but everything corporeal about her lay unmoving on the floor.

Accepting that her consciousness was now elsewhere, I parted the mists to the afterlife and led her towards the river that divided this liminal space from whatever came next.

She faded into the ether to await her turn across, and I stalked back the way I'd come, feeling more like a caged animal than I had since my mortal life.

I didn't know how Kat might be involved, but it worried me. Especially now that Shogaur had returned. The coincidence that he of all demons should be summoned. That he should have found the one other living sorcerer. None of it sat well.

But instead of being there with my sorceress, watching her back and ensuring her safety, I was stuck in this nothingness, this barren wasteland where my only company were the lost souls that had yet to cross the river.

I paced from one leafless tree to another and considered going to Adrian to vent my frustrations, but I knew what my old friend would say. If I wanted to take my place at Kat's side, we needed to find a solution to the problem that kept us apart. Namely, how to stop myself from losing fragments of my soul until I wasted away into an incorporeal wraith.

As it stood, I had no idea what the answer was. What I did know was that I wouldn't find it on my own. And if Shogaur got the better of Kat, I would have no desire to keep going. She was my anchor, my heart. She was the only piece of my soul that mattered.

The spirit's warning echoed in my ears again. If Kat brought trouble, it was only because trouble had found her. I wouldn't let her stand on her own.

Resolve firmed in my blood, and I squeezed my fists at my sides.

Kat would be furious with me, but I could handle her anger.
I could deal with her jibes, her glares, and her fear.

What I couldn't handle was losing her.

My determination set, I summoned the mists and left the
afterlife behind me.

14

Katerina

THICK BLINDS HUNG over the windows along the back wall, dousing the small space in nothing but a pale glow of mid-afternoon sunlight. Just enough to let me make out the blood sprayed across the once-grey paint and pooling on the floor around the chair in the middle of the room.

Just enough to let me see the form sitting on the chair, head bowed, hands and ankles bound to the armrests and legs.

Even in shadowed profile, I recognized the man from the news—medium-length black hair falling over his brow, broad-shouldered, muscular. The sorcerer.

I scanned the room before I stepped in, and when I found it empty, I hurried towards him. He didn't move at the sound of my footsteps, and when I crouched in front of him, I found him unconscious. Not surprising considering the state of him. A relief, even. Not only for me and Barrett, because we wouldn't have to dodge surprise fireballs, but for the man. If he were awake, he would have been in agony.

He was naked, and almost every inch of him was smeared with blood. Someone had sliced the sides of his chest, along his bare arms, and down his legs. It must have been torture.

Confusion nagged at me. Shogaur dealt in whispers and temptation, not physical injuries. On the contrary, he avoided anything that might damage a host body. Had this sorcerer been so stubborn he'd pushed Shogaur beyond the point of patience or reason?

I couldn't wait for the man to wake up so I could ask him who I was dealing with.

I reached out to rest my hand on his shoulder, but at the contact, my magic flared and his rose in response. Fire spiralled over his arms without training or awareness to hold it back. As soon as I released him, the power faded.

"Barrett, you'd better take this one. Free him and get him to the car. See if Poppy can heal some of these wounds without setting him off." I rose and backed away, giving Barrett space to slip around me.

He set to work slicing through the leather straps tying the man to the chair, and as he worked, my nose burned at the unpleasant aroma rising beneath the other stenches.

Sulphur.

The hair on the back of my neck danced, and a cold sweat broke out on my palms and in the small of my back. "I'd work faster if I were you, soldier boy."

"Dammit, Kat, I can only—"

I clenched my teeth. "Work. Faster."

The clever man picked up on my warning. He gave up on the ropes and kicked the legs out from under the chair. The wooden frame collapsed, taking the unconscious man to the floor. With a few more kicks to break the armrests, Barrett was able to hoist the guy over his shoulder.

"Let's go," he said.

"You go ahead. I'm right behind you."

He hesitated only a moment before he saw reason and obeyed. I backed slowly towards the doorway as the sulphuric reek grew stronger.

"I know you're here, Shogaur." I searched the shadows for any sign of him. "Know that whatever you're planning, I will stop you. I've done it before. I'm not afraid of you."

"*Katerina.*"

My name came as a hiss on the air. The sound punctured my veins like shrapnel, and my breath caught in my lungs. I scanned the room again, struggling to catch any hint of red eyes in the darkness, but Shogaur was toying with me.

"If you're so strong, why play games?" I asked. "Are you

too much of a coward to face me after all this time?"

The chuckle that followed twisted the knots in my gut, and two pinpoints of red moved forward from the corner of the room. In the dim light, shadows obscured his face, but I didn't need to see it to remember the horrible grin that had haunted my dreams for so many years.

I summoned magic into my palms and sent the lick of flames up my arms to the elbows. They danced over my gloves, wreathing me in their red-orange glow. A sign of my anger, not my fear.

If I kept repeating it, maybe I'd believe it.

The laugh that wound through my head told me my secret was already out. Dammit.

"You cannot hide from me, my sweet Katerina. Your fear is a fine liquor on my palate. I remember the taste of you. I've craved another sip for all these long years, and now I'm going to drain you of every last drop."

My mouth filled with cotton, and my heart slammed against my ribcage. It took all my effort not to squeeze my eyes shut and pretend I was somewhere else. This wasn't *my* fear. This was him trying to take control of me, and I refused to let him.

"You couldn't get what you wanted from the sorcerer?" I did my best to follow the floating red pinpricks. The bastard was circling me. I'd been stupid enough to stand away from the wall, leaving my back open, but to spin and follow him would give away my sense of vulnerability. It didn't matter if he could read every layer of terror that existed in my blood and bone, I wouldn't give him that satisfaction.

"He was stubborn," Shogaur said. "Even more so than you. I would have worn him down eventually, but you're a far greater gift, *Katerina*."

I wished he'd stop saying my name. Every time those syllables tripped over his hellish tongue, another wave of goosebumps tightened my flesh.

"I remember now why I wanted inside you so badly," he murmured near my ear. I didn't flinch. "You could carry me until the entire world burned and I consumed the fear of every one of these pitiful mortals. Join me. Play with me."

A sharp pain shot into my head. At first I thought it was Shogaur trying to claw his way inside, but I realized I'd clenched my teeth so hard my jaw had gone into spasm.

This standoff was a waste of time. He wasn't going to tell me what I needed to know, and every second I spent in this room increased the odds that I wouldn't make it out in one piece. I tightened my grip around the broken amethyst wand. "Sorry, Shogaur, but just like last time, I don't want to play."

I waited until I felt the brush of him at my back before I whirled around and stabbed the stone shard into the shadows. A hiss slithered through my ears, and Shogaur's humanoid form tumbled into view. He'd changed since I'd last seen him, and not for the better. His grey skin was slick, almost slimy, and his mouth had widened another few inches to reveal even more pointy teeth. Above his glowing red eyes, adding to his towering form, two horns covered in shedding velvet extended from his skull.

He jerked the remains of the wand from his side and threw it to the floor. It didn't matter. I didn't need contact with the blood, only for it to be spilled.

"I hope you enjoyed your visit." I threw myself into the words Emrick had taught me so many centuries ago.

The power of the spell flowed through me, intense and unfamiliar. I struggled to direct it, especially when Shogaur pushed back. Desperation made me send more magic into the words, but they slipped away from me. In so many ways, I was a stronger sorceress now than I'd been during our first encounter, but in every other way, thanks to my time-weakened magic, I was back where I'd started when Emrick first took on my training.

I felt out of control, unable to pin Shogaur down.

My last hope faded when the pain hit—a blood-deep agony that stretched my insides and writhed like snakes. The fire around my arms erupted in defence and flooded the room, catching the chair, the blinds, the empty storage units along the wall, but I couldn't control it as I dropped to my knees.

The words to the banishing spell disappeared, lost, and Shogaur's power surged.

Make room for me, he whispered, his tone coaxing, cajoling, reassuring. *The pain will end. You'll feel no fear.*

"Get out," I ordered, clinging to the lessons Emrick had taught me to guard my mind. "You have no place here. I'm stronger than you'll ever be."

That laugh again, the total disregard for my attempt at fortitude as he wedged his way in.

Gritting my teeth, I curled my hands into fists and imagined steel walls clapping shut around my skull. My magic dried up within me as I locked it away, and chills overtook me where before there had been heat.

Give in. Enjoy the peace and quiet I can offer. The rest you crave.

"Silence, demon. Nothing you say will convince me to make way for you."

We both know that's not true. Why else did you come for me? You could have stayed safe on your island and let me have my fun. You wanted to find me. You want what only I can offer. You fear the loneliness that's overwhelmed your life. You fear the stretch of time ahead without change or end. You fear the drudgery of battle after battle as you take on a war you cannot win. Let it end now, Katerina. Give me your fears. Let me take them from you, and all will be well.

I screamed to drown out his voice and doubled my efforts to remove the tendrils of his power seeping through the smallest cracks in my mind. The pain grew hotter, as though my bones were being consumed by hellfire. My muscles shook, my vision burst with stars, and I vomited my breakfast all over the bare concrete floor.

The steel walls I'd raised collapsed. I replaced them as quickly as I could, but Shogaur was relentless. The pressure on my head felt like a vise, and I was certain my skull would fracture as easily as those imaginary steel walls.

Voices shouted my name from beyond the shop door, but no one came for me. At least I had something to be grateful for. No one else would need to suffer this pain.

Before I could shout for them to get away, Shogaur took advantage of the distraction to slip past my defences.

There, there, he whispered. My heartbeat slowed as my fear was syphoned away by the demon infiltrating my thoughts. *It's almost over now.*

He crept closer, and the chill sank deeper into my blood. Gone was the burn in my bones, replaced by a numbness I couldn't shake no matter how hard I scraped my knuckles against the floor to shock myself back into control.

I had to regain control.

I squeezed my eyes shut, breathed into my power, and just as Shogaur let out a laugh of triumph, I shot my magic through my system, overpowering myself and short-circuiting my brain.

A cry of rage echoed around me. I opened my eyes to see two red dots darting forward, but as the temperature in the room plummeted and my vision went dark, a pair of strong arms gathered me up and swept me away.

15

Emrick

WITH KAT IN my arms, I stopped outside the empty shop just long enough to tell Barrett and the others to leave. There was nothing they could do against Shogaur without a full arsenal behind them, and hanging around would make them easy targets.

Once I delivered my message, I brought Kat to Adrian's house in Ancaster.

Her face was pale, her breathing quick, but the longer she was away from Shogaur, the more she calmed. I laid her on her bed and bowed my forehead against hers, giving space for my heartbeat to slow.

That had been too close.

If I'd been a minute later, we would have had a bigger

problem on our hands. Shogaur possessing an untrained sorcerer was terrifying enough, but with Kat as his host, he would have more power at his disposal than anyone was prepared to handle.

And Kat would have been lost to me. Alive but trapped. Impossible to save unless someone stronger than the demon lured him out without destroying her. Not something that had ever been done, as far as I knew.

My body shuddered on an exhale. I pulled her hand to my chest, relishing her heat and the fluttering pulse in her wrist. She murmured something incoherent, then relaxed into a deeper sleep. I pressed a kiss on her forehead, nestled her hand beside her, and left her to rest.

I didn't want to leave, but I appreciated that sitting around watching her sleep was no longer something I had the privilege of doing. I left her with a bucket for any possible nausea when she awoke and headed downstairs to where the others were coming through the front door.

"Is she all right?" Rhys asked on seeing me.

"She'll be fine. Shogaur tried to get to her, but she kept him out."

He heaved a sigh of relief and sagged against the door. Barrett nodded at me before passing to the stairs, carting the unconscious, bloody sorcerer over his shoulder.

A woman stood behind Rhys with one hip jutted out and

a perfectly manicured eyebrow arched in study. "Who are you and how did you get our sorceress away from Shogaur?"

I stared back at her and was impressed when she didn't cower under my gaze.

Rhys rolled his eyes. "Emrick, this is Poppy. Poppy, Emrick. He's Kat's… I don't know. Something. But he's a spirit-herder. Escorts magical souls to the afterlife."

"Right," she said, but her curiosity didn't fade. If anything, it became more intense.

An awkward minute passed, and Rhys broke it by clearing his throat and heading for the kitchen. "Anyone for coffee?"

"Oh! Me!" Poppy said. "I'll be right back."

She hurried away, and I followed Rhys into the kitchen. While he started on the coffee, I rounded the corner and leaned against the wall beside the patio door.

Rhys shot me a glance as he scooped the grounds into the filter. "You sure she's okay?"

"She's strong, Rhys, she'll be fine. The demon almost had her, but she power-surged her magic and gave him a full taste of it. He'll need time to recover."

The young Seer frowned. "So why did you make us leave? Wouldn't that have been the best time to go in and get rid of him?"

I tried not to smile at his eagerness to get his hands dirty. He reminded me of Katerina on her early hunts, the way she'd been when she first made up her mind to go after Shogaur. In her case, it had ended with her tied to a stake, drenched in oil, and on fire. Rhys didn't have the benefit of her healing ability.

"He still would have been too strong for you. It would take a whole coven of witches to restrain him and put him down, even weakened. Kat might have been enough to best him a while back, but now… well, we might need the coven anyway."

I hated to say anything that diminished her, but my bias for her skills wasn't enough to let me ignore the threat she faced.

"How come Shogaur almost got Kat when he's had the sorcerer for over a day?"

I rubbed my brow. "All I can think is that his familiarity with her made it easier to find her weaknesses. Shogaur's had a long time to sit and plan his revenge."

Heavy footsteps approached the kitchen. Barrett stalked in, his face stormy, and went straight to the cupboard where the chocolate-covered biscuits were hidden. Kat would have laughed at his break in character.

He dumped six of them on a plate and brought them to the kitchen table. "The sorcerer's awake. Nearly set me on fire, so I dropped him in the shower. He says he wants to leave. I told him to shut up and get clean, then we can talk."

A loud scream came from upstairs, followed by a shouted apology and a slamming door. More footsteps came down the stairs, then Poppy returned, cradling a long-haired, grey…

something in her arms.

"*Rowr*," the something said, revealing that at one point it had been a cat.

"Cuddles was a naughty little man and went exploring, didn't you, Cuddles? Did you get into the bathroom cabinet and pop out to give the man in the shower a scare? Yes, you did."

Barrett ground his teeth.

"The man's been tortured by a demon, and now you've traumatized him with your zombie cat?" Rhys asked.

"Cuddles isn't a zombie," Poppy argued. "He's just unalive."

I stared at the cat, now registering its lack of soul. The urge to touch the furry remains and transform it into the pile of dust it was supposed to be tickled my fingertips, but I kept my hands behind me. If Kat hadn't dealt with the cat, it meant she approved of it. Likely to annoy Barrett, which I didn't condone, but I wasn't about to undermine her authority in front of her team.

Poppy sat across the table from where I stood, settled the cat on her lap, and stared at me. "So, spirit-herder, what's your story? How are you and Kat involved?"

"Please don't ask," Barrett said. "I don't have the stomach to hear the whole thing again."

I laughed, and something in Poppy's expression changed from curiosity to awe. She didn't push the issue, just stared at me as the percolator did its job and Rhys set about readying the coffee. Barrett stood to help him gather the various extras, and soon enough the three of them sat at the table, Rhys at one end with an empty chair to his left and Poppy to his right. Barrett sat next to the empty chair.

"Going to join us, or just stand there looking menacing?" Rhys asked me as he nudged a cup towards the empty seat beside him.

I hesitated. I didn't know what drinking coffee with a table of mortals might cost me, but I doubted it would be much as long as I didn't offer to pass the milk. And Rhys was right. I did feel like a goon slouched against the wall.

Making sure my gloves were in place, I took the empty seat.

"What do we do about this demon, then?" Barrett asked.

I sipped my coffee and looked at Poppy, who was still staring at me.

Rhys cleared his throat. "Emrick mentioned we might need a coven. Do we have one of those lying around? Poppy? Do you have anyone?"

She blinked and seemed to come out of her daze. "Uh, no. Not since I was told if I had anything more to do with my old group, I was a dead witch walking."

Rhys licked his lips. "Right. Forgot about that. Barrett? Do you know anyone?"

"I know the people who hunt witches," the soldier reminded him.

"Right. So I guess… we'll wait for Kat?"

The silence was broken by more shuffling on the stairs, followed by the entrance of the sorcerer. He looked haggard. His shoulders were stooped, and he held his arms close to his body. His ill-fitting, borrowed clothes didn't do much to hide some of the wounds peeking out over the neck of his sweater, and I guessed the state of the rest of him wasn't much better. I didn't know what Kat hoped to get out of this guy, but I doubted it would be anything useful. His magic was strong and wild, but he was a broken man. I suspected the best we'd done was save him from a worse fate.

"Coffee?" Rhys asked him.

The man dropped into the chair at the other end of the table with a disdainful glance at the mangy cat, stuffed his hands in his lap, and kept his head bowed. Barrett slid a cup over despite the lack of answer, and I took another sip from mine.

Kat couldn't wake up soon enough.

16

Katerina

I woke up feeling hungover.

I lurched to the side of my bed and vomited everything left in my stomach into the blue bucket that had been conveniently placed there for me.

Once done, I rolled back onto my pillows, closed my eyes, and groaned.

Everything hurt. The effort of raising my arms was too much. Opening my eyes seemed impossible. Even processing the slightest sounds felt like a feat beyond my current capacity.

I hadn't been sick in, well, ever, but I imagined this was what it felt like to recover from the flu. Or maybe the plague.

My responsibilities and curiosity called to me, however, breaking through the aches and pains caused by lying completely still. Somewhere in this house was a sorcerer who had miraculously managed to keep Shogaur out of his head for the better part of twenty-four hours. Impressive considering I'd barely lasted ten minutes.

Focused only on meeting the stranger, I slid out of bed, carefully set my weight on my feet, and stood. The world wobbled around me. I closed my eyes to stop the wave of nausea that nearly forced out my stomach lining and stayed perfectly still until the weaving and bobbing stopped.

Only when I was sure I wasn't about to collapse did I head for the the bathroom. No more nausea. Good start. I took a quick minute to clean up and then, one foot in front of the other, I headed downstairs and followed the low hum of voices into the kitchen, where I swore my vision played tricks on me again.

It wasn't possible that Barrett and Rhys would be sitting on either side of Emrick while Poppy gaped at him from across the table. Nor was it possible that my ex-lover would be sitting so comfortably with these people, as though he'd always been there.

I was so intent on the back of his blond head, it took me a moment to notice the man sitting at the end of the table. His head was bowed, his black hair shielding his eyes. He wore a T-shirt I recognized as one of Rhys's and jeans that appeared slightly too short at the ankle and wide at the waist. Probably Barrett's. At least they'd given him a chance to shower. Though it made me wonder how long I'd been out.

"Hey, kitty Kat," Poppy said, tearing her eyes off Emrick to greet me. "Nice of you to join us."

"How long has it been?"

"About an hour," Barrett said without looking my way.

An hour, and I still felt like garbage that had gone through the trash compactor.

Still, it could have been worse. I could have been harbouring a demon that drained me of all my power and thoughts and emotions and used my body to carry out some ungodly deeds.

So yeah, I'd take the aches and pains.

I slipped into the chair beside the sorcerer and took in all his cleaned-up glory.

The force of his magic was intense. Now that he was conscious, he'd managed to tamp it down, but it surged off him in pulses that triggered mine, and the two of us ebbed back and forth.

If he noticed, he didn't respond to it. He kept his eyes down, but I caught the stiffness in his jaw and the hardness around his mouth. I wondered if he'd said anything since waking up but wasn't about to ask the others in front of him. That would be rude, and Maera had given me more than one lecture about rudeness.

"So. Sorcerer. Who are you?"

By the looks I got from everyone around the table except

Emrick, I still had some work to do on my social graces.

Slowly, the man raised his head. He kept his chin tilted down and glowered at me from under his heavy eyebrows with all the venom of a snake that wished it could wrap around me and strangle me. Friendly.

"I am not a sorcerer."

I snorted a laugh. "We're going the denial route on this? Your magic is about to erupt and blow the entire kitchen into the backyard, but okay, let's take a step backwards." I looked to Barrett. "He give you a name?" Barrett shook his head, and I turned back to the stranger. "Start there, then. What do we call you?"

"Nothing. I want you to leave me alone. I don't care who you are—I want nothing to do with any of this."

I opened my mouth to point out the irrelevance of his wishes when the memory of how we'd found him slapped me upside the head. Shogaur had kept him bound in an empty room. There had been no food that I'd seen, and obviously he hadn't been let out to relieve himself. I regretted that sometimes it took me a while to remember compassion and empathy weren't bad words.

With a deep breath, I met his raging glare and said, "Look, this demon isn't finished with you, no matter how much you want to be finished with him. We're your best shot at getting him off your back. You might not care who we are, you might not want to give us your name, but we're going to keep you safe and send Shogaur back to the hells he came from, all right?"

No change in the glower. After a few beats, I shrugged and stood up. "Barrett, make sure he stays in the house, but otherwise, Not-a-Sorcerer, make yourself at home. Rhys, Poppy, could you help with that?"

Rhys nodded, while Poppy looked skeptical. Barrett gave no sign he'd heard me, but that was fine. I knew he'd carry out the order even if he pretended I hadn't given it.

Maybe I should have pressed the guy harder, but something in his stonewalling told me I'd be wasting time and energy. He'd kept a demon out of his head—what chance did I have of getting in? And when it came down to it, we didn't need his cooperation to stop Shogaur. All we needed was for him not to get possessed. As long as the stranger stayed here and didn't set anything on fire, I could focus on the real priority: the fear-eating demon who had a bad habit of causing national crises.

"About the demon," I said to the others, "any thoughts?"

"Do you know any covens we might bring in to help us with the banishing ritual?" Rhys asked.

I raised my eyebrow, surprised to hear the suggestion coming from him. "I have a few contacts. The survivors from that shop in Toronto—what was it? Rune the Day? They owe me for getting them away from Mikhail, so they might be willing. Unless they're the ones who did the summoning, of course." I tilted my head. "Maybe that's the angle we need to approach here. Poppy, do you know how to track down the summoner? Based on the power remnants of the summoning spell or something?"

She pursed her lips. "Not off the top of my head, but let me think on it. The signature would be pretty potent. Especially bringing through a demon of Shogaur's level."

I looked to Barrett. "Can you reach out to Tony and see if their Hamilton people can keep their eye out? The storefront is toast, so Shogaur has to move somewhere. I want to know where."

He nodded and reached for his phone, and I turned to Rhys. "How about you? Any new visions?"

"Nothing. It's almost like something is blocking me. Is that possible?"

I frowned. "More likely it's a blanket effect. Because they're not from this realm, demons can project a frequency that offsets certain abilities. It's not like anyone knew what was coming the last time he was summoned."

Rhys's question awoke a deeper concern, one I couldn't put my finger on.

That worry piled on top of all the others I'd managed to suppress since waking, and the tunnel vision of an oncoming panic attack teased me. Not wanting to break down in here, I stepped away from the table.

"You guys keep brainstorming next steps. I need to clear my head."

I left the others in the kitchen and made my way into the living room. The warmth of all those bodies sitting around the table had set my stomach roiling again. My head throbbed, my legs wobbled, and I reached the armchair just in time to drop into it.

Rhys had asked if it was possible Shogaur knew about him. I didn't see how he could, but what if he did? Poppy said someone was after her—that was concerning enough, but what if…

The answer hit me like a punch to the gut.

You could have stayed safe on your island and let me have my fun.

Shogaur knew where I lived, which meant he had to know about Rhys and Maera. Had he been watching me? Or had someone else filled him in?

Fear gripped me as I thought of our house, isolated as it was in the middle of the woods. It was warded against any and all magic, which would keep Maera safe as long as she stayed inside, but for how long if Shogaur wanted in?

I pulled my phone out of my pocket and dialled Maera's number. She answered on the second ring.

"Kat? Is everything all right? You never call me." The edge in her voice confirmed her immediate worry—and also made me realize I should make a point of calling her more often.

"Probably? To keep it that way, I want you to stay inside

until you hear from me, okay?"

"Why? Kat, what's going on?"

"Just… trust me. If you see or hear anything unusual, call me straight away, but stay in the house. Maybe avoid the doors and windows."

"All right." Her uncertainty was palpable, but I knew she'd listen and stay put. She was beyond the impetuousness of youth, and she'd known me long enough to appreciate I wouldn't warn her needlessly. "Be careful, Kat. And watch out for Rhys."

We hung up, and I shoved my phone back in my pocket and bowed my head. Shogaur had come too close to possessing me, our one lead about what the demon was up to or who had summoned him wasn't talking, and now my home was on my enemy's radar.

We'd saved the sorcerer, but the clock was still ticking. How big of an explosion would we face when the timer ran out?

17

Katerina

IN THE EMPTY room—away from the overheated pot lights, the people, and the distraction of an unsolved mystery—the stress and strain of my encounter with Shogaur swept over me. A chill cut through my bones, and although I tried to summon my fire to fend it off, my magic was too drained to do anything more than sputter. I wrapped my arms around myself, pulled my knees to my chest, and bowed my head against them, but the shivers overpowered me.

"How are you holding up?"

I jumped at the sound of Emrick's voice. Of course I hadn't heard him come in. The man was literal air when he wanted to be.

I didn't bother raising my head. "Go away."

"You're freezing." His voice was closer now.

"It's my rage that you broke your promise and saved me. Again." Yes, Shogaur had surprised me with how strong he was, and yes, I nearly hadn't made it out of that empty shop, but what had Emrick given up by whisking me away from danger? His ability to grow facial hair? The memory of our first kiss? I couldn't bear thinking about it. My soul sang with love for him because he'd come for me, but he refused to understand that I would rather suffer for a thousand years than live without him for eternity.

"Don't be ridiculous. Sit up."

My body betrayed me and did as he asked, rising out of my slouch to look at him. He wore only a white T-shirt, having removed his sweater, and in a smooth motion, as though he'd done it a million times since yesterday, he popped it over my head and pulled it down my shoulders. His fingers brushed against my cheek, and I sucked in a silent breath at the electricity born from his touch—as powerful and thrilling as it always was. More so for how badly I longed to sink into it. That light touch was a taunting fix for a painful addiction. And that was with his gloves on.

The smell of loam and campfire and *him* filled my nose from the thick cotton blend, and my heart lurched with old pain. I wanted to tear the sweater off and throw it across the room, but again my body rebelled as my arms slid through the sleeves to hug the sweater closer around me.

"Thank you," I grumbled.

He chuckled, his silver eyes gleaming in the dim light. "You're welcome. Now do you want to tell me how you're doing? Shogaur got close on that one. You haven't kept up with your practice."

I scowled and shoved myself out of the armchair to pace the room. He was right, of course. "It's been eight hundred years. I cast him back to hell. How was I supposed to know he would pop back up?"

"He's not the only threat. Not the only demon. The exercises I taught you—"

"I know. I've let a lot of things drop. I don't need you pointing out my failures."

Exasperation crossed his fine features. "Kat, I'm not saying you failed. I'm worried about you. If I hadn't made it in time today…"

"I did get him out on my own."

"At what cost?" he pushed. "What if he'd recovered? You had no magic left. What if he came for you right now?"

I made another attempt to summon my power, and this time fire crackled over my palms. "See? Everything is back to normal. Bring on the demon battle."

Emrick pressed his lips together. His gaze was focused on the flames, but I doubted he was thinking anything positive about them.

A shadow spilled into the room from the doorway, and Emrick and I looked over to find Rhys poking his head in. His attention locked onto the fire in my hand. "Everything all right in here?"

"Perfectly," I said, shaking my magic clear. "We were just settling a debate."

Emrick's eyes trailed over to meet mine. "Were we?"

The words made sense to me—no, we were nowhere close to settling anything between us. None of our problems could be cleared up with a sweater and an expression of concern, but the look in his eyes nearly broke me. A deep, pleading look as though he wished they could be.

I hardened my heart against it, reminding myself yet again that my decision to send him away had been in both our interests. "Yes, the debate of whether I'm capable of dealing with this demon by myself. Answer—I am. I did it before, and I can do it again." A strange expression flickered across Emrick's face that I couldn't interpret, and my defences went up. "I'll admit, I wasn't prepared for how strong he's become. Next time, he won't take me by surprise." Not wanting my confidence to falter under Emrick's doubts, I turned to Rhys. "How's our guest?"

"In his room," Rhys said. "He got tired of Poppy playing Twenty Questions about his name."

"Get anywhere?"

"We know it's not Eugene. Very strong reaction to that one, and not in a good way."

"Fantastic. Eugene it is until he gives us something better. But you came in here for a reason. What's up?"

"Poppy wants to try that tracking spell again. For the demon this time. Tony got back to Barrett—they cleared the store after fire services finished with it, and there was no trace of him."

I wasn't sure what luck Poppy would have chasing a creature from the infernal realms, but if she wanted to give it a shot, who was I to dissuade her?

Emrick and I followed Rhys into the kitchen, and Poppy greeted us both with a smile. She scratched Cuddles between the ears, and the cat closed his eyes in undead bliss. "Lover's spat over, then? Nice sweater, kitty Kat."

Heat warmed my palm, and I crushed it down. *We need the witch. We need the witch.* If I had to remind myself of it a thousand times, I would refrain from firebombing her in the face.

"You think you can find out where Shogaur is?" I asked in lieu of an attack.

Poppy frowned, and I spotted the hesitation lurking in her dark eyes. "No guarantees. There are a lot of barriers in the way. But I got a sense of his energy in that shop, and I might be able to use it the same way we used the sorcerer's blood. At the very least, it could help narrow things down."

I nodded my encouragement. "Maybe I can help with that. He and I got nice and cozy today."

She shuddered. "Better you than me."

She set Cuddles on the chair beside hers and left the room to gather her supplies. The cat's yellow eyes fixed on me. I slid into the chair across from him, folded my hands on the table, and accepted his challenge.

"What are you doing now?" Barrett asked from where he stood leaning against the kitchen counter.

I lifted a hand to shush him. "No one with a soul can refuse a staring contest with a cat." I snorted a laugh. "Must be why you've never tried, Barrett."

Emrick's low laugh sounded behind me. "Are you sure you have the stamina? It's been a while."

"I will prevail."

My silent war with Cuddles stretched on, my determination growing with every watery eye. Cuddles didn't twitch, a sure sign of confidence. Or from being undead.

"All right, I think I have everything," Poppy said as she returned to the room. She bumped into Cuddles's chair as she passed, and the cat jumped down and padded out of the kitchen with a grumble.

I cursed. "I call a draw on that one, cat. Don't think you've won!"

He meowed from the living room, and Poppy nodded in understanding. "Staring contest? Well, at least it's proof you still have a soul."

I flashed Barrett a smug grin, then turned my attention to Poppy as she set up her map and tools.

Emrick settled into the chair beside me, the casualness of the gesture drawing me back to all the years he'd done the same as he, Adrian, and I had planned a hunt. He crossed his bare arms, showing off every thick rope of muscle from where his unnaturally pale forearms emerged from his heavy leather gloves to where his toned biceps disappeared under his T-shirt. My mouth watered, and I tore my gaze away. I refused to think about running my fingers under that shirt and over the planes of his stomach, the ridges of his pecs—

A groan nearly escaped me, but I swallowed it and sank deeper into his sweater. A mistake, of course, as another waft of his delicious scent shot sparks down my stomach and through my core.

Thankfully, Poppy finished her prep and sat down at the head of the table. "All right, here goes nothing. I make no promises that this won't turn around and bite us in the ass, so you better be ready if Shogaur makes a sudden appearance."

Barrett grunted and pushed away from the counter. "If I'm not needed here, I'll make myself scarce and keep an eye on our guest."

I waved my hand to shoo him away. "No one needs your grumpy mug around while we work."

"If you do summon anything, give me a shout."

I saluted, and he left the room. Rhys shook his head at us. "You two give me a headache. You can't really dislike each other as much as you pretend to."

"The day Barrett and I start getting along is the day you know the world has ended. Why would we give up the fun? One day, one of us will snap, and I suspect we're both taking bets on who it'll be."

Purple smoke drifted up from Poppy's mortar, and she edged it towards me. "All right, here we go. Think about his energy, how it made you feel, the nature of it. When you have a lock on it, give the bowl a tap, and I'll pour out the contents."

I set my fingers on the edge of the cool marble, closed my eyes, and took a deep breath.

Emrick's face floated behind my eyelids, and I frowned. That was not helpful. I knew where *he* was. Right at my elbow with those bare arms taunting me.

I dragged my thoughts to the empty store. To the room at the back. To the red eyes boring into me from the shadows. To the pressure building in my head as Shogaur tried to take over. The memory of the pain was nothing compared to the actual thing, but my magic reacted to the threat, fire flaring hot then burning out, replaced by a layer of ice that frosted my fingers and the surface beneath my hands.

"Breathe, Katerina," Emrick's soft voice flowed around me. "He's not here. Go beyond the fear."

I sank into the cadence of his words, letting them guide me past the danger to the remnant of the demon that stained my consciousness. Shogaur was a thorn in my side, but I had to give him props for forcing me to push my magical boundaries.

As soon as I had a grasp on him, I tapped the mortar, and Poppy poured her spell onto the map. The demon's red eyes followed me, flickering in my vision as I watched the powder shift and swirl before evaporating into a rough circle… exactly where we'd left him.

"Huh," Rhys said.

"Seriously," said Poppy. "That's anticlimactic."

I frowned at the map. "And strange considering Tony said they cleared the place."

"Think they missed something?" Rhys asked.

Poppy snorted. "I bet they didn't even check. Cowards."

Whatever my issues were with the witch hunters, I knew if they had a chance to get rid of a demon, they would take it. If the shop was empty, it had to mean our spell had gone wrong. Either our power wasn't strong enough to track him, or…

I couldn't deny my brain had rebelled against thinking too closely about his rancid energy.

Bracing myself for what I had to do, I heaved a sigh, straightened my shoulders, and held my hand over the map. With my eyes closed, I sank deeper into the memory of him, like a greasy hand smeared on a wall. His laugh in my ear, his voice in my head. The pain. The agony of fire licking at my skin as the wooden post against my back grew scalding hot. The sizzle of my hair as it caught, and the puffs of smoke wafting from the edges of my oil-soaked skirt. The way he'd closed his eyes and inhaled as though my terror were an anticipated entrée.

A duo of gasps told me something was happening, and I opened my eyes to watch the lines of Poppy's spell shift, the circle moving away from the downtown core towards the water and off the map in a northward direction.

My phone buzzed on the table. Rhys grabbed it after the third ring. I couldn't answer it myself, too lost in the horror of the past and the lurking dread that threatened to swallow me whole.

Emrick rested his hand on my thigh, but I barely felt it through my disassociation from the present. I had to remember I was here in Adrian's house, not tied to that stake.

Rhys put the phone on speaker. "Hello?"

"Rhys?" Maera's voice filled the room. "Is Kat with you?"

"Mum?"

I didn't blame him for being confused. I wouldn't have

recognized my housekeeper's voice, either. It was hushed, panicked.

"There's something outside the house. It hasn't tried to get in, but it's not leaving. And there are eyes. Red eyes. Staring at me from the woods."

I shoved the chair back with my legs as I rose to my feet. "That'll be our demon. We'll be there as soon as we can. Stay away from the windows. There are some protective spells on the doors that will buy us time if he tries to get in, and I'll be there in less than ten minutes."

The son of a bitch had fled the moment we'd taken the sorcerer away from him. I'd expected him to come after me, but no. Of course not. Instead, he was defiling my home.

Well, he could try, but he wouldn't succeed. I wasn't the same innocent child he'd met in the thirteenth century. I was a woman who was done with his shit, and he'd better be ready for the storm he'd set off.

18

Katerina

I STOOD NEXT to Emrick in the middle of the living room. The others were arrayed around us, awaiting orders.

"It's a six-hour drive to Manitoulin, and we can't afford to wait that long. Emrick and I will go ahead, and you guys can leave as soon as you're ready." I pulled my knife from the sheath on my belt.

Rhys turned his worried gaze on me. "Will mum be all right, do you think?"

"If Shogaur thinks to get past your mother, he'll be staring down the barrel of a whole different type of hell," I offered, needing him to keep hope. "Maera Byrne is terrifying."

"She is that."

Despite his agreement, the tension remained in his eyes,

and I pulled him in for a hug. "We'll be there in a minute. No matter what happens, he won't win, all right?"

Rhys replied with a brave smile as he nodded, and the confidence shining in his eyes—no less afraid for my promise—tightened my stomach. Screams from ages past filled my ears, and I crossed my fingers I would be able to see this through without history repeating itself.

I turned to the others. "Rhys is already keyed to the ward, but I need samples from Poppy and Eugene so you'll be able to get into the house."

Poppy grimaced but held out her hand. I sliced into the tip of her middle finger and collected the blood drop on a tissue. She stuck her finger into her mouth and mumbled something around it. When I stared at her, she popped her finger out. "What about Cuddles? He's technically a magical now."

I dropped my gaze to the cat prowling across the floor. "Grab him."

It took both of us and Rhys to hold him steady long enough to draw a smear of black, sludgy blood. Finally, I turned to Eugene. He'd come downstairs at Barrett's summons, but he did not look happy about it.

"Hand," I said.

"I don't need to get through your *ward.*" His hair fell over his dark, flashing eyes, and my magic rose to match his.

I breathed it back down. "You can't stay here. Shogaur will

track this place down, and no one will be here to watch out for you. If you want to avoid him, you need to go with the others, and the only way you'll get into my house is if I have a sample of your DNA."

He rumbled in his throat and spat on my cheek. "There."

I blinked and, with slow, deliberate movements, used the tissue to wipe it off. "Thank you."

"I think I would have rather given you spit, too," Poppy said, eying her bleeding finger.

"We'll be right behind you," Barrett assured me, and I nodded my thanks. I had no doubt he'd get them home safely and as quickly as he could. Hopefully, if I wasn't with them, Shogaur wouldn't give them a second thought.

I stepped back to Emrick's side, set my hand against his bare arm, and soaked in the buzz that rattled my heart at the contact. The temperature in the room dropped, and I saw Rhys shiver before the mist wrapped around us and the room faded from view.

In another moment, we stepped into my kitchen, and Maera let out a shriek at the sight of us. She slapped her hand to her chest and let out a string of curses I was relieved her son wasn't around to hear.

"Warn a woman before you pop out of the ether like that," she said when she caught her breath. "You nearly dropped me dead where I stand."

"Good thing you'd have died where you love to be," I said, earning a dark look. It was fine—she'd calm down. "Where are the eyes?"

Her hand trembled as she pointed out the floor-to-ceiling windows along the back of the living room. "They were by the trees. Near the beach. I turned off all the lights and stood there watching them, but they never moved. Didn't come any closer, but didn't disappear, either."

"He was messing with you. We refreshed the ward on the house not long ago, so you'll be safe inside. Try not to panic, all right? If he's out there, it's because he's feeding on your fear. Don't let him make it a feast."

She heaved a deep breath. "I feel better now that you're here. I'll bake some cookies while you deal with him. Let him feed on those."

I rested my hand on my housekeeper's shoulder. "Maera, please don't feed the demon cookies. We don't want him to stay."

She rolled her eyes and shrugged off my hand with a dry laugh, then headed into the kitchen to bake her worries away.

I turned to Emrick and crossed my arms. "What do you think? Scout the perimeter or guard the fort?"

"I'll scout, you guard. He can't do anything to me." He brushed my hair behind my ear, and I shivered under his touch. "Everything will be okay, Katerina."

I nodded, and he stepped into the mist. Once he was gone, I wandered over to the back windows and stared into the shadows. It was well after midnight, heading straight into the witching hour, and we had a demon on the property. This was shaping up to be a long night.

After keying the new DNA to my ward, I spent the rest of the early hours watching the property line. Despite the magical barrier, I felt uneasy. The magic had been woven to keep out all supernatural blood, meaning only mundanes could pass through it without their signature being added to the spell, but that didn't mean Shogaur couldn't fight his way in with enough patience and power. Once Poppy got here, I'd ask her to check for any weaknesses in the ward and bolster it if necessary. Almost everyone coming was a magical of some kind, except for Barrett. Unless his loathing for magic was a front for his well-hidden gargoyle blood. I would totally believe it if he turned out to be made of stone.

With Emrick and me in the house, Maera went to bed feeling much more confident she wouldn't be possessed or murdered in her sleep. I opted to crash on the couch for a few hours while time allowed. The others were due to arrive around six, and if we intended to make plans to go demon hunting, I wanted to have at least a few winks behind me.

Not that sleep came easily. At some point Emrick dropped into the armchair beside me. I hugged my arms closer around my body to prevent myself from reaching out and inviting him to join me, aching for the comfort of his strong, familiar body curled behind mine but knowing I would be walking the wrong way down the path I'd set if I gave in.

The next time I opened my eyes, the barest hint of dawn streamed through the windows. Voices reached me from the front of the house, and I rolled off the couch to open the door, expecting to find Barrett's red SUV parked outside.

Instead, I found three trucks and twelve people wearing matching fearful expressions.

Emrick fell into place beside me, his closeness prickling my skin, and I did my best to close myself off from him. My focus had to stay on the mob gathered on my lawn. My neighbours. People I was on good enough terms with to exchange nods when I passed them in town. I had a sneaking suspicion their impromptu visit had less to do with some sudden epiphany about me and far more to do with a certain demon stirring up trouble in my backyard.

I clenched my hands at my sides and pasted on a bright smile. "Doc Emerson? What brings you here so early?"

He was an older man in his mid-seventies. Probably should have retired a while ago, but up here in the quiet community, he said working kept him young. Not that anyone would know it to look at his balding pate and expanding belly, but he was always ready with a smile. Until today.

"We're here to tell you to leave," he said.

"Funny," I replied, proud of myself for maintaining a level voice. "I was about to ask the same of you. This is private property. If you could all get back in your cars and go home, I would appreciate it."

"You're not wanted here," Postal Worker Rita said. Her red hair was tied into a knot on the top of her head, and her pink-and-purple pyjama bottoms shouted *I was relaxing with my morning coffee and suddenly I'm part of a mob.*

I kept my breathing even as I stepped forward, wanting to ensure I put some distance between our guests and the vulnerable human in the house behind me.

"Doc, Rita, come on. You've known me for a few years—you know I'm not one to cause trouble. Whatever you've heard, whatever reason you came here, it's not true. I'm asking you to leave."

Doc reached into the back seat of the SUV, and Emrick sucked in a breath as the man drew out a rifle. I groaned and bowed my head.

"You've been here a few years, all right, but you've never become one of us, have you? Always kept to yourself. You, your housekeeper, and her boy. What are you hiding in there?"

Oh, nothing, just my immortality, my ability to set all your trucks on fire, and Rhys's ability to see into your futures.

I swallowed my response and squeezed my hands tighter to avoid any stray flames from licking free of my gloves.

Doc raised the rifle and aimed it at me, and I scanned the rest of the people who'd arrived with him. There was the butcher, the resident Reiki master, the yoga instructor… Manitoulin Island was full of artists and retirees. It was why I loved it. They weren't usually the violent types. Trust Shogaur to ruin that for me, too.

"I'm going to ask you one more time to leave," I said.

"Or you'll what?" Rita asked.

I didn't know. I wasn't about to blast them out of the sky or set them on fire. They'd been hit by demonic influence. They were afraid. If I didn't deescalate the situation, I'd have a riot on my hands.

"Or I'll call the cops and have you removed."

"Cops are right here, Miss Palon," came a voice from the back of the crowd, and I cursed under my breath at the sight of Officer Bruce Myers.

Of course Shogaur had visited the police station. Most likely, it had been his first stop. Now if I said anything remotely threatening, it would go on public record, and even if I got the rest of this mess sorted, my relationships here would be screwed.

This was why I hated living around people. I missed the days when my nearest neighbours were kilometres away.

The sound of tires crunching over snow reached me from down the road, and I held my breath as Barrett's SUV came into view. I spotted Rhys in the back seat, his expression twisted into confusion at the sight of the people he'd grown up with threatening me on my front porch.

Barrett pulled the car out of the way but left the engine idling as they stayed inside. I sent a quick prayer to the heavens for his practical thinking.

Rhys, unfortunately, let his emotions take over. He threw open the door and rushed towards us. "What's going on?"

Doc swung the rifle towards him. Before I could react, Emrick stepped forward. "Go home. All of you. Now."

His voice was laced with a deep, resonating power that made my insides tingle, and if it had an effect on me, it was nothing to how quickly the mob backed away.

It had cost Emrick to use that particular ability. I knew it had. Even as I watched, his skin became a smidge more translucent, the blue veins on his arm standing out in stark contrast. My heart clenched, and I reached to pull him back, but the damage had already been done.

As we watched, Doc, Rita, Officer Bruce, and all the others climbed into their cars. In another few minutes, they turned around in the narrow lane and disappeared from view.

"What was that?" Rhys asked, his eyes wide. "Why were they threatening you?"

"Because Shogaur convinced them it would be a great idea." My shoulders drooped. "He dug into their minds, drew out the tiny suspicions they have about me and turned me into a villain. If he gets his hooks in any deeper, the next time they come it'll be with a can of kerosene and a match, and it'll take more than Death staring them in the eye to chase them off."

Rhys turned to watch the fleeing vehicles. "You can't be serious. They don't really want us dead, do they?"

"Not in any conscious way, no, but they're not ruled by reason right now. This is what fear demons do. They burrow into people's heads, make them see the worst. Right now, our neighbours think I'm the bogeyman and you and Maera are my minions. If we stay here, someone is going to wind up dead."

Rhys shivered. "I knew this demon was bad news, but to turn friends on each other like that?"

I snorted. "All you need to do is look through history to see that changing the minds of a few people in an isolated community is child's play for him and his kind. Once he gets started, that mob will get bigger. If he wants us out of the way, he'll aim them at us like a weapon and we'll have a real battle on our hands."

19

Katerina

WITH THE INITIAL panic over, Emrick stepped into the afterlife to avoid the crowd, and I ushered everyone into the house. The hullabaloo outside had woken Maera, so she was up and ready to fuss over everyone as they came in.

"I'll get coffee on. There's cereal in the cupboard, or I can make pancakes. Rhys, you need to brush your hair, you look like a slob. James, I'm so glad you're here. Definitely making pancakes. And who is this?"

She landed her warmest smile on Poppy and the sorcerer. It was one of the great things about my housekeeper. She was never thrown by unexpected guests. If they came with me willingly, she assumed they were friends and treated them as such.

"I'm Poppy. Necromancer, kitty Kat's indentured servant,

whatever you want to call me."

Maera threw her arms around Poppy's neck. "You're the witch who gave us the sleeping potion recipe that probably saved my son's life."

Poppy's eyes flared wide, but her surprise only lasted a moment before she returned Maera's hug with extra flair. "Oh, I like you."

"And this is Eugene," I said, gesturing to the surly extra.

"Not my name," he grumbled.

"It's not," I agreed. "We don't know his name. He's the sorcerer you saw on TV who was blowing up Hamilton's underground."

Maera's smile flickered, but she kept it firmly in place as she extended her hand. "Welcome, Eu—um. Welcome. Come in, come in, I'll make sure you all have somewhere to sleep with clean sheets and towels. James, you know where you're staying. If you don't mind, you can bunk with… the other young man. What was all that going on outside?"

I left the others to explain the situation while Barrett and I went to the car to bring in the suitcases the others had left behind. Fetching and carrying wasn't usually my area, but the foyer had become loud and busy, and this early in the morning, before coffee, it was too much.

"How was the drive up?" I asked as I reached for Poppy's bag.

"Uneventful." He frowned. "The sorcerer nearly lit my seat on fire."

"Oops."

"You need to be careful with him, Kat. He's angry, he's afraid, and he's a walking powder keg. Any push on his emotions and he's liable to go off."

"I know. It's why I want him with us. If Shogaur gets him, imagine the damage he could cause. But by the sounds of it, he doesn't want to learn how to control it."

Barrett raised an eyebrow. "Taunting him is probably not the best way to win his trust."

I jutted my hip. "You know I can be sweet and welcoming."

"With people who hate magic?"

"You and I get by."

"I don't have the ability to set you on fire."

I pursed my lips and bobbed my head to acknowledge his point, earning me what I swore was a passing glint of amusement on his face. But I must have imagined it. "I'll take your advice into consideration. We don't have time to treat him with kid gloves, but I don't have the insurance coverage to browbeat him. Maybe Maera will have some luck wearing down those furrows."

We started back towards the house, and I nearly stumbled when the bag in my hand let out a low "*Mrow.*"

"Proserpine!" I stomped up the steps and into the foyer.

"Did you pack Cuddles in your suitcase?"

I dropped the bag, unzipped it, and stared down at the grey cat, who was contentedly wrapped up in an old towel.

Maera shrieked. "What is that?"

"That's my cat," Poppy said with a smile.

"That is *not* a cat," Maera replied.

"He is. He's just…"

"Resurrected," I finished, giving Cuddles a scratch on the head before he pulled back his lips to hiss at me.

Maera blinked, swallowed, and turned away. "Pancakes. I'll get started on the pancakes."

Poppy swept the cat into her arms and gently snuggled him against her chest. "Don't worry, Cuddles, she'll warm up to you. How could anyone not love your little face?" Her perfect eyebrows shot up. "Oh! Kitty Kat, I just remembered—you know that challenge you gave me? About tracking the summoner? I think I found someone who can help us. Her name is Murisa. She lives out in Oakville. I only know her by reputation, but her focus is all about summoning and banishing circles. No one knows demons like she does."

I tugged on my glove to smooth out a crease. "In what sense?"

She rolled her eyes. "She's not a summoner. Well, not that I know of, anyway. But hey, couldn't hurt to ask her yourself. Want me to set something up, see what she can do?"

"Do it. We don't have time for me to be sanctimonious."

Poppy coughed something that might have been, "for a change," but I ignored her and left her to make her calls.

An hour later, the table was covered in empty, syrup-spattered plates. Barrett looked almost blissful in his post-pancake haze, and even Eugene had consumed his weight in carbs.

I'd refrained from partaking, unable to convince myself to squeeze into the space between Rhys and Eugene, feeling too boxed in by the threats weighing down on me. Emrick had returned and stood apart from everyone as well, his gloved hands in his pockets, keeping his distance to avoid making contact. His attention was trained outside, watching the shadows beyond the trees as the sun made its appearance over the horizon.

"I can't believe old Doc Emerson has it in him," Maera said, shaking her head as she rose to clear away the dishes. "Do you really think we should leave, Kat? Where would we go? Aunt Madge might take us, I guess..."

Her aunt lived in Vancouver and hadn't spoken to the family in fifteen years, but hey, miracles could happen.

But my opinion on the matter had changed once I'd consumed the requisite amount of caffeine for daily survival.

"I think you should stay here. This house is protected, and no matter where you go, Shogaur will try to split my attention. At least here, I can keep an eye on everyone."

"I never thought I'd need protecting from Rita," Rhys mumbled.

"That being said," I continued, "Barrett, can you put your skills to use and lay some traps along the property line? We may not be able to ward off humans, but that doesn't mean we can't make it a pain in the ass for them to reach the house."

He wiped his mouth with his serviette and pushed himself to his feet. "I'm on it."

"Poppy, any luck getting in touch with Murisa?"

The witch tapped her bright pink nails on the table. "She wants to set up a call. Says she should be ready around eight o'clock."

"Great. We'll meet downstairs in the rec room, out of Maera's hair."

"Thank you!" Maera called from the counter where she'd already pulled out the ingredients for her next round of stress baking. Scones, by the look of it.

"Do you want to sit in on the call with Murisa?" I asked Rhys.

He shifted in his seat. "I actually thought I'd take a stab at triggering another vision. If something's blocking my second sight from Seeing Shogaur directly, maybe I can See around him? If that makes sense?"

Pride surged through me that he had come so far in the past few months. He'd gone from being afraid of his visions, to not knowing what to do with them, and had finally reached a place where he was learning to control them. My young protégé, who had gone so long with no defined purpose, was finally coming into his own.

"That's a great idea," I said. "But wait for Barrett to come back, all right? I'd rather you're not by yourself when something kicks off."

He grinned at my assumption that he'd be successful, but I had no doubts.

Finally, I turned to Eugene, but he gave me a disgusted look and walked away, heading downstairs to his guest room. Barrett's advice came back to me, nudging me to go have a gentle word with him, but for now I let it be.

"What'll we do until eight?" Poppy asked as she helped Maera clear the table. "I think, kitty Kat, you and me should sit down with mimosas, and you can fill me in on the deal between you and this gorgeous hunk of man-meat."

She reached for Emrick's arm where he stood by the window, and I lurched forward, shouting, "No!" as I grabbed her fingers a hairsbreadth away from her death.

My heart pounded in my chest at what had almost happened, and Emrick turned to stare, stunned. He hadn't realized she was so close or he would have moved faster than I had.

"Uh, okay, what the fuck?" Poppy demanded as she jerked her arm away. I didn't resist her, the danger over. "I didn't take you for such a jealous bitch."

I pulled off Emrick's sweater—my skin immediately turning chill with the missing warmth—and tossed it at him. He pulled it over his head to cover his bare skin. Anger rushed through my veins, but it was dampened by my relief that I hadn't just watched her turn to dust in front of me.

"It's not jealousy, it's self-preservation," I snapped. "I might need your help to kill Shogaur, and if you'd touched him, you'd be dead."

Poppy scoffed. "Never tell me age leads to improved self-control."

"Not because of her. Because of me," Emrick said, more gentle than I was in the mood to be. "One touch of my skin and your cells would have jerked forward in time."

The witch blanched. "How far forward?" she asked, though she had to know the answer.

"As far as it took to decompose your body to earth in a breath." I struggled to slow my racing heartbeat. "He's Death, Poppy."

Terror flickered through her eyes at what she'd almost done—snuffed out her young years in a blink before she had any idea what was happening. Fear morphed into confusion as she looked between Emrick and me.

"But you touched him," she said. "You're still here."

"Yes, well." I looked at Emrick, falling into the swirl of his endless moonlight gaze and the memories of how differently I used to touch him. Not a warning hand on the arm or a thoughtless brush of my fingers. My fingertips had known every inch of him. "He's my Death, isn't he?" I fought the pain that stabbed through my chest and ignored the way so many pairs of eyes bored into me. "Excuse me."

Needing a moment to compose myself, I headed to my room.

I pulled off my T-shirt and yoga pants and tossed them into the hamper, then grabbed a fresh outfit. Identical black pants, because why change perfection, with a forest-green sweater that hugged my neck and fell on a diagonal from left hip to right knee.

I showered, dressed, and was in the process of bundling my black hair into a loose knot on the top of my head when a gentle knock sounded on the door. A familiar knock that set my insides fluttering.

When I didn't order him away, Emrick came in and closed the door behind him. I watched in the reflection as he took a few hesitant steps towards me. In another time, he would have rested his hands on my shoulders, slid his thumbs up the sides of my neck and into my hair. Within minutes, all the effort I'd put into making myself presentable would have been undone, and we would have been naked in bed, grasping at each other as though to let go would be to unmoor ourselves in the ether of the universe. Sweat-slicked skin and ragged breaths, fingernails digging into muscle. The rest of the world forgotten.

Instead, here we were. Him keeping a respectful distance, me doing my best to put those years behind me.

"I did another tour around the house. No sign of Shogaur," he said. "I got the sense he's still around, but he's keeping his distance. If everyone stays within the ward, you'll be safe. Barrett's finished with his traps. He came in a few minutes ago."

"Thank you."

He nodded and shoved his hands in his pockets. Our eyes met in the mirror, and the silence extended between us until I wrenched myself back to the present. "It's almost eight. I should get downstairs to this meeting with Murisa. I'm wondering what our chances are that her spell leads us to Mikhail's patron."

"The mysterious Abigail."

"I need to find out who she is. I have a suspicion my life is only going to get more complicated the longer she's around."

"You will. Nothing evades you for long when you put your mind to it."

Nothing except Emrick's little problem of fading into nothingness with every decision he made outside the afterlife. But I didn't bother to say it. He would already be thinking it.

I rose from my vanity table and walked past him, heading back into the living room. Being alone with him was too difficult. I'd gone to my room for space, but I felt like I couldn't breathe. At least in the kitchen, there were cookies.

Maera puttered around her domain, scrubbing one pot while another simmered on the stove with the mouth-watering scent of garam masala and curry leaves.

"Everyone is downstairs?" I asked her.

"They are. Barrett headed straight down to sit with Rhys. Thank you for asking him to wait."

"Of course."

Maera glanced at me over her shoulder. "Is this demon really going to try to stir the country into some national witch hunt?"

"That's how he usually plays it," Emrick said. "I can only guess how much easier it'll be for him this time with the accessibility of social media. He could spread his influence across the entire continent if he wanted. The entire world."

"Then why hasn't he? What is he waiting for?"

I rubbed my brow. "A face."

"Excuse me?" Maera asked.

"He needs to possess someone before he takes to the cameras. In his current form, he might slip into the minds of a few people before they realize what they're looking at. Get him on camera and he'd start a panic against himself, which would slow down his plans. If he can step into a host body and shield himself from the world, he'll gain far greater traction."

Maera's throat bobbed with a hard swallow. "That's what he was trying to do with the sorcerer, wasn't it?"

I nodded.

"Does the host have to be magical?"

"The host lasts longer if they carry magic," Emrick explained. "Mundane bodies give out too quickly. Kat and Eugene are sorcerers—they would have more than enough strength to host him indefinitely."

I shuddered at the idea, and the pain in my head returned as I remembered Shogaur's latest attempt to invade my mind. I hated that he was somewhere near my home. Ward or not, I didn't trust him not to hurt us. Whoever had summoned him, I needed to know their plan.

I braced myself and turned to Emrick. His silver eyes were intent on me, and goosebumps rose over my arms, a small fire kindling in my lower belly. "I know you just came back, but would you mind doing another patrol?"

"Of course." Two simple words, spoken with the intensity of an eternal promise, and then he was gone, and I was left craving his return.

Damn the man.

20

Katerina

MURISA BHATT WAS not what I expected.

As she stared out from the laptop screen, she looked to be just out of high school, though Poppy assured me she was old enough to drink—a difference of a whole year in most provinces. For another, she looked like someone who made a living decorating cakes or scrapbooking. Not nearly as beribboned as Cyn the Tea Boutique lady, but equally sunshiney and seemingly happy in her own skin.

She was a stunning young woman with a warm bronze complexion and dark eyes. Her thick black hair was smoothed and styled in a braid that draped over her left shoulder and held out of her face by a teal cloth headband. Golden leaf earrings dangled from her earlobes, while a rose-shaped pendant draped from a teal ribbon around her throat.

Behind her, however, were rows of heavy, leather-bound books I could only assume were grimoires and magical reference tomes, and something smoky bubbled on the table against the wall to her left.

"Demons, huh?" she said, her bright smile conflicting with the serious subject matter. "Always makes for a good day. And you want me to track a summoner? I've never done it before, but it sounds fun! I'm always down for a challenge. First off, do you know what we're dealing with?"

"Fear demon," I said. "Shogaur, specifically."

Murisa blanched, her smile fading. "You're serious?"

"Unfortunately," Poppy said from where she sat on the couch beside me. "You should see this son of a bitch. Red eyes. Feels… mucky."

"I'd guess so. That is a serious heavyweight."

Her recognition of both his name and the terrifying significance of his presence in this realm reassured me that we dealt with a professional. Now I had to hope she could help us get rid of him.

"I've only read the stories, of course," she said, "but he and his ilk are mentioned in almost every demonology textbook I own as examples of demons to leave alone. He hasn't been summoned in something like… five hundred years?"

"Eight hundred," I said.

She frowned. "Are you sure?"

"Pretty sure." My skin crawled, and I tamped down the memories. She didn't need to know the details.

"Anyway," she continued, "we might be able to trace whoever summoned him, but we can't pull the information out of thin air. It'll take samples. Rituals. The demon's blood would be incredibly helpful, but the odds are probably slim that we could get something like that?"

She sounded so hopeful I felt bad about letting her down. Emrick had been in too much of a rush getting me away from Shogaur to think of swiping the blood I'd spilled in the empty shop.

"He tried to possess me. Would that work?"

Murisa pursed her lips. "It *might* lead us to the demon. If he's near the summoner, it could work."

Or it might be a big waste of time.

"What about something the summoner might have come in contact with?" she suggested. "A place, maybe?"

There was the store, but what remained of it was hours away in Hamilton. Luckily, we had something—someone— much easier to access. I thought of the cuts all over Eugene's body, damage Shogaur wouldn't have bothered to cause but a human might have if they were trying to coerce him into accepting the demon's offer.

"We have someone who fits that description. He might be

a bit touchy, though. I think they tortured him."

Murisa blinked. I half-expected her to end the call, but instead her features brightened with excitement, and she just about danced in her seat. "That would be perfect! Obviously not for the person they tortured, but yes, absolutely. I can tap into their energy and see if I can follow it to its source. Probably. I can try, anyway. Again, never done this before."

I nodded and rose to my feet, taking the laptop with me. Poppy stood and followed me, peering over my shoulder at the woman on the screen.

"How long do you think it'll take?" I asked.

"It won't be quick. It'll depend on how strong the energy signature is around this person and if I'm able to amplify it from this distance."

"I might be able to help with that," Poppy said.

"Excellent."

The two women exchanged a glance through the screen, and I rolled my eyes skywards. They were of the same ilk, these two. Witches who enjoyed dabbling in fields outside the acceptable standard for the sake of discovery.

That's how blood spells were discovered, ladies.

But I wasn't about to pooh-pooh their enthusiasm when their questionable moral foundations could be exactly what we needed to get rid of Shogaur.

I knocked on Eugene's door, and when he didn't answer, I

opened it anyway.

"Hey, what the hell?" he asked as he bounded off the bed to his feet. He was half-dressed, as though he were getting ready to hop in the shower, and I had a moment to take in the red, healing slices across his muscular torso before he pulled his ill-fitting sweater back on. His black hair swept across his brow, his eyes burning coals beneath his heavy eyebrows.

"We need you." I set the laptop on the bed and gestured for him to sit down. "Eugene, Murisa. Murisa, Eugene."

"That's *not* my name!"

"What is your name?" Murisa asked.

He flushed and pressed his lips together.

"We don't know," I answered for him. "He refuses to tell us. But he's an untrained sorcerer, so please try not to piss him off. He has a habit of setting fire to his surroundings."

I swear his jaw popped at the force with which he clenched his teeth.

"All Murisa needs from you is, well, to tap into the summoner's energy that's probably still hanging around you, all right? No big deal."

His eyes bugged out of his head. "What? No. Leave me alone. Get out of my room."

I crossed my arms. "You won't need to do anything other than sit there and glare. You have the easiest job of everyone." At the panic in his eyes, I realized belatedly that I might have come at this the wrong way. I hated when Barrett was right. Drawing in a deep breath to find my patience, I dropped my arms to my sides. "Poppy, can you give us a minute, please?"

"What? But—"

"Out."

She huffed and left the room, slamming the door behind her.

"Murisa, give us a sec." I leaned over, muted the mic on the computer, and turned the screen so it faced away from us.

Eugene sagged onto the side of the bed and buried his face in his hands. "I don't understand why you won't leave me alone. I told you I don't want to be involved in this."

I leaned against the wall across from him and folded my hands behind my back, aiming for an open posture. "Are you the one who summoned him? Is that why you're ashamed to talk about your magic?"

"No."

"Do you know who did summon him?"

"No."

With each negative, his anger rose, and the warning glow around his hands grew brighter. I swallowed my frustration. Lashing out would escalate matters and increase the odds that I would need to rebuild my house. "The longer you withhold information from us, the more people are going to die. That blood will be on your hands, not ours."

I started towards the door when he shouted, "I don't remember, all right?"

Slowly, I turned around. "Excuse me?"

His face was flushed, his breathing rapid. I wasn't sure if he was about to incinerate me or burst into tears. "I don't remember anything. Not my name, not where I'm from. I don't know anything about any fucking demon except I woke up in that room, bleeding. A woman was there, her face covered in some costume cloak, and this monster with red eyes was trying to convince me to let him into my head. I got away and made it halfway across town before he caught up with me, and then—I don't even fucking know. Fire started shooting out of the sewers. My skin felt like it was about to burn off. And then he had me again, and again he was trying to climb inside my head."

He tapped his temple. "Do you know what it feels like to have someone crawling around in there? Telling you what you want? Promising to make all the pain go away? You say I'm a sorcerer, but I have no idea what that fucking means. I have *magic?* What am I? Some video game character? I don't believe this is fucking real, let alone know what to do with it."

He fell silent. My jaw had dropped, and I stared at him in stunned silence. With an effort, I clamped my mouth shut and took a few slow steps towards him. His breaths came quickly, and his entire body trembled. I was overwhelmed with the desire to hug him, but I kept my distance.

"In that case, I'm sorry. More than you know. There's a lot to explain, and a lot of work to do, but if you put a bit of faith in us, we can try to help you remember. At the very least, we'll keep the demon from trying anything else on you, all right?"

After a moment, he nodded, the barest of gestures, but it was enough to remove another pound of tension from my shoulders.

I sat beside him. "Whether you like it or not, you are involved. We don't know how this woman knew about your latent power, but she must have targeted you because of it. You can run kicking and screaming if you want, but if Shogaur wants you, he will track you down. Do you believe you can stand against him on your own?"

A shudder ran through him, so intense it shook the bed, and he wrapped his arms around his middle. "No." It came out breathless, terrified, and my heart melted towards him a fraction.

"I don't want to push you into anything," I said. "I know how frustrating it is for people to tell you what you need to do when it goes against your marrow to do it. But if you want to save yourself, I'm asking for your help. You just need to sit here and let Poppy and Murisa do their thing. No harm will come to you."

He raised his head, and his eyes shone with doubt. "You can promise that?"

I opened my mouth to do exactly that, then shook my head. "I wish I could, but until Shogaur is back in hell, I can't. Which is all the more reason for us to tap into every available resource to make that happen. For everyone's sake."

His nostrils flared, and for a moment I thought he would refuse again. Maybe push me away and run out of the room. Maybe throw a fireball at my chest. Then his shoulders drooped, and he nodded. "Fine. But I'm not leaving this house until he's gone for good."

"That would probably be best."

After retrieving the laptop and bringing Murisa back into the conversation, I opened the door for Poppy to come in.

"All right," Murisa said. "If anyone needs to pee, this is the time. Once we start, we shouldn't stop until we get what we need. It's possible the summoner will detect the tracking spell and block us if we delay."

Eugene sent me a look, and I nodded my encouragement. This was the best way forward.

"Kat?" Maera called from upstairs, her voice filled with uncertainty. "You'd better hurry up here. Looks like the mob's come back."

21

Katerina

I HURRIED UPSTAIRS to the front of the house and stared through the window as a truck tore down the driveway. The tires were shredded from Barrett's traps, but the vehicle kept moving until it stopped outside the house. A dozen people poured out of the cab and the bed.

"Get out here, Palon!" Officer Myers shouted, gun already in his hands. "We're here to take you in."

It seemed our time was up.

Emrick stepped out of the afterlife and pulled me down a second before the window shattered and glass rained over my head. Maera screamed and ducked behind the dining table to protect herself from any flying projectiles.

"Kat, what do we do?" she hissed at full volume from

across the room.

It was a good question. I didn't want to stay on the floor under a heap of broken window while people stormed my house. I also couldn't let them interrupt whatever was going on downstairs. We needed Murisa to track the summoner, which meant she had to finish her ritual.

That left me to deal with these trespassers.

Angry and inconvenienced, I slipped my arm out of Emrick's grasp and rose to my feet, shaking out the sparkling shards that had gotten stuck in my hair.

"Go downstairs and stay away from the windows," I said to Maera. "If you see anyone going around back, shout."

Maera stayed in a crouch as she hurried across the kitchen and down the stairs to the rec room. Once she was gone, I braced myself and headed for the front door. I'd made it less than five steps before Emrick took my arm again.

"What are you going to do?" he asked.

I lifted my eyes to his silver gaze and held his stare, hoping that somewhere in the pause between my looking at him and opening my mouth, I would find the answer to that question. When I didn't, I clenched my teeth and once again pulled my arm free.

I'd figure it out when I got outside. This wasn't my first mob.

With a final breath, I pulled open the door and stepped

onto the front porch. Officer Myers's gun swung my way, along with a few hunting rifles that appeared in my neighbours' hands. I ignored the threat. A gunshot would injure me as much as the next human, but unless they were really lucky, it wouldn't kill me.

"I asked you to stay off my property."

"And we told *you* to get off our island," shouted elderly little Mrs. McCreary from down the road. "You're a menace, bringing nothing but trouble. Hikers going missing. Drownings. Rabid animals. You're a blight on our home, and it's time to show yourself out—or we'll make it happen."

Officer Myers nodded. "I've got a cell at the station with your name on it, and if you don't come willingly, I can make sure you never leave it."

"Would you mind repeating that? I'm sure your superiors would be interested in hearing you threaten bodily harm."

Was taunting them the best way to get us out of this predicament? Probably not on the list of Top 10s, no, but my mouth wouldn't stop flapping as my brain worked to come up with something more effective.

Shogaur had gotten into their heads. The only way to get him out was to kill the demon. The demon was nowhere in sight, which wasn't an insignificant obstacle, but if I didn't get them away from here, there would be violence.

"This is your last warning, officer." I clenched my hands at my sides.

I wasn't used to dealing with mundanes in conflict. I couldn't summon my magic. Couldn't wrap them in ice or consume them in a fireball. I would have to use my wits, and right now they felt as rusty and out of reach as my magic had a few months ago.

"This is yours, Palon."

I rolled my eyes and pulled my phone out of my bra—the only storage space I had in my pocketless outfit. With a few flicks of my thumb, I brought up the camera and hit record. "Say hi, guys! You're live! Doc, care to wave? I've got over a million followers watching you point that gun at me right now."

A total lie, of course. I didn't do social media. I didn't even know if the words coming out of my mouth were correct— they just sounded like something I'd heard during Rhys's phone scrolling.

For the first time, doubt crept into my neighbours' eyes. A few of them lowered their weapons, the aim of a few others wobbled. Satisfaction gave me a warm squeeze. Their falsified fear of me might be strong, but rational thought and self-preservation existed somewhere beneath it. Shogaur hadn't accounted for the power of the internet.

I didn't have much time to gloat, however. Officer Myers had only just dropped his aggressive stance when a cry from downstairs rattled through my marrow.

"Rhys, stop!" Meara shout. "Where are you going?"

I stepped backwards to go find out what the hell was happening, but the moment I moved, the mob moved with me. I froze, trapped between whatever Rhys had done and needing to prevent this crowd from ambushing my home.

Emrick slipped to my side, grabbed the phone out of my hand, and took my place. "I'll hold them back. You go."

Despite knowing what it would cost him, I didn't hesitate. I turned on my heel and ran downstairs only to find the rec room empty and the back door open.

Where the hell had everyone gone?

The fear that gripped me also grabbed hold of my legs, increasing my pace as I tore through the trees towards the snow-covered beach.

The unnerving silence of the scene brought me to an abrupt stop.

Barrett, Rhys, and Maera stood on the edge of the water. Not panicking, not battling any embodiment of evil. Just standing. Staring at each other. Outside the ward.

I scanned the area for any sign of Shogaur, but all was quiet. What the hell had I missed?

"Guys, come back inside the house," I called, inching towards them and watching the trees, the bank. "It's not safe out here."

The faintest stench of rot hit me, and I wrinkled my nose

to block it out as my heart galloped against my ribs. I might not be able to see him, but the demon was close. "Barrett, what are you thinking? Get back here."

He didn't even turn to look at me, his entire body tense.

I closed the rest of the distance between us, the alarm bells in my head shrieking as the reek of sulphur grew stronger. We had moments before Shogaur appeared. What were they waiting for?

A passing thought struck me that Rhys was caught in a vision. Were they waiting for him to finish before they dragged him back? If so, that was a huge risk to take for a few glimpses of the future.

Now that I was closer, I saw that not all was as calm and quiet as I'd believed it to be. Tears ran in rivulets down Maera's cheeks, and terror filled her green eyes. Barrett's jaw was tight, the line of his mouth grim, and his brow furrowed. He'd rested his hands on the hilts of his blades, but he hadn't drawn them. Maera's hand on his arm had stopped him.

They both stared at Rhys.

Dread wrapped around my insides, and I turned slowly to face him. As I did, my fear transformed into an overpowering, breath-stealing horror.

He was smiling—the bright, victorious smile he saved for the greatest moments of his life. Beating a difficult video game boss. Watching an internet person do something ridiculous.

Getting permission to accompany me on a wyvern hunt.

But his eyes weren't happy. They were triumphant. And they weren't green or white but a deep blood-red.

"Everything is wonderful, Katerina," he said, and it was his voice but not. It was a voice that ran its sharp edges down my spine and tore my world in half. "I'm so glad you joined us."

22

Emrick

THE LAST OF the mob disappeared among the trees minutes after Kat left the porch. I hadn't done anything beyond stand there with her phone, and they'd cleared out as though they'd been chased away. The terror in their eyes made my skin crawl—not only because of what they might have imagined was chasing them, but because of what their abrupt exodus might mean for the people inside.

Free from my promise to protect the house, I stepped through the mist in my hurry to get to Kat.

I returned to the world just in time to watch a red-eyed Rhys extend his hand towards her. My stomach dropped, and without giving myself time to think, I pulled her through the mist and out of his reach. We popped up a few feet away. For half a breath, my vision went murky and I experienced an odd sensation, like something inside me had gone numb.

Everything returned to normal as Rhys came at me, hands out. At the last moment, he realized his error, turned on his heel and fled. The shadows of the trees consumed him until all sign of his red hair was gone.

Kat launched herself after him, but I grabbed her shoulder and jerked her back. Her eyes were blue fire when she turned on me, but I didn't back down. "You think he'll be satisfied with Rhys? If you give him the smallest chance, he'll kill the kid and take you."

I refused to let her go until my words sank in. I wouldn't let her take that risk on herself, no matter what it cost her to watch him flee.

In the breaths that passed, I considered the strange feeling I'd had, and a coil of unease wrapped around my heart. A quick assessment showed nothing of me missing that I noticed, but that didn't mean nothing had been traded for my decision to save Kat. I'd lost enough fragments of myself over the centuries but it had been a long time since I *felt* it happen. Did that mean the pieces I traded were getting larger? More significant? Or was the problem that I had so few pieces left to give that they were becoming more obvious.

I couldn't worry about it just yet, not while the woman I loved was on the verge of breaking down in my arms, but I couldn't afford to disregard it, either.

It took a few breaths, but Kat's body sagged with defeat as she accepted I was right. She nodded, and I released her, ready to go after her if this was a feint.

Tears sprang into her eyes, and she turned to Maera. "I am so sorry. I made you a promise, and I let you down. Again. But we'll get him back. I won't stop until we do."

Maera stared in the direction Rhys had gone, her face slack and her hand half-raised as though pleading with her son to come home. I worried what it would do to her if he never did. I sympathized with the woman. I liked Rhys. He was a good kid—kind, caring, doing his best to find his way. He didn't deserve this.

But I had no idea how Kat thought we could save him. In all my years, I'd only seen a handful of cases where the host survived this kind of possession. The only way to banish the demon was to draw his blood. The only way to draw his blood was to get him out of his host. And rarely did a demon abandon his host for any reason other than the body's death.

Kat knew that as well as I did.

When Maera finally let her hand drop, Kat stepped towards her, but her housekeeper turned her back and shambled towards the house.

I longed to put my arms around Kat and assure her none of this was her fault, but in a flash, her grief disappeared and she whipped towards Barrett.

"What the hell just happened? I told you to stay inside and keep an eye on him. Why the *fuck* are any of you beyond the ward?"

He flexed his jaw, and a spark of fury flared in his eyes. But I caught the flicker of remorse in there as well, which he quickly hid under his usual stoicism.

"Rhys triggered a vision. His eyes were already white by the time I got downstairs, and he was saying something about danger in the woods. He got hooked on whatever it was and kept repeating it. Danger in the woods. Whatever it was scared the crap out of the kid. Then his eyes cleared, and he looked straight at me and told me to tell you not to worry about it. To do whatever you have to do. After that, he got up and ran. I tried to stop him, but he was too damned quick. I spotted Shogaur waiting for him a second before he crossed the ward. By the time I caught up…"

Kat wavered on her feet, but she stopped me when I made to steady her. "What about the crowd out front?"

Her blue eyes still burned, and I prayed she didn't lose her anger. She would need it and so much more to survive whatever came next.

"They left," I said.

"Just like that?" Her shoulders slumped. "I knew they were a distraction, I just didn't realize from what. Me or Eugene would have been the preferred catches, but a Seer will do nicely in a pinch."

Barrett crossed his arms. "What do you think Rhys Saw in that vision that made him run out here? I didn't see any danger other than the demon, but he wouldn't have been in such a rush to meet *him*."

Kat scowled. "He Saw what someone wanted him to See."

I dropped my hands to my sides. "You think the summoner interfered with Rhys's visions?"

"I almost guarantee it. He hasn't been able to See anything about Shogaur, which already struck us as odd and made me wonder if someone was blocking him. Now, the first time he sits down and tries to push his way through the fog, he winds up a target? It's too much of a coincidence. The summoner had to be waiting for the opportunity. She must have sensed him scrying for Shogaur, and she manipulated him into going outside where the demon could reach him. If his eyes cleared before he went, he must have really believed leaving was the only way forward."

A sob caught in her throat, and by the way her body trembled, I knew how much she was holding back. She needed to get it out or she would burst.

Barrett stared over the water. "What do you think he means to do with Rhys?"

"Carry out whatever plans he and his summoner have

in mind," Kat said. "With Rhys's innocent baby face behind whatever social media press he gets, Shogaur will have an easy time winning people over to their mob mentality." Her lip wobbled. "His magic will help him survive for a while, but how long before Shogaur's power starts draining him? How long before his body gives out?"

I crossed my arms to hold myself back from offering whatever comfort I could. "We always knew the timeline with Shogaur was tight. This might make it tighter, but you haven't been dragging your feet. We'll find him."

I couldn't promise her we'd find him in time. To do so quickly enough—and with a way of bringing Rhys back safely— would require more miracles than I was willing to bank on.

Kat drew in a deep breath and pulled her shoulders back. "Barrett, go get Poppy. And get Murisa here. In person. If that witch knows how to deal with demons, we need her on site and ready to go to war with us. Rhys belongs to this family, and I'm not going to let some demon take him away from us. *No one fucks with my family.*"

Never again.

She didn't say the words, but she didn't have to. I knew only too well how she carried the loss of her birth family every single day of her long life.

Barrett went into the house without another word, and Kat drew in a shuddering breath.

Then she cursed and launched a fireball over the lake. "I should have put more protections on him. I should have guessed what someone might do if they knew about his second sight. I fucked up, Emrick. I fucked up, and Rhys is paying for it."

"You didn't. You've been protecting everyone since you found out Shogaur was back. You're strong and you're powerful, but you can't be everywhere."

"I have to be. At least for the people under this roof, I have to be. I promised I would keep them safe. They're relying on me."

"They're here to help you take down a demon, Kat. All of them know there are no guarantees." I hesitated to say what worried me, but staying silent served no purpose. "You know getting him back will be… difficult."

I couldn't bring myself to say impossible. Besides, Kat had proved often enough that, for her, nothing was impossible.

"His green eyes and winning smile are going to cause a lot of problems if we don't find him soon," she said, "but believe me, Emrick—I will find a way to bring him home."

I prayed she was right.

But she wouldn't be able to do it by herself, and I knew she'd never put the others at risk to fight with her. Which meant I would be by her side until the crisis was over, because there was no way in the afterlife I would let her face him alone.

I'd have to be aware of my limits and force myself to stay on the right side of them, but if it looked like Kat was about to fall, I would be there to pull her back—even if it cost me a century of memories.

She threw two more fireballs with a yell, then spun on her heel and started back to the house. "Shogaur has had me on the back foot up until now, but goddammit, that ends here."

23

Katerina

O NCE I RETURNED to the house, some of the fire that had pushed me into action ebbed into cold uncertainty, and I wrapped my arms around myself as I headed up the stairs to the living room.

Emrick had disappeared to offer me space, and I both appreciated his consideration and hated that he'd left me to prop myself up alone. But no, this was good. I wasn't supposed to rely on him to prop me up. After everything we'd faced over the past few days, I was starting to forget he wasn't supposed to be here at all.

A peek through the front windows confirmed what Emrick had said. Although the truck with its shredded tires was still there, the mob was gone. I wished it made me feel better that one of our problems had resolved itself, but it didn't. Not even a little bit.

I would have taken on the entire goddamned island if it meant Rhys was here, safe within these walls like he was supposed to be.

Guilt and worry burrowed into my chest, and I knew as sure as I saw the runes on my gloves that they wouldn't leave until he was home and Shogaur was back in hell. If he was lucky—because if I found a way to ensure his demonic remains were torn into pieces and left to flutter aimlessly in a void some-where, I would do it.

Someone cleared their throat behind me, and I turned to find Poppy picking at her bright pink talons, her brown eyes wide and her dark skin drained of blood.

"I heard about Rhys," she said.

I shook my head. "Don't. Sympathy and commiseration won't get him back. Is Murisa on her way?"

She crossed her arms and leaned against the wall. "Just bought her ticket and will be heading to the airport within the hour. Barrett is getting ready to drive to Sudbury to pick her up. She should be here a little after noon."

She flinched as though expecting me to be angry at the delay, but there wasn't much we could do about the distance. Unfortunately, I was the only one who could take advantage of Emrick playing chauffeur.

"That's fine, we'll make do. There has to be some way to get ahead of this while we wait. Did you get anywhere on the video call?"

"We did…" Her hesitation made me want to shake her, but I hugged myself tighter and bit my lips until I tasted blood. Shogaur's win today was my fault, not hers. It wouldn't be fair to take my anger out on her when I needed her to help me fix it. "The spell she cast pinpointed somewhere in Toronto. Close to the warehouse where you fought Mikhail."

A chill wrapped around my heart, and my palms grew clammy. "Another coincidence that can't be a coincidence. It has to be Mikhail's patron. Abigail. What I don't understand is why." I rubbed my eyes and did my best to shake off the exhaustion weighing me down. "Who is this woman? How can she have amassed so much power, yet no one knows who she is? She has access to spells that should have disappeared a thousand years ago. She summoned a demon that hasn't been seen in eight hundred years. She—"

My lips went numb and prickly as shock coursed through my system, and I dropped into the chair in the corner.

"Kitty Kat? What's wrong?"

Poppy pushed off the wall and came to sit on the couch across from me.

"The ritual Mikhail used, Shogaur… Are they coincidences, or is everything meant to draw me out? Why would this woman be targeting me?"

The witch snorted. "It wouldn't surprise me if you're on the shit lists of covens across the world."

"I'm no stranger to death threats, Pop, but this…"

I found myself searching the room for Emrick, needing his support, needing him beside me as I worked through the revelation that was on the tip of my thoughts.

"That ritual slaughtered my community and stole my son from me, and Shogaur burning me alive is the closest I've come to my final death since I became immortal. Who could know those things about me? Everyone who was around back then is dead."

A low *mrow* sounded through the room, and Cuddles waltzed in, his kinked tail in the air. At some point, some-one—I suspected Maera—had given him a bath, and although he smelled a lot better, the clean fur hadn't done much for his looks except showcase the missing patches. He jumped onto the couch beside Poppy, curled his paws under his scrawny body, and stared at me.

I didn't have it in me to stare back.

Poppy stroked his fur and offered a slow shrug. "Cuddles is right. Not everything stays dead that's supposed to. Especially knowledge. If this Abigail woman has it out for you, it's possible she's dug deep into your history to learn what she needs to bring you down."

I curled my hands into fists to crush the fire threatening to rise. "If she thinks shoving my past in my face will stop me, then she's pulled the wrong lessons from her research."

There had to be more to it than me getting in some coven's way, but I wouldn't find out until I tracked this woman down and demanded answers face to face.

Going to Toronto would mean leaving the safety of the ward and making myself vulnerable to Shogaur's attempts to take over my mind, but I couldn't hunker down here and wait for the demon's return. Rhys needed me on the offensive.

"All right," I said, breathing through my rising anxiety, "we need to move fast. As soon as Murisa gets here, I want you two working together on a charm or a spell or a goddamn peanut butter sandwich that will protect our minds from Shogaur. Then I want you to focus on how to draw him out of someone without hurting the host. If I find Abigail, I can get her to order Shogaur to release him, but if I can't, I need a solid backup plan."

The thought of Rhys being trapped with that monster inside him—I forced my mind away from that line of panic. I didn't have time to lose my mind. "I'll also need you on social media duty until Barrett gets back, then put him on it. See if he can get the witch hunters to help us out. Twenty-four-seven coverage. Now that he has a host, Shogaur won't delay much longer to start feasting on the world's fear, and I want to know the second he bites. It might take me a while to boot him off this plane, but I can at least ruin his meal. I know I'm putting a lot on you, but I also need you to watch Eugene—"

"Gavin."

The deep voice drew my attention to the top of the stairs, and I looked over to find the sorcerer standing there. For the first time since I met him, he wasn't cowering. The fire of fury and loathing still burned in his eyes, but beneath it was a degree of confidence that had been missing.

"Gavin?"

Poppy tugged on one of her curls. "In the process of using the summoner's energy to track her, we tapped into a few of Gavin's missing memories."

"They're not all back," he said, "but at least I don't have to put up with you calling me Eugene."

I checked his expression again to see if he was joking, but he was nothing but a stone wall. All right, so he hadn't warmed up to me yet. Good to know.

"I don't need anyone to watch over me," he said. "I'm not a child."

"Then make yourself useful and help Poppy and Barrett monitor the social media feeds."

"You shouldn't go on your own," Poppy said, and she sounded so different from the woman who'd yelled at me in the cemetery about wanting to run and hide that I had to do a double take. At my surprise, she rolled her eyes. "Whatever issues I have with you, kitty Kat, I don't want them to be resolved by you dying or being taken over by some freak who gets off on people's nightmares. Wait for Barrett to get home. I know the two of you are matches and gasoline, but at least someone'll have your back."

"I'll be with her."

When had Emrick returned? I hadn't noticed him stepping into the kitchen, but now I couldn't see anything else, as though he'd sucked the entire space between the living room and kitchen into himself. My eyes locked on his silver stare, and my heart pattered.

I opened my mouth to argue with him, but his expression grew steely, his eyes sharp as flint. "I've already made up my mind. Even if all I do is drag you away if things go to shit, I'm going. Besides, can you really afford the time it would take to drive all the way to Toronto?"

We stared each other down, and I realized something had changed for him. There was a current of fear beneath his determination, which only made me worry more. What was he not telling me? I silently begged him to back off, but his conviction never faltered.

Soon enough, we would need to have words, but he was right that I couldn't afford to waste time. "All right. Give me three minutes to pack."

"Three minutes?" Poppy asked, sounding far more like her usual self. "I don't think I've ever packed in three minutes. And for the record, don't think I've forgotten about our plans for mimosas and girl talk. The tension in this room is thick enough to choke on. Whatever's going on between you two is worth at least a bottle of bubbly, if not six."

Her nervous babble followed me to my room as I grabbed my duffel bag and stuffed in a few black T-shirts and two pairs of leather pants, my usual hunting uniform. I hesitated over my comfier sweaters but ended up ignoring them. If I had the opportunity to enjoy a moment's comfort, I would be home again. A few hygienic items followed the clothing, along with the wooden case for my leather gloves. After changing into my hunter garb to prepare for whatever we might find, I enjoyed a single moment to breathe and returned to the living room.

Emrick hadn't moved. His eyes trailed over me, his wide frame inviting me to join him. My mouth went dry as the butterflies in my stomach danced, and I cursed my body for betraying me. When I got close enough, he plucked the bag from my hand and slung the strap over his shoulder.

"You're really not going to fill me in? You two suck, you know that?" Poppy grumbled as she crossed her arms.

I turned to face her. "Keep me updated on what you and Murisa find out. As soon as I know anything, I'll check in with Barrett. Under no circumstances are any of you to leave the protection of the ward once Barrett and Murisa return. Poppy, have Maera give you access so you can key her into the spell."

Poppy saluted, while Gavin glowered at me from the doorway, his brown eyes so full of rage the back of my neck prickled. I didn't care. He was free to hate me—as soon as this was over, he would be out of my life. Right now, my only priority when it came to him was preventing him from going the same way Rhys had.

Sorrow pinched my heart, and I dropped my gaze. "Tell Maera where I've gone, all right? Tell her I'm going to get Rhys back."

A soft hand rested on my shoulder, and I closed my eyes at the sensation of Emrick's bare thumb brushing against the side of my neck. My whole body sang at the electricity of his touch, and I breathed into it with all my seventy-five years of longing.

A familiar tug on my stomach told me we were sliding into the afterlife, and I raised my head in time to watch the room fade into a white fog. Poppy's mouth fell open, and then she was gone. Emrick and I skimmed along the edge of the mortal world and returned to the realm of the living at the remains of the burned-out warehouse.

24

Katerina

MY STOMACH DROPPED as I took in the scene in front of me—the place where, not that long ago, I'd prevented a whole room of witches from having their blood drained through their skin. Even now, weeks later, the reek of sweat and burned corpses lingered in the air.

Though maybe that was my memory playing tricks on me. More people would have noticed if it were real. I hoped.

Police tape fluttered in the wind where it had been left behind, but nothing else appeared to have been touched. Enough debris remained that wading through the room was a pain in my immortal ass. I stepped over a fallen beam and kicked a few half-burned crates out of my way until I reached the circle that had been drawn in blood in the centre of the concrete floor.

Overhead, a large chunk of the roof was gone. The magic let off during our battle had eaten through the beams until parts of it had collapsed to join the rest of the clutter on the ground, and the bright afternoon sun shone through the gaping hole to illuminate my view. The cheerfulness and warmth of the sunlight contrasted sharply with the runes scrawled before me, belying the seriousness of the fact that someone had brought forth a demon that was prepared to whip the entire world into a fear-based frenzy.

I knelt and ran my fingers over the markings, scowling as the energy of the spell rippled through me. The magic itself was neutral, but knowing the intention twisted it into something bitter and acrid that soaked into my skin and left a burning sensation in my throat.

"I thought Murisa's spell was supposed to take you to the summoner, not the source," Emrick said as he walked the edge of the circle.

I stood up and walked in the opposite direction, trying to find some clue about the person who'd drawn it. "That was my understanding. I suppose the summoner might have been here when Murisa cast the spell. She did say whoever it was might sense the magic."

"If that's the case, they can't have gotten far."

"Would you mind taking a look?"

I asked the question without looking at him, hoping he would understand what I wasn't saying. I needed space. Being alone with him was becoming increasingly difficult. When he was close, he left my head in such confusion I couldn't see straight—and I needed to get a grasp on what was happening here. Rhys didn't have time for me to be confused.

Emrick rounded the circle to reach my side, and my blood sang as his fingers brushed against mine. He dipped his head so his lips were close to my ear. "We'll find her."

The deep timbre of his voice vibrated through me, and I closed my eyes to savour the sensation. When I opened them again, he was gone.

My breaths came easier, and I took another lap around the circle, but nothing in the summoner's signature struck me as familiar. There was a notable wobble to the runes, though, as though whoever had written them had done so with a shaking hand.

Or an aged tremor?

Abigail's hunched form popped into my head, and my frustration rose that once again she'd evaded me. But was it by coincidence or collaboration?

Red flashed in my vision as I reached for my phone and brought up Poppy's number.

"Meow meow," she greeted.

"Are you talking to me or Cuddles? Because neither answer

is okay."

"Just trying to speak your language."

"You left out the hissing." We were getting off track. "I need your help."

"That was quick. Did you get her already?"

I kicked at the dried spell circle. "I found the circle, not the witch. Tell me, how well do you know Murisa?"

Poppy hesitated, and when she spoke, it was with a note of surprise. "Like I told you, not that well. By reputation, mostly. She's not part of any coven—she has to keep her magic on the DL to avoid her parents finding out she practices. From what little she's told me, they'd lose their shit and burn all her stuff. Why? You don't think she fucked up the spell to let the witch escape, do you?"

"It would be a rookie mistake to rule it out. Now that you've seen Murisa cast the tracking spell, do you think you could replicate it?"

"I could give it a shot. She walked me through it, so I understand the basics. It's not so different from the one we did with the maps. I don't have all the ingredients she used, but enough of them that it should work, though the results might not be as exact."

I cursed. We didn't have time for me to wander around Toronto searching for this woman. At the speed with which Abigail was moving, she'd be gone long before I found her.

Unfortunately, without this spell, I had nothing. "How long would it take to try?"

"Fifteen minutes? Twenty?"

I ground my teeth. Every minute lost was galling, but if Poppy could make this spell work, I could get Rhys back within the hour. "Do it. Ask Gavin to help you again. Anything come up on your social media watching yet?"

She groaned. "Nothing but people being obnoxious levels of death-defying and millions of other people lapping it up. My brain is literally oozing out of my ears right now, kitty Kat. You owe me for the therapy I'll need."

"You owe me for your life."

"Eventually you'll consider us even."

She hung up, and I stuffed my phone back in my thigh pocket.

As though he'd been waiting for me to hang up, Emrick stepped into view. "No one's here. I found footsteps in the snow leading towards the road, so she must have had a car ready."

I felt the telltale symptoms of tears threatening to rise, so I turned my back on him and made another tour around the summoning circle. "Poppy's going to try the tracking spell again. If this Murisa woman is screwing with us, I'll find out. When she and Barrett get to the house, I want him watching her until we know where she stands." I bit the side of my thumb as my head raced with all the things we needed to do and all the time we didn't have to do it. "There's no sign of Rhys on the internet, but it won't be long. Shogaur got what he wanted—for now—and he'll use it. Poppy says it'll take twenty minutes for the spell, but I can't stand around until she calls back. I need to move. I need to do something to get Rhys home, because if anything happens to him—"

Strong arms wrapped in a soft sweater bundled me against a broad, warm body. "It's all right, Kat. It's going to be all right. Breathe."

But when I took in a breath, it caught on a sob.

I buried my head against Emrick's chest, and he held me closer as the temperature dropped.

25

Emrick

I BROUGHT US to Adrian's house in Toronto's Kensington Market. If this Abigail woman had been at the warehouse, she wouldn't be too far from Toronto. I would be able to take Kat anywhere she needed to go, but I knew she'd prefer staying close. The last thing she needed was to feel like she was running away.

I tugged off my other glove, tucked it in my pocket, then stroked my fingers through her long black hair as she trembled against me, working so hard to hold back her tears. She didn't have to—I would never judge her for them—but I understood why she was. It had nothing to do with being embarrassed to show her emotions in front of me and everything to do with not wanting to lose control. If she slipped now, she would struggle to pull herself together, which would waste precious moments if the opportunity came to act.

I knew all this without her having to say a word. There had been a time when I'd known the woman in my arms better than I knew myself. By every look, every gesture, I could guess every thought passing through her head.

Over the better part of the last century, Kat had built a wall around herself to protect us both from the inevitable, and as the seconds ticked by, I wanted to tear that wall down and crush it into dust.

Involuntarily, my fingers curled into her hair, and I drew her tighter against me. My heartbeat raced at her faint Kat-like aroma of aloe and wisteria, and my body reacted despite myself.

Kat stiffened in my arms and pulled away. I let her go, though the distance between us when she was so obviously distraught shattered something inside me.

She lifted her blue eyes to meet mine, and the mingled pain and desire shining through them stole my breath.

"You should go." She said it softly but firmly, and a few weeks ago I might have obeyed, but not today. Not when that demon was out there and some witch had painted a target on Kat's back.

"I won't."

She frowned—the faintest of creases on her flawless brow. "Emrick…"

"I won't, Kat," I repeated, my tone as firm as hers had been but not nearly as soft. "I refuse to walk away as long as that monster walks this earth. I know you're scared, and I know you're stressed, but do you have any idea what images live in *my* head with him around?" Anger and the terror of long-held memories sparked through my blood, and I shoved my hand through my hair. "From the moment I learned Shogaur was back, I haven't been able to get rid of the sight of you tied to that stake. Your clothes on fire, your flesh blistering, roasting. I can't forget how close he came to stealing you away from me. I *will not* give him a second chance."

Her lips parted as she stared at me, the pulse in her throat fluttering though her chest remained still, as if her breath had gotten trapped somewhere along the way. I longed to claim her mouth with mine. My fingers twitched with the need to touch her, and I clenched my hands at my sides to hold myself back. There were a few promises I would happily break and risk Kat's wrath, but even if it killed me, I would not ignore her wishes for me to keep my desires to myself.

After a moment, she released her breath on a shuddering exhale. "I have Poppy, I have Barrett. I'm not alone in this. Any help you try to give will only make things so much worse. You can't save me, Emrick. Not anymore."

Frustration shot through me, wiping away the burn of my longing. This infuriating woman. Stubborn. Clueless. I adored her. I wanted to shake her. "If it comes down to saving you or losing you, Katerina, you better damn well believe I'll do whatever it takes to keep you here."

Her eyes flashed, her frustration rising to match mine. "That's the problem, Emrick. That's always been the problem. Why can't you understand that?"

"Because you're the one who refuses to understand," I shot back. Seventy-five years of holding my tongue and letting her lead the way, and I was done with staying silent. "Not having you breathe the same air as me would break whatever sanity I have left. I am trapped here, Kate, and the only part about my existence that makes it bearable is that you're trapped here with me."

"Kat," she whispered.

Holding her gaze, I closed the gap between us until there were only a few centimeters of space.

In the way she tensed, it may as well have been a chasm.

"If you keep helping me, you'll disappear, Emrick. Maybe not this time, or next time, but what about the time after that? Or the time after that? You say you can't breathe without me? Imagine what I would endure having you exist but not know who I am? If I died, you would serve your time and join me in whatever life comes after this one. If you became a wraith… I'd be trapped here without you forever."

The desperation in her voice was a knife slash through my

heart. I tucked her hair behind her ear. "If I'm forced to stay away from you, I may as well be a wraith already."

My heart beat in time with hers where my palm rested over the pulse in her neck. My anger washed out of me under a wave of new-sprung need, and I swallowed hard as I inched closer towards her. She tilted her head back, her gaze never leaving mine. A single tear streaked from the corner of her eye, and I brushed it away with my thumb. The contact of my skin on hers sent fire through my entire system, and goosebumps rose on the back of my neck.

I anchored her to this world, but she anchored me to my humanity. She was my passion, my heartbeat, my sense of adventure. She was my only reason not to slip so deeply into my role as Death's servant that life no longer had meaning.

"What you said to Poppy earlier," I said. "When you called me your Death. It's true. I am yours, Katerina. Wholly and completely." I tilted my head, willing her to see me. Desperate for her to claim me again as her own.

I caught every warring emotion as they battled across her features. I watched how hard she fought to keep the walls up. I spotted the exact moment they fell. Still, I didn't move. I kept my promise. If she walked away right now, I would let her, even if it left my soul bleeding.

My breath caught when she reached for me. Slow. Hesitant. Still debating, fighting, trying to convince herself to stop. Her fingers curled into the front of my sweater, and a whimper escaped her as she pressed her lips against mine.

With that simple contact, my restraint snapped.

26

Katerina

I WAS A fool.

A masochist. An addict.

But I couldn't help myself.

At the touch of Emrick's bare palm on my neck, my blood had begun to sing, my cells bouncing through time, always landing in the present because my anchor to this life was right here in front of me.

And then he'd said all those things and my lungs forgot how to work. My heart forgot how to beat. I could only stare and wonder how it was that the gods could be so cruel as to offer me such a gift as this magnificent man and wrap him up in such a curse.

I'd felt my resilience crumbling. All those lectures I'd given myself—all those nights staring into the darkness yearning for him, reminding myself over and over why I'd made the only decision I could—faded into whispers that drifted away on the breeze flowing through the open window.

One moment I was standing statue-still in the middle of the room, looking at the person who had once been my entire world after the rest of it lay rotting around me, the next I was on my toes drawing him closer, needing his kiss like a fish needed water.

After that, all thought vanished. My back hit the wall. Emrick's hands encircled my wrists, and he slammed my arms over my head as his lips crashed down on mine, as if he were afraid I'd pull away from him again. I gave him everything I had, all resistance gone. His body rolled over me like a wave hugging the shore—chest, stomach, hips—until the only gap between us was created by the clothes I wished were gone.

My skin burned, my magic so close to the surface I was certain flames would engulf the whole house. Lost in this universe of desire and passion, I didn't care. Let us burn. Let us be so consumed by our need for each other that nothing and no one else mattered.

"I've missed you, Kat," Emrick moaned against my lips. "Gods, how I've missed you."

Then his mouth was on me again, his tongue searching, tasting, savouring. My body arched against his, offended by the barriers between us, desperate for more contact, more heat.

He released my wrists and skated his fingers down my sides, over my shirt. He slipped his hands beneath it and curled his fingers around my waist. I wound my hands through his hair, pulled his head down, and clasped him to me, terrified that if I let go, he would vanish into smoke. That this fleeting reunion would be nothing more than a single flame doomed to go out at the first punishing draft.

My phone buzzed against my thigh, and my galloping heart leapt into my throat. My hands stilled, and my body stiffened.

What the hell was I doing?

Rhys needed me to stay focused, and I'd allowed myself to be distracted. Yet even as my guilt gave me a solid thumping, even as Emrick gently slid his hands from my waist and smoothed down my shirt, I panted for more.

Emrick's eyes were black with desire, but on an exhale, he bowed his forehead against mine and glided his hand down my thigh to grab my phone.

I squeezed my eyes shut, did my best to centre myself, then convinced my fingers to release their hold on his hair so I could answer the call.

Seeing Poppy's name on the screen poured a bucket of cold water down my back.

"What have you found, Pop?" I asked, my breath thick with interrupted lust.

Emrick kissed my forehead and backed away to give me space, and my soul complained at his absence. The bedroom suddenly felt too small and contained, too filled with what-ifs and almosts. I needed air or I'd collapse.

I headed downstairs to the living room, Emrick close behind me.

"I had more luck with the spell than I expected to," she said. "Gavin's like a living, breathing amplifier. It's amazing. Hmm… I wonder if it would work for any magic or just involving Shogaur…"

I huffed with impatience. "Proserpine."

"Right. Sorry. We narrowed it down to a hotel on Adelaide, so she's still in Toronto. I looked the place up. It'd cost my right arm, a leg, and probably a kidney for a single night in the place. This chickie-pie you're hunting must be rolling in it."

If Mikhail had thought Abigail worthy enough to follow her lead, she had to be powerful. And with that kind of magical power, gaining wealth wasn't a far stretch.

A hotel like that would mean lots of security, but I was no pauper myself. With Emrick's skills, my resources, and a few favours, I was confident we'd get through the front door.

"Thanks, Poppy."

"And Kat? There's something else."

The lack of nickname and the sudden edge to her voice set off an uncomfortable rumble in my gut. Emrick looked at me with concern, and I held his gaze in an attempt to find comfort as I readied myself for the worst.

"A new trending video flooded my social media accounts about ten minutes ago," she said. "It's Rhys. He doesn't say much, but I guess he doesn't have to. It's racking up views pretty quick."

A shiver ran through me. "Send me the link."

I hung up and sank onto the couch, burying my face in my hands. The corner of my phone dug into my cheek, and I leaned into the pain. It kept me grounded against the intangible discomfort playing cat's cradle with my innards. I'd put too much faith in wards and humans. I'd underestimated how far Shogaur was able to go to manipulate people into giving him what he wanted, and it hadn't even occurred to me his summoner might know how to maintain control of him.

The last time I'd faced him, his summoners had been mid-level witches, arrogant in their belief that they held his leash. They hadn't. Shogaur had twisted them around his finger from the moment he'd risen from the depths.

Abigail—assuming that's who we were dealing with—either had a grasp on the reins or had agreed to some sort of partnership. I doubted Rhys was her endgame, but it was a solid move on the board if her goal was to fuck with me.

Emrick settled on the couch beside me, close enough that his shoulder brushed against mine. As we waited in silence for Poppy's text message, I fought an emotional war between throwing myself at him to pick up where we left off—in desperate need of a distraction and of *him*—and acknowledging how bad a decision that would be.

When my phone buzzed, he rested his hand on my thigh in silent support, adding fuel to my internal battle.

I clicked the attached link, and all my remaining lust vanished as a video opened on a familiar handsome face and flapping red hair as Rhys walked through a park.

"Do you notice how common these new age shops are becoming?" he asked the camera. Casual. Confident. Just shooting the shit, sharing his thoughts with the world as he wandered through it. "I feel like every time I turn the corner, there's another one. This one focusing on books that'll 'change your life' or 'empower you,' the next one offering crystals or massages or needles in your head that'll help sort out all life's problems by fixing your emotions." He laughed lightly. "And who knows, maybe they're right, you know? It could be everything they're promising will come true, but I can't help but think there's something darker going on in those back rooms. Because you know what else I've noticed? The people who come out of those stores, suddenly it's all they talk about. How their lives are so much better. How they want to put what they've learned into practice to help change the world. Sure. You know how my girlfriend changed the world? She dumped me."

He shook his head as he rolled his eyes, and I caught the flare of resentment in his emerald glower.

What resentment could he possibly have? Rhys hadn't had a girlfriend since that movie date two years ago, and as far as I knew, he and the girl were now good friends and texted each other about video games until three in the morning.

I didn't know why I was surprised Shogaur was making up stories. He had to be pulling details from Rhys's memories and mixing them with whatever narrative he wanted to spin.

That was where he excelled.

"It's not right, is it?" Rhys continued. "These people who promise their customers the world when it comes at the cost of other people's lives. Am I way off base? You tell me in the comments."

The video ended, and against my better judgement, I scrolled down to see what people had to say.

I should have known better. Rule number one of the internet: never look at the comments.

Over a hundred people had already left their opinions, and my only point of relief was that, so far, the viewpoints were fairly moderate. The milder comments called the owners of these stores frauds. A bunch of people called Rhys on his bullshit, but they were rudely shouted down by some of the harsher voices. A few of the louder ones bandied the word *witches* about.

"You've got to be kidding me," I said. "Witches? Again?"

"Are you surprised? It's always worked for him and his kind before."

"Of course it has. Women with power never fail to light the powder kegs." I ran my palms over my hair. "Shogaur will be able to influence every person who watches this video. He'll feed his fear through every spoken word and latch on to every latent worry. This is going to get real bad real fast."

I sank into the couch. Emrick leaned back with me and crossed his arms, his brow creased, his lips pressed into a thin line. He understood what was coming as well as I did. All anyone needed to do was look in the history books to recognize the path Shogaur was taking.

Fear was powerful.

It was stronger than any magic I possessed.

This video might have been tame, but it would take root where it needed to. More videos would pop up, the grumbles would get louder, and like-minded people would band together and stir themselves into a frenzy. And once the fear spread far enough, penetrated deeply enough, there was very little the average person wouldn't willingly do to protect themselves.

Still, the side of reason and practicality was armed with something it hadn't been during the last big witch hunts in the sixteen hundreds or the Crusade against the Cathars in the thirteen hundreds: forewarning. Rhys's video gave him a wider reach, but it also meant Shogaur's cards were on the table from square one. That had to give us an advantage.

"Right." I threw my phone onto the cushion beside me and slapped my thighs. "First things first, we need damage control. Then we need to get into that hotel and find our summoner. Let's see how the witch hunters feel about destroying a demon *before* he clears out the witches."

27

Emrick

"You won't want the witch hunters to get involved with Shogaur," Barrett said.

Kat had called him to ask if he'd play middleman with Tony, but he was still en route to Sudbury. For everything that had happened since we'd left Kat's place, it was only just past nine-thirty in the morning.

"Why not?" she asked as she paced the length of the living room. I tucked my feet closer to the couch to keep her from tripping on them, though what I wanted to do was pull her into my lap. After what had passed between us upstairs, my skin tingled with the need to touch her—to soothe her if I could. "Aren't they supposed to be my stand-in? Or am I right that they want to wait until Shogaur does their job for them in paring down Toronto's witch population, even if it comes at the risk of hurting non-magicals?"

Having witnessed the witch hunters in action, I wouldn't put it past them to do exactly that. Kat had her reasons for not liking them, but my experience with the organization wasn't any better. I'd escorted many magical souls to the river who'd been taken before their time, caught in the crossfire of one of the hunters' operations.

Barrett grunted, which I didn't take as an objection to her statement, but he followed it up with, "Because if they get within firing distance, Rhys is as good as dead."

Kat drew to a stop. "Yeah, I guess that's true. What's an eighteen-year-old to them, right?"

The soldier sighed. "If it means stopping Shogaur before anyone else dies, they won't hesitate. Which is why I plan to tell Tony you have the demon covered and that any movement from the witch hunters will fuck up your plan."

My surprise at his response was great, but it was nothing compared to Kat's as she staggered on her feet. "You would do that? James Barrett, that's almost decent of you."

"Yeah, well, I'm not doing it for you," he grumbled.

A shadow of a smile ghosted across Kat's lips. I licked mine in response, remembering the feel of hers.

"What about the rest of it?" she asked. "That video needs to come down. Until we're able to track him, we need to play whack-a-mole with his social media career. It's the best way to keep his power in check."

"That shit is Tony's bread and butter. It'll take him minutes to squash the video and any others that come up."

Kat glanced at me in relief, and I nodded my agreement. One less stress.

"What about the hotel?" she asked.

"That'll be a bigger pain in the ass, but I'll see what I can do. I'll use Abigail as incentive. I bet the hunters are eager to get their hands on Mikhail's patron."

"Can I ask you to do one more thing?"

"You're bothering to ask?"

I smirked at the way her eyes lit up with amusement. "Get a read on Murisa when you pick her up, all right?" she said. "I want to know what team she's playing on."

She hung up, and I crossed my arms. I wished I had a clearer idea of what was going through her head—regarding her plan, regarding me, regarding Shogaur. She was focused on the middle distance as she put her thoughts together, and I found myself needing to be involved. Whatever existed between us now—stuck as we were in this interrupted middle ground—I couldn't bear to be shut out. "I thought you trusted Poppy."

Her gaze cleared as her mind came back to the room, and she pinned me with a look that spoke of years of shared experience. "Come on, Emrick, you know better than that. Trust is never a guarantee of loyalty."

I arrived at the hotel around nine-thirty that evening. Poppy hadn't been exaggerating about the swankiness of the place. From where I sat in the lounge just off the lobby, I had a good view of the paparazzi as they followed the minor celebrities from the front door to the elevator bay before security stepped in. Finance moguls, CEOs—the place reeked of money, and I couldn't wait to leave.

Unfortunately, Kat was nowhere to be seen.

While we'd waited for Barrett to get back to us with information about where we were going, I'd convinced Kat to get a few hours' sleep. The woman was in desperate need of rest, and I had some patient souls waiting for me to do my job.

With each soul I'd escorted, I'd scouted the scene for any connection to Abigail, Shogaur, or the seemingly rising threat against Kat, but today there had been nothing shocking or tragic—only the natural course of lives fully lived.

A relief in many ways, but a large part of me wished for my own way to help Kat find answers. A way that didn't threaten my soul or break my promise to stay uninvolved.

Something in my gut told me the answers would come soon enough—likely too quickly for us to keep up with them. Until then, the witch and her demon worked solidly in the shadows.

Though at the moment, Kat's continued absence was pushing me to tear through said shadows.

When I'd returned to the house, I'd found a note from her saying sleep wasn't happening, so she was going shopping. She'd suggested I get to the hotel ahead of time to assess our options if things went wrong upstairs. Since my purpose tonight was to play chauffeur and watch her back, I was grateful to have something else to offer other than standing witness. If all went well, by the end of the night Kat would have the summoner under her boot. Once we had them, she could persuade them to order Shogaur to release Rhys and return quietly to hell. I was under no illusion that the persuasion would be neat or tidy.

After half an hour waiting for her to arrive, my patience had reached its limit.

Plenty of other women walked into the lobby, many of whom shot me appraising stares as they passed. I'd dressed to fit in, wearing a tailored charcoal suit and white shirt, leaving off the tie and keeping the top button of my shirt undone. With every passing minute, I itched to throw off the jacket; the collar scratched my neck.

Though when Kat walked through the front door, all thought of comfort vanished. All thought of anything vanished. The women watching me may as well not have existed as my attention homed in on the vision in sapphire blue.

Her black hair was down and swept over her right shoulder, covering the single sleeve of the silk-and-sequin dress. The neckline cut downwards across her chest, leaving the other shoulder exposed, and a peek-a-boo slit revealed a hint of cleavage. The waist hugged in tight and followed the line of her hips, ending just above mid-thigh on the left and draping down to the floor on the right. She'd topped the whole outfit off with a pair of black, heeled sandals that I hoped would slip off easily if she needed to run. She wasn't wearing her leather gloves, but as long as she wore that dress, I hoped she had no need to summon her magic.

Everything about her was perfection. I rose to my feet, leaving my drink forgotten on the table as I made my way towards her. I couldn't look away. It took everything in my power not to take her in my arms and disappear with her, to tease her out of her dress and leave it a shimmering pool at her feet.

Her blue eyes—almost the exact shade of the dress but deeper, more vibrant—sparkled with amusement when she met my eye, but I didn't care. Let her laugh at me for the way she'd brought me to my knees. I doubted there was a man in this room who hadn't turned to gawk.

"Sorry I'm late," she said when I reached her. "I was in the middle of getting ready when Barrett called back."

"Any news?" My voice came out husky with want. Kat's eyes turned dark, and her gaze dipped to my throat and my undone button.

She licked her lips and blinked, centering herself. "Plenty. How about you? Learn anything while you waited?"

"We're dealing with a lot of security, but they seem focused on stopping people from coming in who shouldn't be here."

"Good, then let's get moving before we attract any unwanted attention."

She turned her back, and a groan escaped me as she revealed the extra surprises this dress had to offer—two wider diagonal slits that revealed more milky skin from shoulder blade to waist. As though some beast had clawed at her back.

Or maybe I was projecting my desires.

"Where are we headed?" I asked as I followed her.

I prayed someone else got into the elevator with us, because I didn't know how long my self-control would last.

"Room 2314," she said. "Tony's people hacked the system and found a booking confirmation under A.D. Palon."

She looked at me over her shoulder, all teasing gone, and the heat in my blood evaporated, replaced by a bone-deep chill.

If we'd had any doubt that all of this was for Kat's benefit, they were gone now. I took her hand and tugged her towards me, overpowered by an irrational need to keep her close. The sooner we found this woman, the better I'd feel.

And my soul be damned, if she made another move against Kat, she would be dust before she took her next breath.

28

Katerina

MY HEART HAMMERED against my ribs as I made my way to the elevators. I told myself it was the anticipation of finding Abigail and saving Rhys, but my lies fell flat even to myself.

Part of it was undeniably the thrill of the hunt. My quarry was skilled at evading me, but I was no novice, and the opportunity to exercise my long-forgotten abilities offered a much-needed jolt.

And unlike the masquerade where I'd sought out Mikhail, where everyone had hidden themselves behind their frivolous costumes, the hotel offered a more dangerous type of illusion—one of normality. The only way anyone could get past security standing at every turn was if they gave the impression they belonged here.

Fortunately, I'd planned well with my blue number. Every male gaze in the room swung my way as I stepped past them, and I garnered more than a few appreciative female gazes as well.

Though they were only caught by me for so long.

Thus lay the true reason behind my racing heart. With Emrick behind me in a suit that flaunted the span of his broad shoulders and a white shirt that hugged his chest and hinted at his tapered waist—the loose button at his throat that teased me with the possibility of unbuttoning the rest of them—how could I not be distracted? His blond hair was styled in a loose tousle, with a few strands falling over his brow, begging me to brush them aside. A dusting of stubble covered his jaw. A Norse god would have appeared lacking next to him.

Maybe.

I couldn't swear to it, not having met any myself, but I imagined there would be a good amount of envy in Thor's eyes if he could see my *gàst-ladman* now.

My mind tumbled back to our kiss this morning, and I wrestled with myself to gain some perspective. A large part of my motivation in dressing the way I had was to get us to the elevators without security giving us a second glance, but an equally large motivator had been the thought of Emrick's reaction when he saw me.

He hadn't disappointed.

I'd thought to put myself on even ground with him

again and bolster my confidence so I could rebuild the walls I'd worked so hard to put up between us. All my plans had shattered the moment his eyes had darkened. Everything he'd wanted to do to me had played out in my head as clearly as if he'd whispered them in my ear.

This man would be my ruin—but until then, I had no doubt I'd enjoy every moment we spent together.

He stayed close to my side as we reached the elevator, his large hand splayed across the small of my back. His touch wasn't the possessive gesture it appeared to be but a trick we'd learned centuries ago. He wouldn't make a move against anyone until I was ready, and the contact would give him an extra second of notice before I acted.

We were a team. For many centuries, we were *the* team.

There was a rich bittersweetness that we'd stepped into those roles again. Especially since our foe was such an old acquaintance.

I knew Emrick being here in person was a bad idea. He could have swept me upstairs into Abigail's room as soon as we were out of sight of the people in the lobby, then disappeared to safety… but I couldn't deny his presence steadied me. His touch raised my belief that I was ready for whatever lay ahead, and as the elevator doors closed behind us, I felt more like my old self than I had in a long time.

"I asked Poppy to recast the spell again before I left the house," I said, doing my best to recentre my concentration on the hunt instead of on the yearning pulsing between my legs. "According to her, the summoner hasn't moved. Everything points to this hotel."

We'd have to move as quickly and as quietly as possible. I knew a little bit about who I was dealing with—despite her seeming age, Abigail was quick, strong, and cunning. That she'd used my chosen surname for her hotel booking made it more than a little likely we were heading into a trap, but as long as I remained aware of my surroundings, I could best her. It wasn't like she could kill me easily.

I would do everything I could to take her down alive if it meant getting Rhys free of the demon, but if she pushed me, I would kill her first. With Emrick here to clean up the mess, security would never need to know what happened.

And if the room was empty, I'd know someone was playing the same game we were, constantly rolling the dice to stay an extra step ahead.

The elevator stopped on the twenty-third floor, and I drew in a deep breath as the doors slid open. Emrick scratched his index finger gently across the bare skin of my back, and a thrill ran through me. I leaned into the press of his palm and, just for now, appreciated how right it felt to be in the thick of the excitement with him.

With Emrick at my side, I was unstoppable. As Abigail was about to learn.

29

Katerina

As we stepped out of the elevator, I summoned a low-level flame into my palm. I had no idea what to expect when we reached the suite, and I wanted to be prepared.

If Abigail waited for us inside, she would throw her whole arsenal at my head—and she'd shown just how strong her arsenal was more than once during our fight with Mikhail.

But as we approached the suite, I sensed nothing.

No magic, anyway.

I considered knocking but doubted anyone inside would be foolish enough to open the door, and we had no key card, so no letting ourselves in. Once again, Emrick would have to be my ride.

My phone buzzed in my clutch, and I cursed as I tugged

open the snap and pulled it out. I was ready to blast whoever was calling me, but instead I found a text from Poppy with a link to a video.

I shifted so Emrick could watch over my shoulder and made sure the volume was all the way down before I clicked it. As the page loaded, there was Rhys. This time he sat in what looked like a comfortable living room filled with house plants and bright natural light. He was still smiling, but this time it looked bitter. The expression was out of place on his youthful face but natural enough that no one looking would notice the demon shining out from behind his eyes.

As he spoke, captions popped up along the bottom of the screen.

You know, they read, *the more I think about it, the more I'm annoyed by what these new agers are doing.* He put "new agers" in air quotes, his mouth twisted into a sneer that was nothing like my poor, sweet friend. *Convincing people they're better than they are. Talking them into leaving the people who care about them in the dust while they go in search of power. What exactly do they expect these people to do with whatever power they find? Not take care of their loved ones, obviously. What do we matter anymore when they have a chance at learning magic?* He wiggled his fingers as he said the word, and I could hear his disgust through the silence. *It's bullshit is what it is. I think someone needs to tell these witches where to go, don't you?*

Fanaticism burned in his eyes. Just like the last video, the words themselves were tame, but Shogaur's influence poured out of every syllable, his insidious whispers travelling through the air waves to lodge in the brains of his viewers, clawing at their deepest fears. I could only imagine the damage he'd done in thirty seconds.

Again I scrolled down to see what lovely points of view his audience had contributed. The video had only gone up ten minutes ago, and already hundreds of people had added their calls to action. The moderate voices were quieter this time; the more hostile suggestions claimed all the attention.

It had been less than twelve hours, and already Shogaur was gaining traction. I liked to think that without the demonic influence, a video like this wouldn't have picked up speed, but maybe that was naïve. I'd seen what damage a few pointed posts could do.

Poppy had followed up the link with a message that Tony was already working on taking the video down. I doubted it would be down soon enough.

I tucked my phone in my clutch and pinched the bridge of my nose. Time was getting too tight on this. We had to get moving.

Emrick quirked an eyebrow and jerked his chin towards the door. I nodded. We had to see what was inside. If the comments on Rhys's videos continued to double as Shogaur's influence spread, then by the end of the night, we would have thousands of angry Torontonians storming every new age, yoga, and crystal shop in the GTA. By tomorrow afternoon, it would be all of Ontario, and from there we'd be looking at a national crisis before it spread across the border.

Eight hundred years ago, it had taken years to stir up enough hatred against the Cathars for anyone to make a move, but here we were in the glories of the modern age, watching it happen in a matter of hours.

Emrick extended his hand to me, and I slipped my palm against his. Everything around me faded to white, the mist obscuring my vision except for the shadows of something *other* and *beyond* that extended past the fog, and then we were back in the here and now, standing in the tiny foyer of a stunning open-concept suite. A full modern kitchen abutted a cozy living room that overlooked the heart of downtown Toronto. Comfortable and lush, without a single touch of personality.

Emrick disappeared, presumably to check the other rooms, and I stepped farther into the living room, extending my awareness to pick up any lingering magic and sensing none. Nothing of anything.

Had we missed the summoner again?

I cursed under my breath. They were always a step ahead. If Murisa had given the summoner the heads up, she would regret all her cheerful smiles and eagerness to help. I didn't handle being made a fool of well.

And if Poppy was part of it?

I considered the necromancer, thought of the fear in her eyes when I'd caught her summoning her *guard* in the cemetery. Had she been surprised by my unexpected arrival, or was she a part of whatever the summoner's ambitions were in bringing forth Shogaur?

I prayed I was wrong. I didn't want to believe the worst of her, but if my suspicions proved true, I would carry out every threatened punishment a million times before she begged me to end her life.

Anger simmered in my blood as I wove through the furniture, searching for any clue as to who might have stayed here. Whoever was playing with me had dragged Rhys into our game, and there would be no forgiveness, no deals, and no mercy for anyone involved.

Only once before had I been fooled by my belief in the safety of family and community. Alodie, Mae, and Blythe had deceived us all. They'd been our teachers, our healers, our leaders. The day they'd turned on Palonia had been the day my faith in loyalty had expired. There were only two people in the world I trusted now, and nothing I'd learned over the past eight centuries had motivated me to change my mind.

The temperature around me dropped as Emrick returned through the mist. "The bedrooms are empty. No one's here."

Like the mature woman I was, I stomped my foot against

the fancy carpet to vent the frustrations building within me. Shogaur's plans were gaining momentum, his summoner remained out of my reach, and every hour that passed was another hour Rhys lost. With the magic in his blood, he might be able to withstand Shogaur's possession for a few days, but the thought of him rotting away with that demon inside him…

I set my hands on my hips and firmed my jaw to keep myself from succumbing to my fear. "Give me one reason not to burn this whole place down on the chance the summoner is hiding somewhere in it."

"Even your life savings wouldn't cover the liability?"

I huffed and spun in a circle to take in the empty room. "That's hardly an argument."

He smiled at me, but beneath his attempt to raise my spirits, I sensed his frustration was equal to mine.

"We need to find her," I said.

"We will. We knew it was a possibility she wouldn't be here, but that doesn't mean she's far. Let's go upstairs and check the bar, then I'll take a tour of the street. You can wait here in case she comes back."

I doubted anyone would step foot in this suite again until housekeeping came to clear it out. Shogaur was on the move now. He had his host, his target, and access to the entire world on Rhys's phone. Abigail had summoned him with a plan in mind, and she would want to capitalize on the chaos the fear demon evoked. I didn't see her sitting at the bar nursing a cocktail and watching the view. She would want to be close to where the action was.

Struck with inspiration, I pulled out my phone and searched for new age shops in the neighbourhood. Sure enough, there were three within a five-block radius of the hotel.

Damn. Rhys—Shogaur—Rhyshogaur was right. It really was a booming industry.

"I think we should take a walk." I started towards the door, navigating around the length of the couch. "It's possible Abigail—the summoner—whoever—wants to watch—"

A click sounded in my mind as the hum of magic filled the air and prickled over my skin. I froze and looked down. There was nothing under my feet except the ugly, trendy carpet. Was something hidden underneath it?

But the magic didn't feel like it was coming from under me. If anything, it felt…

I looked up at the ceiling. At the spell circle filled with runes glowing above me, growing brighter.

"Kat!"

Emrick leapt over the sofa in my direction, but he was still too far away when the spell burst and bolts of purple lightning shot straight for my chest.

30

Emrick

ICAUGHT KAT before she hit the floor, covering her body as more lightning bolts shot from the spell circle we'd both missed. One struck my back, and my muscles twitched so badly I nearly lost my hold on her, but I tightened my arms to keep her with me.

Smoke filled the room as fire spread, and alarms blared in my ears. I ignored it all, focused only on the woman on the ground in front of me.

The summoner had been clever hiding the circle where she had—not only out of sight but keeping the magic hidden until triggered. By going around the couch, Kat had stood in the exact right place to wake up the runes and set off the waiting spell.

"Kat, are you all right? We've got to get out of here before security shows up."

I brushed her hair out of her face, and fear lurched in my chest to find her unmoving, pale, her eyes slightly open as she stared blankly at the ceiling. "No," I whispered. "No, no, no. Come on, Kat, wake up. Wake the fuck up!"

But no matter how loudly I called for her, how firmly I gripped her, she remained still in my arms. I rested her on the floor and pressed my fingers into her neck. No pulse thudded against my fingertips. Panic threatened to take hold of me, but I kept it at bay long enough to rest my hand on her chest. Her dress was destroyed, the lightning having struck her right in the torso, which allowed me direct access to her skin—to the place where her heart should have been beating.

The gestures were meaningless. As soon as she'd hit the ground, I'd felt the tether between us snap. Felt my heart bleed into the void where she should have been. The ground gave out from under me, and I braced my hands on the floor to stop the world from spinning.

I couldn't breathe. I couldn't move. I was trapped in this moment of torment as my future—my humanity—wavered in front of me. An eternity of emptiness. Of loneliness. Of the pain of missing half my soul.

My vision blurred, and I blinked away the tears that threatened to fall. I wouldn't let them. This was far from over.

Hating to leave her but not believing this was the end, I slipped into the afterlife and shouted for her. There was no spark of her soul waiting to be called. No hint of her anywhere.

"Katerina!" I bellowed her name with as much force as my body could produce. Loud enough that the lost souls drifting through the wasteland stuttered, stalled, spun towards me in lazy circles as though summoned by my desperation.

I rushed to the river, the line in the sand not even I was allowed to cross, but there was no Kat waiting for me to say goodbye.

My grasp on my panic slipped, and I threw myself into the still water.

Not once in my fifteen hundred years serving Death had I dared dip a toe in this barrier between planes, but tonight, I didn't care about rules or boundaries. If Kat was anywhere in this place, I needed to find her.

Ice closed in around me as I dove into the depths. The more I kicked my legs and tried to surge forward, the slower I moved. My thoughts turned hazy, but I didn't care. What did I care about anything except either bringing Kat back to me or joining her wherever she'd gone?

Something grabbed the back of my shirt and threw me onto the riverbank. I landed with a jarring thud that clacked my teeth together and stole my breath, but when I looked around, I saw nothing. Nothing at all—not even the wasteland that had become my home. Only a deep, dark fog. It enclosed me, with shapes moving beyond the limits of what I could see, indecipherable forms swirling in circles.

I'd stepped where I wasn't allowed. If I did it again, I would never make my way back, never make my way forward. I would be stuck in the river as another lost soul, condemned to remain in this liminal space for the rest of eternity.

The thoughts dropped into my head one warning at a time as though someone were speaking the words, and I understood that Death itself had stopped me. Not only had it taken Kat from me, but it hadn't allowed me to be the one to escort her. After all I'd done in Death's name, it had stolen that last, precious moment from me.

"Please," I whispered. "You can't take her from me. I've given you so much. I've served you as I swore I would. I'll give you anything."

Gabrielle's face swam through my mind, the woman for whom I'd traded my soul. The woman who had left me the moment she'd been well enough to do so, while my body had wasted away and become this being that straddled life and death.

The message was clear—I'd already made my deal and was living the consequences. I was in no place to make any more bargains.

I waited for resignation to hit me, but the agony was relentless. If Kat was lost to me, I wouldn't be able to endure it. Not as I was. If she was gone, I would give up the rest of myself. I would become the wraith I was already on my way to becoming and serve the rest of my debt without feeling.

The only other option was to lose my sanity and drift into madness.

The fog swirled again, and something in the way it cradled me soothed the pain. A warm balm on an aching muscle. No visions accompanied the sensation, no words dropped into my head.

A moment later, I was shoved out of the afterlife back into the destroyed hotel suite. Kat was just as I'd left her, surrounded by the spreading fire. I crawled to her side but hesitated before reaching for her. If I touched her and she turned to dust, the strained fractures in my heart would burst. I pulled on my gloves, lifted her head so it rested on my lap, and took her limp hand in mine. If this was her end, then let it be mine, but I wouldn't release her until she'd gone. I'd take as much as I could get, knowing it would never be enough.

31

Katerina

MY HEART STOPPED.

For a long moment, almost like someone had hit pause on the universe, I remained in the cold, impersonal living room, and then, as though that same person had hit another button on the obnoxious remote control pointed at my life, I stood in the grey fog of the afterlife.

Dead?

After so long, I'd honestly begun to wonder if it was possible for me to die. Yet all it had taken was a well-aimed lightning bolt.

At one time I would have been relieved to know it, content to have an ending after all that... continuing.

But not now. Not when so much rested on me to set it right.

Beyond the fog, the shadows shifted, seeming to come closer, and I watched, expecting to feel afraid. The fear never came, only a deep curiosity. What sort of creatures lurked in this place? Could they harm me or were they simply observing?

I'd never actually been to the afterlife before, for all the times I'd passed through it at Emrick's side. He only ever took me along the fringes. I'd asked him why once, and he'd told me it was no place for the living. That even if I were to see it, I would forget it the moment I stepped back into the mortal world.

But he'd told me about the creatures that lurked in the shadows and preyed on any lost soul unlucky enough to drift too far from the river. For the most part, he said, he forgot they were there. They were the bacteria floating in a glass of water. He knew they existed and probably had some purpose, but he didn't have to worry about it.

At the thought of Emrick, my heart squeezed, and I whirled around in the fog. Where was he? In my confusion on arriving here, I hadn't registered his absence, but if I was dead, shouldn't he be at my side? Shouldn't he be here to tell me what to expect and to guide me towards what came next?

Something moved in the fog ahead of me, and this time fear pinched at me with irritating little pincers. Was my physical body actually here with me, suffering the pangs of panic, or was it somewhere else? Lying inert on the carpet in that room?

Where was Emrick?

I wanted him beside me when I faced whatever this shadow was. I didn't want to be by myself if this was the end of eight hundred and seventy-seven years of existing. It wasn't fair. To be taken out because I'd missed something as simple as checking the ceiling.

A rookie mistake had taken me down in the end. How humiliating.

The shadow came closer, towering over me in the mist, and my fear grew. It squeezed my throat and twisted my stomach into coils of snakes.

My body had to be here with me, right? I couldn't be feeling these things if it was lying dead somewhere. Unless this was death. The act of dying. My insides reacting but no longer functioning.

I thought of Rhys, trapped inside a tiny corner of his mind while Shogaur controlled the rest of him, and anger consumed the edge of my terror.

It wasn't right.

This couldn't be my end when that monster was still out there. When the evil witch who'd summoned him had escaped me.

I had to get back into my body and continue this fight. I wouldn't leave Emrick to face his future alone. I wouldn't abandon Barrett to hunt Shogaur without me. I'd promised Maera I wouldn't stop until Rhys was home safe, and I wasn't about to let anyone stand in my way. Not even Death.

He'd had thousands of chances to take me. This time, the decision was mine not to go.

"Put me back," I shouted at the moving figures beyond the fog.

Thoughts swirled through my mind—of rest. Of peace. Of putting down the mantle I'd worn since stepping out of Palonia. I shoved them all aside. A few months ago, thoughts like that might have tempted me, but not anymore.

"I'm not done here," I said. "Put me back."

The fog pressed in more closely until everything was shrouded in darkness. I felt nothing, saw nothing. This had to be the end. Everything I'd worked for wasted because I hadn't been careful enough.

Resignation leached into me like a chill, and I closed my eyes. With a last thought for Emrick, an apology that I hadn't had a chance to say goodbye, I readied myself for Death to finish what it had started.

Visions floated through my head of me standing on a riverbank, of a choice. An opportunity—not now, but soon. Very soon.

Something tapped my chest, and a sharp burn coursed through me, an avalanche through my veins.

My heart beat once.

I sat up with a gasp and looked around the room that only minutes—seconds? Hours?—ago I'd talked about burning down.

It had been destroyed. The beige couch smoked, the fancy carpet was a charred mess, and the windows had blown out in a spray of glass. I was grateful it was so late at night. The streets of Toronto were busy regardless of the hour, but they would be less busy now than in the middle of the day.

All around me was fire and smoke, and immediately after I sucked in that first breath of new life, I started coughing, my airway going into spasm.

Alarms screamed throughout the room and down the halls, and I was certain that within seconds, fire services would break down the door and half the on-hand security would be waiting in the hallway.

I turned towards Emrick and found him sitting back on his heels. His gorgeous suit was in tatters, his hair was oddly damp, and streaks of drying tears stained his face. His expression was filled with awe and a touch of fear. I reached for him and flinched when he pulled away from my touch.

I waited for an explanation, and when none came, I struggled to get to my feet. "We should leave before someone shows up."

Emrick rose beside me, his gaze still locked on my face, but he stood with his gloved hands behind him, something he never did when it was only the two of us in a room.

Discomfort at his reaction trickled through me, but I didn't have the strength to push him about it. Not yet. First, we had to get out of here.

I held my hand out to him, and he eyed it as though it were something foreign. Finally, he closed the distance between us, but instead of taking off his glove, he pulled a knife from where it lay hidden under his jacket.

"Emrick, what are you—"

"I'm not taking chances," he said, his voice hoarse.

He gripped my wrist, and I hissed as a sharp pain sliced across my forearm. A pool of blood swelled to the surface of the cut. As we watched, the wound sealed, leaving my skin flawless except for the blood.

His jaw flexed as he released me and tugged off his gloves. When he pulled me to his chest, his arms were like vises around me. I sagged against his solidness, a relief after the drifting emptiness of the afterlife. His chest stilled as he held his breath, and, with the lightest touch—barely making contact—his fingers brushed the back of my neck. My cells jerked forward in time even as time forced me to stay right where I was, and we transported out of the room as the door flew open.

32

Emrick

I DROPPED KAT at Adrian's house in Kensington Market, waited until she was in the shower, then left.

Part of me longed to stay with her. The look she'd given me when I'd rejected her touch after she'd woken up had punched me in the gut. I sensed her confusion and horror over what had happened—though I didn't think she understood the full extent of it—and I wanted to comfort her. But I couldn't. Not yet. Not while I was reeling with too many of my own feelings to have space for hers.

Instead of torturing myself by staring at her, terrified she'd disappear again, I took myself to Adrian's house in Muskoka.

I found the vampire in his garden, his personal paradise behind the house, clearing paths around the beds he would clean up when the snow finally melted.

He didn't look up when I arrived, though I knew he was aware of me. The subtle stiffening and relaxing of his back gave away his registration of my trespass and his dismissal of the threat. His vampiric instincts were well honed after two thousand years.

For a while, I said nothing. I followed him as he first shovelled a path, then knelt to shove some of last year's garden debris into a large black contractor bag.

Anyone who saw Adrian in his library might be shocked to discover he engaged in such manual labour, but though he loved his books and his armchair, my friend was far from idle. He'd been a Roman tribune in his mortal life, and he'd never lost his restless energy.

Tonight, I was especially grateful for it. I would have hated to be cooped up inside the house staring into the crackling fire. Outside, the air was clean and brisk, smelling sweetly of the coming spring. After feeling as though my lungs were caught in a vise for the past hour, it was a relief to take a full breath.

Adrian stood up, tossed the bag onto the next path, and turned to face me. The sleeves of his burgundy shirt were rolled to the elbows, and mud marred the knees of his slacks. The sight almost coaxed a smile out of me. While Adrian might not be afraid of manual labour, he was terrified of casual clothing.

"So," he said, "are you going to tell me why you stopped

by, or will you continue to follow me around like a spectre?" He frowned as he looked me over. "Because I have to say, you're looking very spectral tonight. What's wrong?"

The words lodged in my throat. I couldn't come out and say them, so I talked around them. "There was an incident."

Adrian canted his head. "At the hotel?"

Barrett must have told him where we were headed. Good. It saved me from having to explain the whole disaster.

"Yeah. The summoner wasn't there, but they—she—left a present for Kat."

"Is Katerina all right?"

"She—" Again the words stuck, and I cleared my throat. "She'll be fine. But it was close, Adrian. Too fucking close. I thought I'd lost her."

It was the closest I could come to giving him the full story. My hand trembled as I shoved it through my hair and cupped the back of my neck. Adrian watched me, waiting patiently for me to get whatever was bothering me off my chest. The part of myself determined to protect my wounds wanted to snarl at him for being nosy in his silence, but I pushed the instinct aside. I'd come here for this exact reason. To gain perspective. I had to get past this.

Kat was safe.

She was breathing.

Our bond was securely back in place.

I had to hold on to that.

"Something happened while she was… gone." I stuffed my hands in my pockets. "I tried to go after her, and Death pushed me back. I always thought…" Again I trailed off, struggling to put into words the thoughts that had needled me since my dive into the river. "The odds of Kat being bound to me in that ritual were so slim, and the coincidence of my being there early enough for it to happen at all… I thought it was the gods' way of—I don't know. Making up for what happened with Gaby? Acknowledging the shit position I'd found myself in, being stuck half in this world, unable to connect with anyone? If not for you, I would have lost my sanity centuries before I met Kat."

Adrian bowed his head at the acknowledgement, and I stared off over the garden towards the melting lake. "I always thought the bond between us was a gift to me. That no matter what I had to endure, she would be there. Mine. And when the time came for her to pass on, I would be the one who took her—and maybe have the chance to go with her. Tonight, Death made it clear that's not the case. He tore her from me. Ripped the bond from my chest and separated us. I thought forever."

I don't know what I expected from Adrian, but it wasn't the faint smile I was so used to seeing when he knew something I didn't.

"You mean you discovered how fragile and precious your connection to Katerina is?"

By his tone, he was laughing at me, and I riled. "It shouldn't be *fragile*, Adrian. Not after nine hundred years. It should be as permanent and solid as the foundations of the fucking earth."

He held up his hand. "I meant no offense, caro amico. All I meant was you've realized you're the same as everyone else. Life is precious, Emrick. *Love* is precious. Do you care for our sorceress any less because she's her own person, not some Galatea sculpted just for you?"

"Of course not," I grumbled.

"And is your bond any less of a gift for not being permanent? Or does knowing it's not make you want to protect it all the more fiercely?"

I didn't think it was possible for me to want to guard our bond any more than I always had.

"How am I supposed to protect it when she won't allow me to involve myself?" I asked. "The woman frustrates me beyond belief. Because I would, Adrian. I would enter the infernal realms and destroy the source of Shogaur's power. I would scour the earth for the summoner and turn them to dust without a second thought."

"But then you would run the risk of leaving Katerina in the same position you found yourself in tonight."

My strength seeped out of me. "Exactly."

"How does she feel about all this?"

"I don't know. I left her to change and heal up in the shower." When Adrian quirked an eyebrow, I waved him off. "I'm going back. I just needed a minute to—to—"

"Come to terms with how human you still are?"

"Something like that." I kicked a clump of snow near my boot. "She let me in, you know. Before we went to the hotel. I don't think she wanted to, but she did. It gave me hope that maybe we could try to find some new balance. Something that let us be together without me walking such a precarious line. Now I don't know. Knowing what I do, I don't think I'd able to hold myself back if she came as close to her end as she did tonight."

Adrian rested his hands on the top of his shovel, giving the casual pose an otherworldly grace. "You'll make it happen. That's the nature of love. Bond or no bond, immortality or no immortality—you find a way." He returned his attention to his garden. "What's your next move?"

"She wants to hit the streets outside the hotel. After Rhys's latest video, she expects violence and thinks the summoner will stick around to watch it. After that, I'm not sure. We might return to Manitoulin. There's a witch at the house who knows something about demons. It's possible she can give us some insight into how to stop Shogaur while keeping the kid alive."

"Do you think my presence would be appreciated?"

Something in me relaxed, and I realized what the other half of my purpose was in coming here. "Kat values your counsel. And she might have a few things to talk about that she'd rather not discuss with me."

I hoped so, anyway. I also hoped Adrian would nudge her in my direction. I hated to think all the strides forward we'd made had been lost.

He nodded. "I'll be there. Let me know when you're on your way, and I'll head out directly. Now, if you'll leave me to my gardening, I'd like to get this section finished before the sun comes up."

I left him to it and returned to Toronto, feeling lighter if no less uncertain of what the future held.

33

Katerina

AN HOUR AFTER leaving the hotel room, Emrick and I stood outside the building. Emergency vehicles clogged the street as first responders attempted to put out the fires caused by the spontaneous interior electrical storm or treated the injuries of people who'd gotten caught under the shower of glass.

I wished the arson investigators the best of luck determining the cause of the destruction. The case would be a thorn in someone's paw for the rest of their career. Or their introduction to a world they never dreamed existed.

At the sight of the devastation, I hugged my arms around myself and wished I'd packed a cozy sweater after all. After what had happened—and everything that had happened after—I needed the comfort. Especially since it seemed Emrick wasn't about to offer it.

He stood beside me wearing a knee-length peacoat, worn open to reveal his white T-shirt and jeans. A far cry from the tailored suit, but he still attracted gazes from more than half the EMTs and quite a few of the injured.

I was surprised any of them dared to gawk given Emrick's grim expression. His jaw was set, the lines around his eyes and mouth were hard, and his posture was so stiff Barrett would have given his stamp of approval. Everything about him screamed restraint, and I was sure that if I rested my hand on his arm, I would shake with the vibration of his emotions.

So I kept my hands to myself. Whatever he was upset about, it would have to wait until we'd dealt with the summoner. Which I prayed would be tonight. If Abigail or whoever had progressed to leaving random spell circles behind, she posed more of a danger than summoning demons or encouraging ambitious blood witches. She was going to kill someone—a lot of someones. I was determined to be the last casualty of her cruelty.

Trusting Emrick would follow me, I left the chaos in front of the hotel and headed towards the largest of the three new age shops that had come up in my internet search.

"What are you hoping to find?" he asked.

"I wouldn't say *hoping*. I'm expecting angry people with stones and, close behind them, a suspicious person lurking in the shadows getting off on the stone-throwing."

Anyone else might have asked if I really thought Shogaur's manoeuvrings would work so quickly, but Emrick knew better. The magic in those videos had been palpable. Any mundane watching them—heck, any magical who didn't know to brace themselves—would be pulled into Shogaur's madness. Suspicion, paranoia, anger. All the nuances of fear that first set people on edge and then made them lash out.

I hadn't heard from Barrett or Poppy thanks to my phone being fried by the lightning, so I could only hope Tony had taken down the latest video by now.

"There are a lot of new age shops in the city. What makes you think they'll stick around here?"

"That spell circle wasn't set for the cleaning staff. If Abigail—or whoever—expected me to come, she would have wanted to stick around to see the spell go off. Besides, why wander the city when there are shops right here?"

Was I being short-sighted?

Even as I asked the question, I felt a prickle on the back of my neck. The sensation of being watched. I continued down the street, using my peripherals to take in the traffic, both vehicular and foot, and the shadows leaching out of the alleys. This area was busy even in the middle of the night.

I missed my island. Whoever was watching me would have been easy enough to detect among the trees.

Emrick grabbed my arm and pulled me into the darkness between buildings to avoid being trampled by a man running towards the new age shop. As he passed, he drew his arm back and flung something through the window. The ringing smash of glass was followed by the peal of an alarm inside.

"There's our first stone," I said.

I wished I'd been wrong. If we were already at the stone-throwing, how much longer would it be before we reached incendiary devices?

At the burst of flame that shot through the window into the street and sent the nearest cars veering into each other to escape the scorching heat, I had my answer.

The man who'd thrown the bomb darted away from the building, but I kept my eye on him as he circled back. He stuck close to the stores on the other side of the street and tried to hide himself among the crowd that had gathered to watch the shop burn. He would reek of smoke, making him easy to catch, but hey, I wasn't here to tell him how to engage in proper criminal behaviour.

Most of the people in the crowd stood in stunned shock, their cameras out so they could put their amateur videography skills to work, but my gaze homed in on the person standing on the fringes of the group. He wore a manic smile on his young, handsome face, and his red hair was hidden beneath a black tuque, but I recognized him.

"Rhys."

I stepped forward, then stopped. Everything in me longed to go after him, to chase him down and tackle him. But for a rare change, rational thinking held me back. After I tackled an eighteen-year-old to the ground, how was I supposed to drag him kicking and screaming back to Adrian's house, especially with his demon-imbued strength? The mob would be on me before I got to my feet.

Even if, by some miracle, the crowd stood by and did nothing while I kidnapped a struggling teenager, I'd failed to pin down the summoner. Without the summoner to order Shogaur out of Rhys, there was no safe way to banish the demon. Until Poppy got back to me with a solution, any confrontation would risk my friend's life.

There was also the fact that the moment Shogaur noticed me and got close enough, he might kill Rhys to mess with my head before he targeted me. Given my current question-able state of mind, I doubted my attempts to keep him from possessing me would end well.

Although it tore at me to stay where I was, hidden behind the growing crowd, I made the smart decision. A minute later, Rhys adjusted his tuque and walked off. I swore I caught the purse of his lips as he started whistling.

"I can't imagine how hard that was for you," Emrick said, his lips close to my ear to ensure I heard him over the buzz of the crowd and the clamour of more emergency vehicles arriving at the scene.

"Hardest thing I've done in a while," I said. "And that's saying something, all things considered."

I would have thought facing Death would be my greatest challenge for the night.

Emrick stroked his gloved hand along the side of my face to turn me towards him. "As soon as we find a way to protect you, we can move on him directly, but until then, you have to keep your distance." His gentle fingers tucked my hair behind my ear, and his silver gaze bored into mine. "You have to keep yourself safe."

His jaw flexed, and he tucked his hands into his pockets as he released me and stepped back. I forced myself to turn away from him and return my attention to the crowd, needing a moment to gather myself after the intensity of his stare.

There was so much I wanted to say to him, so much we needed to talk about after the events in that hotel room, but our relationship problems had existed for seventy-five years. They could wait another day until we'd sent Shogaur back to hell, and stopped the summoner, and saved Rhys, and…

Fatigue weighed on me, and my eyelids fought to stay open. I needed to sleep and process everything. If Abigail was here, we wouldn't find her in this crowd. Already the police were shutting down the street and ordering all bystanders back behind the barricade. We'd lost our second shot at finding her tonight, and I'd have to hope Murisa and Poppy were up for a third round of Track the Witch. If either woman was alive by dawn.

I was so distracted by my rising disappointment, I almost missed the person standing on our side of the street on the other side of the flames. She'd lingered after the rest of the crowd had dispersed, her figure obscured by smoke. With the ripple of heat in the air, I might have believed her to be an illusion if I hadn't felt the weight of her stare.

I stared back, squinting to make out her features in the darkness, but she'd pulled up the hood of her coat, hiding the top half of her face.

This had to be our summoner. Was I right that it was Mikhail's patron?

The corner of her wrinkled mouth curled up in a haughty grin, and the expression struck me as painfully familiar—a memory from so long ago I couldn't tell if it was real or a dream.

I closed my eyes to chase the memory, and when I opened them again, the woman was gone. With my heart in my throat, I broke into a run, pushing through the smoke, ignoring the cries of the firefighters as they jumped out of their trucks and rushed to put out the flames before the fire consumed the entire street. As I tore down the block and skidded to a halt on the corner, I had to accept I'd lost her.

But I'd seen her. I knew she existed, and I knew she was watching for me. I couldn't help but take her presence as a challenge—one I was more than ready to meet.

34

Katerina

AFTER PASSING OUT for the better part of the next day, my energy too drained for me to move, I stepped through the mist into the woods behind my house in Spring Bay. Lights shone through the windows, and I pictured everyone sitting inside waiting for news.

As Emrick and I approached the back door, I found myself slowing, stopping, overwhelmed by the idea of having to go inside and fill everyone in on my lack of updates.

In a rush, my solo jaunt through the afterlife returned to me. My mouth went dry, my legs went weak, and Emrick caught me before I crumpled to the ground. I latched on to the lapels of his coat to hold myself up and stared into his eyes, which still burned like molten silver. "I died, didn't I?"

The question slipped out before I could stop it.

He didn't need to answer. The anguish that passed over his face told me enough, but he nodded as he swallowed. His arms tightened around me. "You did."

If anyone would know for sure, it was the man who escorted souls to whatever came next.

"Where were you? I searched for you, but there was only fog." I didn't mean for it to come out as an accusation. I wasn't angry with him, just confused. Afraid. Alone.

Ever since we'd discovered the bond between us, I'd come to see him as my personal Death. The last face I'd see when the time finally came for me to cross over. A foolish part of me hoped that when that happened, he would find a way to come with me so neither of us would face the future by ourselves.

Emrick didn't blink—didn't move—but his eyes burned that much brighter. "Death came for you directly. I couldn't reach you."

There was more he wasn't telling me. Perhaps he couldn't. Perhaps the answer was too close to the secrets of the afterlife. Or he simply didn't want to. I didn't have any particular desire to push. It was enough to know I'd been alone—that I *would* be alone if I ever came that close to the end again.

For the first time in a very long time, I found myself afraid of dying. I was also more certain than ever that without Emrick my world may as well be empty.

I blinked away the tears welling in my eyes and turned towards the house. There would be time later to process what it all meant. For now, I had a witch to meet and interrogate. Only after I cleared both Murisa and Poppy could I ask for their help in finishing this.

The back door was unlocked—thankfully, since I'd lost my keys somewhere in the hotel disaster. We walked in and headed up the stairs to the living room. Poppy was laid out on the couch, one arm resting on her bent knee to better see her phone as she scrolled through her social media apps. Cuddles lay curled on her chest.

"Anything new?" I asked.

She jumped with a shriek, and Cuddles hopped to the floor with a baleful look in my direction. He'd lost another patch of fur behind his ear.

Poppy pressed her hand to her chest as she sat up. Her nails were now a shocking purple with a sparkling gem on every other nail, and I wondered when she'd found the time to give herself a manicure while we were gone.

"Hell on earth, kitty Kat, you scared the crap out of me. It's your couch, so your risk, but seriously, give a girl some warning next time. No, no new videos. Not with him in them anyway. But he did share footage of the attack on that shop. I don't have to tell you which attack, because I know you had a front-row seat."

My eyebrows climbed up my forehead, and I held out my hand for her phone. "Can I see?"

She frowned and angled the phone away from me. "Where's your phone?"

"It suffered an unfortunate accident. Why? Are you afraid I'll steal yours?"

Poppy let out a groan but passed it over. She was right—there I was standing next to Emrick on the street near the shop, shielding my face from the glow and heat of the explosion.

I let the video play out, then hit pause on a clear frame and stared at the figure standing opposite me. Unfortunately, the angle of the footage offered no additional highlights to the woman's face. It had been a long shot, but I was discouraged.

"Where's Murisa?" I asked. "Has she settled in all right?"

Was that a faint blush I noticed on Poppy's cheeks? "She's probably still with Gavin. She's got a knack for clearing auras, so she offered to help him get rid of some of the lingering demonic energy."

I crossed my arms. "Won't we need that energy to track the summoner again?"

Poppy grimaced. "We seriously thought you had her. We kept the spell active long after we passed you the information, and it stayed right where we said. But I'm sure we can cast it again without him if you need us to."

The suspicions that had risen when I'd walked into the

empty hotel room spiked. "It doesn't look good that I've missed her twice, Pop. Not for either of you."

Her brown eyes flashed, and she rose to her feet, her hair bouncing around her shoulders. "We're doing everything we can. It's not our fault you keep missing the mark. I've looked into Murisa, Kat. She's solid. I trust her. And if you don't trust me, why am I here? You use people when you need them, but you never let anyone in. You twist people's arms to get what you want, and when the results don't make you happy, you think they're against you. Well, I've had it, kitty Kat. I'm done proving myself to you."

Her words hit me like a blow, leaving me staring slack-jawed at her.

Getting slapped in the face with your flaws was never a fun experience, and lately it had been happening so often, I felt more than a little exposed and vulnerable. But just as Barrett had been right about me running into danger like I didn't care anymore, and just as Maera had been right that I'd given up, Poppy had it spot on. Since I'd spared her life three years ago, she hadn't crossed me. Aside from a few toes nudging the line, she'd kept within the confines of grey without passing fully into dark. I'd brought her here because I needed her and because, of all the witches I knew, there was no one I trusted more. And if she believed Murisa deserved a chance, I would give the other witch the benefit of the doubt until I had more of a reason not to.

"You're right, and I'm a bitch," I conceded, the closest I could bring myself to an apology.

"Yes, you are," Poppy said, seeming to accept it for what it was.

I nodded. "Let's get everyone in the kitchen and make a game plan. I don't want Rhys playing host to that monster another day."

Voices reached us from the basement, a cheerful female lilt overpowering deeper masculine tones. "No, no, I got this, I swear. It's nothing at all. A bit of a spell and… see? Right over these stairs. Cool, isn't it? It's one of the first spells I created when I started out. Take *that* stores that refuse to make their entrances wheelchair accessible. Assholes."

Barrett reached the top of the stairs first, and behind him, Murisa wheeled herself around the couch and stopped by the armchair. She greeted me with a wide smile. "Katerina, hi! It's so great to meet you in person. You have a beautiful home. Is that a basilisk fang on your mantel? Maera said you'd tell me the story."

The woman was as bubbly as a bottle of freshly popped sparkling wine, and considering the seriousness of our situation, I might have expected it to be grating. It wasn't. Maybe it was her eagerness to help—and the fact that she'd already proved she *could* be helpful—that made her cheerfulness more of a balm than an irritant.

And being in her presence, I had to agree with Poppy—I didn't sense any darkness around her. I wasn't much of an aura reader, but dark magic came with an acidic tang that always left a film on my tongue. Everything about this woman was sunshine.

Her outfit was equally bright and colourful, even more so than it had been on the video call. Her purple long-sleeved tee matched Poppy's nail polish, her washed out jeans were covered in heart-shaped, rhinestoned pink patches, and her running shoes had been decorated with neon hearts and flowers. The same rose necklace I'd noticed earlier hung around her neck, but her earrings were now sunbursts, and a purple headband with a pink fabric flower on the side adorned her thick brown-black hair.

Poppy dropped into the chair closest to Murisa and grinned at me. "See what I mean? This woman wouldn't summon a demon if someone held a melting potion over her head."

I waited for Murisa to look horrified or offended, but although her smile faded, it was into an expression of seriousness. "I totally understand why you'd suspect me after missing the summoner twice after my help. Especially when your friend is possessed. I didn't have anything to do with summoning Shogaur, but I promise I'll do everything I can to help you bring Rhys home."

Her gaze strayed over my shoulder, and I turned to find Maera standing on the threshold between the kitchen and living room. I hadn't noticed her coming out of her bedroom, but she looked as though she'd aged a decade over the past twenty-four hours. Dark circles ringed her eyes, and her hair was frizzy where it hung in its loose braid. She was dressed, but her sweater was inside out.

I took a few hesitant steps towards her, then stopped. Guilt wouldn't let me close the distance. If she wanted to scream at me, I would take it. If she wanted to launch some pots and pans at my head, I wouldn't raise a hand to block them.

But when she approached and threw her arms around me in a hug as tight as an elastic band, I couldn't help the tears that streamed down my cheeks. Everything from the past few hours welled up inside me, and although I couldn't let myself break down yet—not while there was still so much to do—I sank into this moment and used it to strengthen myself. Maera hadn't lost faith in me, and I swore to live up to it.

Keeping hold of her hand, I turned to face the rest of the room. "Okay," I said, drying my cheeks with the pads of my fingers, "so this is where we stand. When I saw Rhys tonight, he looked to be in good shape. I think we have about forty-eight hours before that starts to change. I want Shogaur out of him within the next twenty-four to stay within the safe zone. The summoner has evaded us twice, and I can't help but think we'd be wasting time if we kept going after her. She's playing with us, and so far we've let her. Now that Murisa is here, it's time to focus on Shogaur." I looked to Barrett. "Where are we with the videos?"

He crossed his arms. "Tony's team has removed every video he's put up. They closed his account, but he created a new one. It's an ongoing process, and he's getting ahead of us, but we're staying close on his heels. Murisa's helping with that."

I raised an eyebrow, and the witch's smile brightened. "I know a lot about demons and summonings and all that stuff, but I'm actually a tech witch. That's my focus. I was able to enchant an alert on Poppy's phone. Every single time Rhys's face appears, we get a pop-up with all the information we need to remove it, which speeds up our ability to take it down."

"That's impressive."

"Isn't it?" Poppy asked, her eyes shining as she looked at Murisa.

Murisa blushed under the necromancer's attention, then cleared her throat. "Give me a list of what else you need, and I'll get started."

"*We'll* get started," Poppy corrected. "If you're going against Shogaur, you need all the firepower you can get."

I really did, but more important, I needed to keep everyone here safe. I held up my fingers to count off the priorities. "One—we need a way to keep Shogaur out of our heads.

Two—we need something to get him out of Rhys without risking Rhys's life. Three—we need a way to pin the bastard down so I can get his blood and send him back to the infernal realms."

None of those items were small beans, but neither Murisa nor Poppy appeared daunted.

"I've already started putting the protection spell together," Poppy said.

Murisa nodded. "Give us a few hours, and we'll have something for you."

With no way of knowing what she was basing her confidence on, I'd have to put some faith in this tech witch I'd never heard of before yesterday.

"All right, you witches start working on that. Barrett, you keep watching the internet. Let me know if anything new comes up. Maera, do you think you're up to making dinner? I haven't eaten all day, and I'm starving." She nodded, looking relieved to be given something to focus on. I turned to Emrick where he stood against the wall staring at me. "Would you mind keeping an eye on the perimeter? I don't trust Shogaur or the summoner not to send something else our way to keep us busy."

He held my gaze for a long while, and in those few passing moments, I read his preference to stay close at my side. In the end, he nodded and stepped through the mist to take his tour.

Finally, I turned to Gavin, who'd snuck into the room

behind Murisa and was lingering near the top of the stairs, attempting to stay out of the conversation. "You, my sorcerer friend, are coming outside with me."

He stiffened and clenched his fists at his sides. "Why?"

"Because Poppy is right. We'll need more firepower once we get Shogaur out of Rhys's body. You're it. It's time you learned how to control your magic."

35

Katerina

A N HOUR LATER, I rested my forehead against the locked bedroom door. "Come on, Gavin, we've been through this. You can't hide from what you are forever."

"I can," he said from inside. "I have no interest in learning how to use *magic*. I don't want the damn stuff. If you could make it go away, that would be great."

"Unfortunately, that's not how genetics work. Your options are to learn how to use it or wait until the day you set yourself or someone you care about on fire, and then won't you be embarrassed."

I drew in a deep breath and reminded myself who I was dealing with. Before a few days ago, Gavin had no idea magic existed, let alone that he possessed any. As far as he remembered, anyway. He'd been tortured by a demon and was now suffering a huge identity crisis. Pointing out all the ways he was a danger to people would not put him at ease.

"Getting a handle on your power will give you a fighting chance against Shogaur if he gets close to you again. Wouldn't you like the opportunity to blast him in the face with a fireball? After we get him out of Rhys, of course."

"I'd rather not have to see him again. I told you I wanted to help, but not with *magic*."

My patience slipped again. "Stop saying it like it's a bad word. You're a sorcerer, Gavin. Magic is as innate to your blood as the colour of your hair or your ability to metabolize carbs." Deep breath in. "This will protect you from yourself as well. I'm not saying you need to reach your full potential, which, believe me, would be incredibly strong, I'm just suggesting you learn the basics to keep yourself safe."

A knock at the front door made me jump. I considered ignoring it, knowing Gavin had to be my priority, but when no one else made a move to answer it, I decided to give both of us a break.

When I climbed the stairs to the foyer, I found the main floor empty. Something was cooking in the oven, but Maera was nowhere around, and Barrett was gone. Murisa and Poppy, I knew, were in Poppy's room downstairs working on those protection spells, and Emrick was still wandering the property.

He hadn't appeared to warn me about whoever was at the door, which suggested he knew our visitor, and by the fact that the ward hadn't kept them out—and by the recent sunset—I could guess who it was.

Sure enough, when I opened the door, I found Adrian standing on my porch. He wore a dark green dress shirt rolled to the elbows and tucked into a pair of form-fitting black pants. His brown hair was brushed neatly to the side, and his eyes were ringed with red.

"Here for a snack?" I asked, stepping aside to let him in. It was rare the vampire left his house. Even rarer that he came to mine when he knew trouble was on the horizon. Adrian was far from a coward, but he'd lived his days of fighting and battle, and all he wanted now was to retire with his books and, for whatever reason, Barrett.

He looked me up and down in a way that confirmed where Emrick had gone while I'd washed off my near-death experience. "I came to see you, tesoro."

I huffed and led him through the empty living room to my bedroom. It was the only place I could be certain we wouldn't be interrupted or overheard. The rest of the house didn't need to know what I'd gone through in Toronto.

"What did Emrick tell you?" I asked after Adrian nudged the door shut behind him.

"That there was an incident. A rather alarming one."

My confidence wobbled, and I dropped onto the stool in front of my vanity table. "He says I died. Like, actually actually. Heart stopped, hello afterlife." I swallowed. "He says he couldn't reach me because Death collected me himself."

Adrian slid onto the edge of my bed so he sat facing me. "That must have come as quite a shock."

"Nothing like being in the presence of Death to make you appreciate life," I grumbled. "Since Alodie, Mae, and Blythe's spell bound me to Emrick, my run-in with Shogaur in the thirteenth century is the closest I've come to a final end. The idea that he might succeed this time… I'll admit, it scares me."

Adrian nodded. "It's human nature to want to survive. It doesn't matter how long you've lived, there is always a wish for *one more day*."

I leaned forward to rest my elbows on my knees. "Even for you?"

His dark, crimson-filled eyes turned up in a smile. "Even for me. Two thousand years—more—and I still wish for another night to savour the life I've created for myself. I'll carry no regrets when that wish is no longer granted, but until then, the desire is always there. So to fear this demon is natural. One might even say that to fear a fear demon is wise. So why are you ashamed of it?"

A laugh bubbled out of me, and I pulled my knees to my chest. "Arrogance, I guess. After all I've seen, I didn't think I was afraid of anything anymore. And Death, well, I thought when the time came, I would run into that fog, eager to be with my family again."

The door creaked as Cuddles padded into the room. He dodged my hand when I reached out to pet him but rubbed himself against Adrian's leg. Rude.

"But?" Adrian asked.

Cuddles hopped onto the bed and butted his head against Adrian's arm, demanding attention. The vampire wrinkled his nose—either at the smell or the long grey cat hair—but complied.

I propped my chin on the tops of my knees. "I don't think it was the *end* that scared me so much. It was that there I was, standing on the edge of the afterlife, straddling this world and the next, and the only thing around me was fog. I guess I realized that, for all my griping, there were people here I would miss."

I didn't specify anyone, though a pair of intense silver eyes hovered in the front of my mind. But it wasn't only Emrick. It was all of them. Even grumpy Barrett.

"What of Emrick?" Adrian asked, and I frowned.

"You really won't leave it alone, will you?"

He held out his hands, offending Cuddles so badly the cat jumped off the bed and left the room. I rolled my eyes at everything I suspected Adrian was about to say but lowered my feet to the floor and set my palms on his.

"He came to me after it happened, tesoro. He was beside himself. Like you, he experienced what his world would become without you, and it broke him. You know my opinion on the matter, cuore mio, that there must be a way forward for you, but I repeat it now more emphatically than I have—you *need* each other. One without the other is a shell. You are the balance you so desperately fight to protect. If anything were to happen to me, I would feel better knowing you both had someone to lean on."

I narrowed my eyes. "What would happen to you? You're retired. All that awaits you is peace and quiet and, well, Barrett."

Adrian chuckled, but something lurked in his eyes, and the way he refused to look at me told me he was holding something back. Dread coiled in my heart, but I set it aside. My old friend wouldn't keep anything serious from me for long. When he was ready, he would tell me.

In the meantime, I would be here to support him as much as he did me.

I squeezed his hands. "I can't make any promises, Adrian, but I'll think about what you've said. I've had my eyes opened to a few things over the past few weeks, and it's put a lot into perspective."

The fact that my life wasn't over yet. The fact that, on my own, I felt like half the sorceress I was born to be. Emrick made me feel whole. I just wasn't ready to accept the consequences of that revelation.

"I'm sure Shogaur's return has played its part in that as well," Adrian said.

I swallowed a rise of bitterness. "No doubt."

"I remember the first time you and the demon became acquainted."

I forced out a dry laugh. "I'm sure you do. I took up the guest room in your Italian villa for months while I recovered."

It was how we met, when Emrick had whisked me out of the flames and taken me to Adrian's. Those two men had nursed me through the agony as my burned flesh healed. I remembered how uncertain Adrian had been to have me there, how hesitant to accept me—and how completely he'd embraced me after I agreed to let him teach me to dance. From the ashes had grown the friendship of ages.

"I'm hoping we don't have a repeat of *that* misadventure," I said. "I like to think I've learned a little since then."

"I like to think we all have."

I turned my head towards a knock at the door and called for whoever it was to come in.

I expected Barrett with an update, or maybe Emrick looking to join in on our conversation, but it was Gavin who stood there glowering at me.

"Yes?" I prepared myself for any amount of vitriol he

intended to spew.

"Fine," he said. "I'll take you up on your offer. Help me not set myself on fire."

I exchanged a small smile with Adrian, then pushed myself to my feet. "Come on, then. Let's get started."

36

Katerina

G AVIN STOOD AT the edge of the beach, his feet hip-width apart, his hands at his sides. We were beyond the ward, but I didn't expect Shogaur to return. Now now that he had what he needed.

I stood a few feet behind the sorcerer, close enough that I didn't have to yell, far enough to avoid any unplanned bursts of flame. There had already been one incident, albeit small and only costing me the belt on my sweater, and I preferred not having to heal from intense burns when I was supposed to be preparing to battle a demon.

"When I was first learning, my teachers used to tell me to picture the fire in my blood as embers. Close your eyes and sink deep into the flow of your body, imagine your heart pumping, pushing your blood through your veins, straight to the tips of your fingers."

I allowed the cadence of teachers past to spin through my mind, drawing on memories I thought I'd forgotten.

I'd hated those lessons so much. I'd never mastered my skills back when my community in Palonia had been alive. Every day had been a fresh hell as I'd struggled to tap into the power that filled me. I'd only been able to cast my magic through direct contact, never able to project it outwards. Fireballs from my palms were nothing but a dream, lightning a laughable idea. I'd been a disappointment to my teachers and, although they never said it, a frustration to my parents. My siblings didn't have the same troubles I did. The only person to falter had been little Katerina, who could create ice as well as fire but couldn't do anything with it.

Not until Emrick had agreed to train me. It had taken a hundred years to break through the blocks I'd built and unleash everything I was capable of, but the day it happened had been the day my future had taken form.

My family was gone, I was stuck with this immortality I hadn't asked for, and finally I'd found purpose.

Maybe I should have asked Emrick to take this fledging sorcerer under his wing. Maybe he would have more success transforming Gavin from reluctant magical into someone who, with time, could help me protect the world.

First step first—protecting my friends and furnishings.

With seeming effort, Gavin relaxed his shoulders so they no longer crowded his earlobes and let his hands fall loose by his sides. His fingers remained extended, as though he were reaching for something out of sight.

"Once you're aware of those embers, I want you to guide them towards your hands. Imagine them waking up, glowing, growing warmer as they move."

My own magic flared within me, a thrilling power surge as it spread through my blood and searched for a way out.

A shout filled the air, and Gavin wriggled in pain as smoke plumed from his pores—not from his hands but from every-where. His shirt caught fire, and the flames threatened to grab hold of his hair. I reversed my heat and focused on the water in the air, cooling the temperature until snowflakes danced around Gavin's head and frost crept over his skin.

Once the small flames were out, I released my magic and dropped my arms. Gavin stood still, chest heaving, staring at his hands as though he didn't recognize them as his own.

When he lifted his head to look at me, his dark eyes burned with rage and desperation.

"I can't do this," he snapped. "I don't know why I thought I could. This power—it's too much. I feel it crawling around inside my head. I don't want to listen to it. If I start, it'll get louder, and I can't—*Argh!*" He shoved his fists against his temples and bent into a crouch.

Do not get frustrated. Do not *get frustrated.*

I breathed through my desire to grab his arm and force him to stand and face me. All that would earn me was another loss of clothes and another door slammed in my face. For so many reasons, he needed to grasp these concepts—and not only because I wanted him at my side to face Shogaur—but he wouldn't learn any faster if I pushed him.

We also didn't have time for him to fight against picking up the basics. We had a summoner and a demon who had both proved they could put me in my place. I needed reinforcements.

Adrian's words echoed in my ears—it was wise to fear a fear demon. Well, here I was, full of wisdom. I didn't want to get lost in that fog again for Death to sweep me away without giving me a chance to say goodbye.

I stood frozen, caught between lashing out and giving up. I was on the verge of telling Gavin I was done. He could go live his life and good luck.

Movement caught the corner of my eye, and I half-turned to find Barrett walking towards us in the deepening twilight. His skin tone looked a little grey, leaving no guesses as to what he and Adrian had been up to since the vampire had left my side. His palm rested on the hilt of a knife hanging off his belt, his thick arms stretching the fabric of his black thermal shirt. His expression, as usual, was grim, but for a change it was focused on Gavin instead of me.

"Magic is the bane of our existence," he said, and I opened my mouth to tell him to disappear. That was the opposite of what Gavin needed to take away from this. He didn't give me a chance to cut in. "But it's also useful against the enemies that exist in it. If it's used properly."

"I don't *want* to use it," Gavin spat, straightening and facing off with him.

"Unfortunately, you have no choice." Barrett's voice was calm, matter-of-fact, lacking his usual disdain for the subject. "This world is at war. A constant, never-ending war of magical against magical and magical against mundane, and more than half the planet's population has no idea. The second your power woke up, you became a soldier. You can bury your head in the sand if you want, but the only result will be that you get your ass kicked. People more powerful than you with a better grasp of that power will recognize you for what you are and tear you apart. Or worse—use you."

Gavin's throat bobbed, and his expression flared with anguish. "I'm not a soldier. Thanks to Murisa, I remember more of who I am. I'm a nurse. That's what I do. I help people. There's no room for destructive magic in that life."

"Then make room," Barrett pushed, closing the distance between them. "Magic users crave power for themselves and hate other people having any. They'll try to take it from you, or they'll try to wipe you out. Either that, or your power will grow so uncontrolled that someone like Kat will have no choice but to put you down. There is zero benefit to you not learning these skills as you'd learn anything else. That's the option you face—you learn or you die. The only question will be when and how."

The two men stared at each other, Barrett looking everything like a soldier in command, and Gavin appearing more like a trapped animal searching for an out.

I was impressed that Barrett of all people had come to deliver this speech and wondered if Adrian had given him a nudge in the privacy of their bedroom. He wouldn't have been my first choice as champion. His hatred of all things magical was ingrained in his personality. Frankly, I was surprised he hadn't gone off to march behind Shogaur against the witches.

But he must have struck a nerve because Gavin staggered backwards to the edge of the water.

"I feel like the world is spinning out of control, and I can't get it to stop," he said, sounding more broken than he had since I met him. "I don't know how to do this."

I approached him, my hands loose at my sides, while Barrett leaned against a tree trunk and crossed his arms.

"I can't stop the spin for you, but we can try to slow it down," I said. "You've got allies here, Gavin. We'll do everything we can to keep you from getting hurt—or hurting anyone else."

I nodded to Barrett, who scowled at me, but it lacked the heat it usually carried. I fought the smile threatening to tug at my mouth. Was he warming up to me? Perish the thought.

I refocused on Gavin. "All right, let's try again. Close your eyes, tap into those embers, and imagine them moving towards your hands. Know that you're safe, know that you're in control of them. They are a part of you, no different from your fingers or toes."

A cold wind blew my hair and ruffled my untied sweater. The sweet scent of campfire and loam wafted around me as Emrick appeared, and I wondered if he approved of the way I'd handled my student.

The first student I'd ever had. A responsibility I never dreamed I'd experience after watching the last sorcerers die out.

"When you feel your palms getting warm, raise your hands and push it outwards. Project it, as if you were throwing a ball."

The air between us pulsed with magic, and I mirrored Gavin's movements, ready to fend off another stray burst of flame if things went wrong. Barrett didn't move, though his eyes narrowed a fraction as he watched.

Gavin's arms trembled, and we held a collective breath, waiting.

Then a stream of fire lit from his palms and puffed into smoke over the melting ice. Hardly an impressive display, but I grinned despite the tiny flame.

Gavin turned to face me, the depth of his shock nearly as strong as the shining self-loathing. The sight pained me, but nothing I said would change his mind. He was what he was, and he could either accept it or he couldn't.

My chest filled with the compassion that had been missing since we'd started our practice. "Give it time, Gavin. Your world just got a whole lot bigger. You need to decide how you want to grow with it."

As the words fell from my lips, I realized how true they were for me as well. With every new person that tumbled into my growing family, the umbrella of my protection expanded. Like Gavin, I was faced with a choice. I could stand in front of them and be the sword that kept them safe, throwing myself into this fight against Shogaur and the summoner, or I couldn't.

And with every passing hour, I knew my window to make that call was nearly closed.

37

Katerina

GAVIN AND I trained for the next few hours, working on the foundations of his starts and stops, with only a short dinner break to interrupt us. Barrett settled into one of the Muskoka chairs at the back of the house and watched from a distance. I questioned his motives in staying but saw no malice in his expression. If anything, he seemed to be studying our movements. Learning how to counter them just in case?

Emrick stuck around as well, leaning against the house with his hands shoved into the pockets of his coat. Although I did my best to ignore him, his gaze became a physical presence—a hand on the small of my back, breath fanning the side of my neck. My skin tingled as though he were right behind me, taking up the space he had during our training days, and I breathed through the sensations stirring within me.

By the end of those few hours, I was less concerned that our guest would set fire to my linens. He still slipped more often than not, but he'd shown a knack for fighting fire with fire, extinguishing the stray flames before they had time to spread. Baby steps. I could tell he hated every second, but he'd kept his complaints to himself.

I was about to walk him through another set of exercises when Barrett called me over. The tone of his voice made the hair on my arms stand on end, and I stalked towards him, braced for bad news.

Sure enough, his phone was in his hand, and he gave it to me without comment.

Emrick pushed away from the house, and I turned up the volume so everyone could hear Rhys's latest video.

"Did you guys see that fire last night?" His smile was cheerful, his eyes wild.

Gavin joined us on the patio and stood at Barrett's elbow to watch the screen.

"I'm not encouraging violence against these witches," Rhys said, "but I gotta say, the flames bursting out of that store were awfully bright, weren't they? Hopefully the other shop owners and the people who give them their money will shut their doors and stay safe at home. But there are still the people who buy into the philosophy. The bullshit."

Emrick came around Barrett's chair to stand beside me. His palm settled in the small of my back, right where I'd sensed it earlier. I sank into his touch, grateful for the support that steadied my shaking legs as Rhys's smile faded into anger and his stare grew more intense. Because I was ready for it, I was able to block out the waves of fear emanating from Rhys's voice, Shogaur's influence at work. How many thousands watching would fall prey this time?

"I heard from a reliable source that these *witches* are behind the rising housing costs in this province. All their 'do-gooding' and fighting for touchy-feely peace and granola crap is making it impossible for the rest of us to get anything out of life. These people need to learn their so-called self-empowerment is not wanted here. They go against what is normal and safe and *right*. Maybe it's time we get a bit louder about that."

The video cut out, and I held my breath as I scrolled through the comments. Fifteen minutes and thousands of people had shouted their agreement. Shogaur knew what he was doing. A few short words, barely any call to action, and a good segment of Ontario's population was gathering forces.

A groan rolled out of my throat, and, almost of its own accord, my thumb moved to the news app. Sure enough, the top local story was about a poor woman who'd been swarmed in the park for doing a tarot reading on her lunch break. She was in hospital in critical condition.

We were out of time. With or without Gavin, with or without Murisa's talismans, we had to move now. I prayed we would find a way to get Shogaur out of Rhys's body before we moved against him, but if it came down to my friend or the rest of the world…

I bowed my head and tried to breathe through the tightening of my throat. How much of Rhys remained in his head? How much was he suffering with every word his body uttered?

I hated this job.

We stepped into the rec room to find Poppy and Murisa sitting near the door to Poppy's room. Maera sat on the couch, her face buried in her hands. Adrian stood behind her, his hand resting on her shoulder.

I didn't know what to say.

The heaviness of the silence filled my mouth with cotton, and my eyes burned with tears I refused to shed while there was still hope we could overcome the threat bearing down on us.

I licked my lips and stared at each one of the people standing with me. Drawing in a shaky breath, I focused my gaze on the wall straight ahead, unable to look any of them in the eye. "Shogaur made a mistake when he took one of our own." My voice trembled. I squeezed my hands at my sides and stepped forward. "He made a mistake when he returned to this plane believing he could get the better of us again. The person pulling his strings underestimated the power standing against them. Every one of us in this room is capable of opposing them, but together we're a force they can't match."

I took another step forward, this time meeting Poppy's gaze, then Murisa's. "We will send this demon back to hell." I looked at Maera. "We will get Rhys back. This demon and the woman who summoned him have pissed me off, and they'll regret it."

Adrian nodded over Maera's shoulder, and I caught the pride in his eyes. Not at my words, but that I was taking a stand and embracing the role I'd once held as master of the hunt.

I pulled my shoulders back and turned to where Emrick stood beside me. "I won't run away scared because of who or what he is. Or because something might happen to me. I'm going to fight—*we're* going to fight. Tonight. And we're going to win."

He hesitated only a second before he nodded.

I returned my attention to the witches. "Have you finished the talismans?"

Murisa and Poppy exchanged a look, and Murisa grimaced as she held out a necklace with a rose made of black tourmaline hanging from a simple silver chain. "This one is finished. The other is… useable, but I don't know if it's strong enough to hold up against a demon of his level. I'll keep working on it. It might come in useful later."

"Thank you, Murisa." I accepted the necklace and slipped it into my pocket. "I appreciate the quick turnaround."

"As for sending Shogaur back to hell, I made you something else."

I frowned. "What do you mean? Once I get Shogaur out of Rhys, I spill the demon's blood and speak the words. What tools do I need?"

As far as I knew, banishing demons hadn't changed that much over the years.

Murisa shrugged. "You could do it that way, but it means rushing through the words, and if you don't get it right, or if the spell is interrupted, you risk losing your chance."

That wasn't wholly true. I'd passed out before finishing Shogaur's banishing ritual the first time, but he was gone when I'd woken up. But I wasn't about to argue with the witch if she offered some form of Easy Mode.

Murisa pulled another necklace from the satchel draped over the back of her wheelchair, this one less subtle and more thrift-store-costume-jewellery gaudy. The large red dome in the centre of the heavy silver setting caught the ceiling lights. The whole thing was about two inches in diameter, the dome rising half an inch from the setting, and I crossed my fingers I wouldn't need to wear it. I'd hate for anyone to see me with it and think it was an accessory of choice.

Murisa must have noticed my distaste because she laughed, the sound light and merry despite the tone of the room. "I know, it's hideous, isn't it? Sturdy, though. You don't want anything that'll shatter during the spell. The dome in the middle is thick glass. Stones and gems are too dense to hold anything in them, so an empty sphere is the way to go. The setting is the magical part. All you need to do is cast the spell to tether the demon to the amulet, and the magic will ensure he can't wriggle free. I've even added an enchantment to collect his blood as he passes into it, so you'll have everything you need to banish him. The sphere will explode when he leaves it, though, so keep your distance."

"Exploding sphere. Got it." I frowned. "How close do I need to get to tether him?"

She grimaced. "Closer than you'd like. Direct contact is best. And not through the host, or you'll risk capturing Rhys's soul in there as well."

A sound escaped Maera's throat, and she pressed her hand over her mouth. Her eyes swam with tears she didn't let fall. I wanted to promise her I wouldn't do anything to put Rhys in greater danger, but as I stared down at the amulet, as I thought of the speed of Shogaur's spreading influence, I realized I couldn't.

I swallowed the lump in my throat. "All right." It came out croaky, so I coughed and tried again. "The timing on this will be dicey."

"I made this for you, too." Poppy handed me a satchel. "Emergency healing salve. Just in case. As for getting him out of Rhys…" She shot Maera an apologetic glance. "We couldn't figure that out. Not without harming him."

I breathed out slowly. "Then we work around it. By now, Rhys's body should have started breaking down—not too much and not permanently," I rushed to reassure Maera, praying I was right. "Just enough to make it appealing for Shogaur to leave if he's offered something better."

In other words, use me as bait and hope we trapped him in the amulet before he forced his way into my head. It meant I couldn't wear the talisman Murisa and Poppy had made, or Shogaur would sense it and not make the leap. It also meant I'd have to pray the barriers around my head were strong enough to keep him out when he charged me—or that whoever came with us made quick work with the amulet if I failed. My death would be worth it, no hesitation, but the rock of dread weighed heavy in my gut. I didn't want to consider the option that we all failed and Shogaur took over my power.

"Not a chance in the afterlife," Emrick growled, staring at me as though he'd read my every thought.

"If that's the choice we're left with, that's how it'll play out." I left no room for argument, but his glower told me he wasn't finished with the conversation. Whatever. He could say as much as he wanted; I wouldn't change my mind. Not if it meant saving Rhys. I looked at Adrian. "That's always been the rule, hasn't it? The hunt comes first. Whatever it takes to protect the balance."

His expression was pained, but he nodded. "Whatever it takes."

"I can't ask you—" Maera choked on a sob, unable to finish.

I gave her my most reassuring smile. "Fortunately, you don't have to ask. Rhys is coming home."

Barrett's face hadn't twitched once with all my talk, but I noted the way he raised his chin. In approval? Well, goodie. Nice to know I'd earned that from Mr. Grumpy-Pants.

"What about me?" Gavin asked.

A laugh escaped me. "For all the progress you made today, it looks like you get to sit this one out after all. We have one talisman, which means you'll be at risk of Shogaur taking you over."

"Unless we use him as the bait," Emrick suggested.

"No," I said over Gavin's horrified protest. "I did not free him just to throw him back into Shogaur's reach."

"Thanks for that," Gavin grumbled.

"Kat—"

I turned on Emrick. "I said no. I'm not putting someone else's life in danger just because you don't want to risk mine."

A few years ago, I might have given a different answer. But now I had my friends—my *family*—to protect. None of these people had witnessed how far I was willing to go for that.

"Gavin, you'll stay here with Poppy and Murisa. You two, I want you tracking the summoner. I don't want any surprises while I'm dealing with Shogaur. Barrett, Adrian, Emrick, you'll come with me to Toronto. We'll stand a better chance of closing in on the demon if we can flank him. Barrett, you'll be Poppy and Murisa's point of contact. I want texts incoming every ten minutes once you tag Abigail, whether there's changes to her movements or not."

"You got it," Murisa said, and Barrett nodded. I was grateful he didn't argue with me about taking point, though I had reservations about him being there at all. While I doubted Shogaur would attempt to take him over, his mundane body being even less use to him than Rhys's slightly stronger frame, Barrett's hatred of magic would make him an easy target for Shogaur's influence. How much would it take for the demon to convince him I was better off dead?

Hopefully the vampire blood running through him would offer some protection. Otherwise, I had to trust Adrian would keep him in line.

"Do we know where Shogaur is?" Adrian asked.

"We cast a tracking spell on Rhys's phone while we worked on the amulets," Poppy said.

She pulled out her phone, then frowned at me, and Maera passed her a pad and pen from the end table for her to scribble down the address. I really needed to replace my phone.

"This is his last known location," she said as she handed me the paper. "It's a small apartment building in Oakville."

"Thanks, Poppy. All right, everyone. We leave within the—"

The sound of car doors slamming interrupted me, and a sense of foreboding cut through the room as the roar of voices and the reflection of fire through the upstairs windows floated into the basement. On numb legs, I headed up to the living room and stared outside.

"Fuck me sideways," I said on a groan. The mob had returned, this time armed with literal torches and pitchforks. "Shogaur must have guessed we're ready to make our move. He's sent them to keep us busy."

Adrian came up beside me. "Then you should go. Stop him now before he takes another step."

Barrett took his place on the other side of the window, peering out around the curtain. "We can't get through them to reach the cars."

"I believe our role in stopping Shogaur ends here, James," Adrian said, and I clenched my teeth. He was right.

"Everyone, protect the house," I said. "Protect Maera. Keep them busy."

I turned to Emrick, who'd appeared near the back windows. His jaw was tight, but he made no move to argue with me.

Poppy's eyes widened as she realized what I was saying. "You're going after the demon alone? It was bad enough when it was only the four of you going, but at least there was the chance of splitting Shogaur's attention."

I ignored her concern. It didn't change anything except make my stomach wibbly with fears of my own. "Anyone have a phone I can borrow?"

Murisa drew hers out and tossed it to me. "We'll text you the information on the summoner's location as soon as we have it."

Her confidence was a welcome contrast to my escalating dread.

I stopped next to Emrick. Dark clouds passed over his moonlight eyes, his gaze full of silent questions. I nodded in answer, and he replied with a subtle sigh before he pulled off his glove. Without looking away from me, he rested his hand on the back of my neck and pulled me towards him. My skin tingled under the contact, my body at once striving to zip through time and put itself back together. I closed my eyes as the room faded.

We were stepping into the past, Emrick and I. Last time, I hadn't been enough to face the fear demon and had wound up first in a dungeon and then burning at the stake before I'd cast him back to hell. I had to hope eight hundred years had prepared me to get the job done before the fires began.

38

Emrick

WE STEPPED THROUGH the mist and were immediately slapped in the face by an overwhelming sense of terror. It emanated from the apartment building in front of us with such intensity it was almost visible, like a dark grey cloud obscuring the moon.

Kat stiffened in my arms, her muscles braced, ready to run, and I had to stop myself from encouraging her to do it. I didn't want her going in there against that demon. Not again. Not when there was a chance she would wind up in the same place she'd been the last time she tried to stop him.

But she'd never forgive me if I prevented her from taking action. Especially not if Rhys died because of it.

I swallowed the fear that was all my own and held her steady as she screwed up her courage. "We still have time to come up with another plan. One that doesn't pit you directly against Shogaur. We know where he is, we know what he's doing. We could wait for him to leave the apartment and lure him somewhere we have more advantages."

Kat's nostrils flared as she summoned her anger to snuff out the other emotions threatening to break her down. I'd seen her do it hundreds of times over the centuries and knew that once she reached this point, there was no stopping her.

If I ever could have.

"I'm not giving him another minute." The lines around her eyes softened a smidge as she turned to face me. "I know you're afraid for me, and I promise not to take any unnecessary risks. But you know I have to do this."

Her blue eyes begged me to understand, and I bowed my forehead against hers. "I hate it, but I know. Whatever you need from me, you've got it."

The need to kiss her wrapped through my thoughts. If everything went to hell in there—more than they were supposed to—I didn't want to miss this opportunity to show her how much I loved her.

But that would be too much like saying goodbye, so I released her and tugged my gloves on.

She pulled the talisman out of her pocket and held it out to me. "Your job will be getting this to Rhys as soon as he's free so I can focus on trapping Shogaur." A furrow formed between her brows. "No. Wait. You can't—it might be considered involvement. Fuck, Emrick, why is this so hard?"

Tears filled her eyes, but she huffed out a breath and brushed them away as she stuffed the talisman back in her pocket.

"I know my limits," I said, holding myself back from touching her.

She nodded without looking at me and marched towards the building. Flames crept over her fingers, up her gloves to the elbow, her fury unleashed. I followed behind her but slowed when movement caught the corner of my eye. I turned my head and spotted a crowd of people marching around the side of the building towards us.

"We might want to hurry."

Murisa's phone buzzed in Kat's pocket, and she extinguished her magic and pulled it out without breaking her stride. "Well, shit."

She handed me the phone, and I read Poppy's message.

He knows you're outside. Just sicced his mob on you with another video.

"That would have been good to know two minutes ago," I mumbled as I returned the phone.

We continued towards the door, watching the growing throng as it closed in on us. How many had answered Shogaur's summons? From my quick glance, I counted around three dozen—young, old, many of them armed with bats and knives and frying pans—and that was just the people coming up the street in this direction. How many waited for us around back? How many waited inside?

I shoved my hands in my pockets to remove the urge to take off my gloves. These people weren't the villains here. They'd simply been caught up in whatever story the demon had spun. Any aggression they showed stemmed from deep, irrational fear that had pushed them firmly into mob mentality, and the only way to get them to see reason was to destroy the source.

The door to the building was locked, so I pulled off one glove and passed us through to the tiny lobby-slash-mail room. Inside was eerily silent, as though everyone in their apartments had hunkered down, waiting for something to happen.

The stink of sulphur wafted from upstairs. Kat and I followed the stench and had reached the first floor before someone from the mob attempted to open the lobby doors. We were halfway up the second flight before someone smashed through the glass.

I shoved Kat forward, urging her to up the pace. Any hesitation she'd shown before disappeared, and she took off at a run to close the distance to the top floor.

From there, it was only a matter of following the reek of

demon to the unit at the end. So far, the hallways remained empty, but already we heard shouts coming from the lobby, and I was certain people would be spilling from their apartments by the time the crowd reached the top.

My heart thundered with my desire to protect Kat, but all I could do was watch her back and warn her of what was coming.

The fire around her hands spread, and my teeth buzzed as she drew more magic into herself. Once it reached its peak, she raised her foot and kicked the door open.

39

Katerina

RHYS STOOD IN the middle of the living room, his smile wide, his green eyes flickering red.

The living room was the same one from the video, and I wondered who it had belonged to before Shogaur moved in. I doubted the demon had decorated it himself before taking over Rhys's body. Or that Abigail had taken the time to set up this cushy pad.

Likely, it had been the home of one of Shogaur's earlier hosts. Some human whose body hadn't lasted a day before he'd burned through it.

The area rug was a worn burgundy that stood out against the green couch and faded red-and-gold wallpaper. The curtains were a cream organza that had browned around the edges, which made sense given the reek of stale cigarette smoke permeating the air. On the side table next to the couch was a stack of mail, one letter half-opened, the letter opener still sticking out of the top.

Katerina…

Shogaur's voice wormed its way into my head, weaving through my grey matter and tugging at my amygdala, making me want to turn and run.

I stood my ground and clenched my fists at my sides. Murisa's banishing amulet dug into my palm through my leather glove, where it would hopefully remain unseen until I needed it. If Shogaur threw himself off the balcony to escape me, the demon would survive the fall, but Rhys's mortal frame would suffer serious damage in the landing.

"Looks like you've made yourself comfortable," I said, stepping farther into the room. Emrick remained by the door, blocking Rhys in and preventing any of the mob from interrupting me. I hoped his tall, muscular frame would overshadow Shogaur's influence, but I had to be prepared to fight off more than the demon if they broke through.

"The world has changed since I was last here," Shogaur said. "I must say, I enjoy it. Everything is so *easy*. It used to take months to convince a small group of people why they should fear the simplest things, but now?" He laughed. "There's no challenge. It's almost not worth it."

It didn't matter that I'd watched a bunch of his videos and had heard the disgusting ideas coming out of my young friend's mouth, to hear him in person raised goosebumps on my arms. There was nothing of the demon in his voice except for his creepy cadence. It was only Rhys. Sweet, innocent Rhys who until a few months ago had remained on the outskirts of the magical world. Now here he was in the thick of it, his body no longer his own, his sense of self crammed into a small corner of his mind as a powerful demon controlled him.

How much time remained before the last spark of him extinguished? And if—when—we got Shogaur out, how would he cope with what had happened? With what his face and voice had made happen?

Rage bubbled inside me, and the fire in my hands flared. I redirected the magic to my right hand, not wanting to accidentally melt the amulet in my left, but kept it reined in. I didn't want to have to deal with the building burning down around me as I wrestled Shogaur back to hell.

"Maybe you should call it quits and head home. I'm sure your fellow demons give you the challenge you want."

His smile widened. "They do, you're right, but the feed isn't nearly as satisfying." He closed his eyes and drew in a deep breath through his nose. "So much fear." His eyes opened, and he nailed me with his green-red gaze. "Do you know what the people in this building fear right now, Katerina? They fear you're going to assassinate the one person who tells it like it is. They're afraid if you kill me, they'll have to go back to pretending they're all right with other people gaining power while they get left behind. That they'll get in trouble for what they've done to reset the balance. That they'll never again have the courage to fight for their beliefs. Right now, they're empowered to act for the first time in their pathetic, irrelevant lives. Isn't that wonderful?"

"It's disgusting. They're empowered to act out of fear-induced hatred. Instead of fighting for a cause that might benefit society, they're targeting people who are just trying to live their lives. They see themselves as heroes, and your online babbling is inflating their egos past the point of reason."

"Exactly!" He smiled as though I'd paid him the greatest compliment, and I supposed, in a sick, twisted way, I had. He was doing exactly what his nature demanded and was soaking up every minute of success.

I knew all that, but I didn't know everything.

"Why were you summoned?" I asked.

He tilted his head. "What do you mean?"

"Don't play games with me, Shogaur. The woman who brought you here, she must have had a reason. What was it?"

"Ah, my saviour. My liberator." He shrugged. "I have no idea. One minute I was bored in the sulphuric confines of my prison, and the next I was here, taking in the sights and sounds

I haven't enjoyed in centuries. There was no one to greet me, no one to order me about, just an open circle and free rein in the new world."

"You're saying it's a coincidence our paths crossed?"

"A delicious one, don't you think?" He walked a circle around me. "I would have loved to get my claws in that untested sorcerer, his power untapped and full of potential, but bringing you to me was a gift I never anticipated."

Emrick snarled and stepped out of the doorway, his silver eyes glowing with fury, but Rhys raised his hands and stepped back.

"Don't worry, spirit-herder, I haven't forgotten you. Your bite still stings."

I looked between them. "What the hell are you talking about?"

As far as I knew, he and Emrick had never met. Back then, Emrick had refused to get involved, far more willing to follow Death's rules than he was now.

Shogaur's eyes sparkled. "Did you never tell her? Oh, that's perfect. All these centuries, and she still thinks she's the one who sent me home?"

A shiver ran down my spine, and the chill only spread when Emrick flexed his jaw and said nothing to contradict him.

I told myself it didn't matter. I'd been the one to get Shogaur out of his host and spill his blood. I'd been the one to start the incantation. If Emrick had finished it because I couldn't, that just meant we made a good team, not that I'd failed.

But Emrick couldn't step in this time. Not without sacrificing part of himself. What would happen if Shogaur struck me down and I didn't get a chance to end this? Everything about our plan hinged on every part of it going well. One slip—one misjudged move—and that mob outside the door would be the least of our worries.

My heart raced, my palms grew clammy, and I tuned out the rising voices down the hall. So much rested on me. Rhys's life depended on me. If I played this wrong, Shogaur might kill him just for fun before he played musical host.

The protective talisman was in my other pocket. The second Shogaur relinquished his hold on Rhys, I had to get it around his neck. Which meant I had to be a lot closer than I was right now.

Filled with fear about the million ways the next few seconds might go wrong, I stalked towards Shogaur until we stood toe to toe. I readied myself to catch the stink of decay from Rhys's withering frame, but nothing met my nose except lingering traces of soap. A rock of apprehension formed in the pit of my stomach, but I forced myself to stay focused. "You think you're so fucking clever? You think there aren't a million witches across the world preparing themselves to take you down? Your social media plan might work great to form your defences, but you've also given your enemy a target. How do you plan to stand against them in the failing body of a psychic? I give Rhys a day or two before he can't carry you anymore, and then what? You'll be forced to start over. No more pretty face to flaunt in front of the camera."

He laughed, the sound drenched in smugness. "That's where you're wrong, sorceress. This body still has juice. For one so young, he's strong. Stronger than you realize, I suspect. With time, he might have become someone to be reckoned with. I can wear this skin for years without worry."

The rock dropped from my stomach into my feet.

That wasn't what I wanted to hear.

As my fear grew, Shogaur's smile grew broader. He leaned down to whisper in my ear. "Nice try, sorceress, but you've lost. Again."

I squeezed my eyes shut against the tears threatening to fall. He was right. I had lost.

But that didn't mean Shogaur won.

He told me to tell you not to worry about it, Barrett had said when he'd explained why Rhys had left the ward. *To do whatever you have to do.*

Rhys had Seen this moment. He'd known what had to come next.

My heart nearly broke under the pressure of my acceptance, but I couldn't give myself time to consider it.

Without thinking, without doubting, I threw myself at the end table covered in mail, snatched the letter opener, and drove it into Rhys's stomach.

Only then did I raise my gaze. His eyes widened, fear and rage, anguish and hate fighting for dominance in his expression as both Rhys and Shogaur registered what I'd done.

"I'm so sorry," I whispered.

He slipped off the blade and collapsed to the floor. His back arched as Shogaur struggled to escape before Rhys slipped too far from this world for the demon to claw his way free.

Black smoke drifted out from between Rhys's lips and coalesced into Shogaur's demonic form on the burgundy carpet, his soot-stained boots soaking in Rhys's blood as it pooled beneath him.

I drew the talisman from my pocket and rested it on Rhys's chest. I wouldn't take the chance that Shogaur might try to take him from me while any time remained.

"Fool," the demon hissed. "You're a weak, pitiful child who thinks you can stand against me. Now you'll stand *for* me."

With a cry, he broke into a run, his form fading once more into smoke as he leapt from the carpet. His fingers brushed my mind, and I dropped to my knees with a scream as pain lanced through my skull. The banishing amulet dug into the palm of my hand, but I'd lost control of my muscles. Shogaur swarmed my defences, pressing in on all sides of the barriers around my mind, fingers creeping, clawing, slashing to take them down. It took everything I had to keep him out.

Suddenly, I was back in the year 1209, my flesh burning, muscle and sinew cooking. The pain was just as intense, the stakes just as high. If I didn't find my way past this agony, the entire world would burn.

I forced my eyes open and tried to focus on the room to ground me. Screams spilled from the back of my throat, and blood dripped from my nose. The ugly carpet beneath me was turning from burgundy to crimson between my offering and Rhys's, and still I couldn't find the strength to push Shogaur out.

Which left one more option. Murisa had warned me the amulet might grab the host's soul as well as Shogaur's, but getting rid of him was all that mattered. Once he was in the amulet, the witches could recite the incantation. My soul would go with his to the infernal realms, but the world would be safe.

I squeezed my hand around the amulet and pushed the words to activate it through my clenched teeth.

Emrick dashed into my line of sight. I tried to shout for him to get back to the door, but his gloved hand snatched the talisman off Rhys's chest, and he pressed it against my forehead.

The protective magic doused me in cold water, and I sucked in a breath as my head cleared. Shogaur's grip slipped, and his smoky form drifted out of me, beginning to reform into its physical shape.

I looked up at Emrick to find his silver eyes blazing. He dropped the talisman around my neck, hauled me to my feet, and pushed me into the smoke. I squeezed the amulet in my hand and shoved it into Shogaur's centre before he finished taking shape.

The silver setting warmed in my palm as the spells activated. Shogaur tore at my guard, his whispers and threats filling my ears, blocking out everything else in the room. Despite the protective magic, his energy closed in on me. The light behind my closed eyelids grew dark, then light, then so bright I had to turn my head away, and still those screams continued. Mine? Shogaur's? Rhys's? I couldn't place them, couldn't orient myself outside this galaxy of torture.

The agony turned into a strange, sickening, sucking sensation, followed by a deafening *pop* that rattled inside my skull.

For a moment, everything went black, and when I opened my eyes, I found myself lying on my back in the unfamiliar apartment building.

"Kat?"

Emrick's panicked voice—close to me but not right beside me.

"Here. All right."

It was all I could manage. I rolled onto my side, taking it inch by inch to let my spinning head settle before my stomach revolted. When the room stopped its roller coaster, my gaze fell on the amulet lying on the floor beside me. The red sphere pulsed with a sick glow, and I sensed the darkness emanating from it.

So far, Murisa's spells had worked. Now it remained to be seen if they would be enough to send the demon back to the infernal realms.

I shoved the amulet into my pocket, then let out a breath and rolled onto my hands and knees, groaning as the nausea came over me again. But when I looked up to find Emrick kneeling next to Rhys, his gloved hands applying pressure to the open wound in Rhys's side, all thought of my own discomfort vanished.

I threw myself across the stained carpet. After shouldering Emrick out of the way to stop him from sacrificing more than he had, I pulled the pouch of healing salve Poppy had given me from the satchel draped over my shoulder. I dipped my fingers into the muck, spread it over the wound, and pressed my hands down to stop the blood from spilling out of him. The salve soaked into his skin and vanished.

"Rhys?" I called. "Can you hear me?"

"What's going on?"

"Is he all right?"

"Was he *stabbed*?"

The voices from the doorway made me look over my shoulder at the crowd standing confused in the hallway outside.

Some of them stared at the various weapons in their hands with dazed expressions, and I was glad they'd come to themselves before they'd had a chance to use them.

"Does anyone have a phone?" I asked. "Call an ambulance. Hurry!"

More than one snapped to attention, and I looked back at Rhys. His eyelashes fluttered, and I pressed a kiss to his forehead. "It's all right, Rhys, we're going to patch you up. Your mother will kill me if you die, so don't do that, okay? Hang on."

His lips parted, and a ragged breath passed through them, filling me with an intensity of fear I was sure would have given Shogaur a hard-on, but then a raspy laugh left him. "Wouldn't… want that."

I laughed and bowed my head against his.

He would be all right. He had to be.

His vision had come true, but it didn't have to end the way he thought it would. I would keep my promise, and he would go home.

I wanted to stay with him and make sure he was all right. I wanted to ride in the ambulance and be a familiar face when he woke up. But if we stayed much longer, the police would want to speak with me, and Shogaur was burning a literal hole through the pocket of my ruined sweater.

Although it pained me, I kissed Rhys's forehead with words of encouragement, then left his side and stepped towards

Emrick. Sirens filled the air as the first responders arrived, and I breathed easier knowing in a few minutes, Rhys would be in good care.

Emrick took my hand and led me into the tiny bathroom, away from the prying eyes of the people still gathered in the doorway. I was certain most of them would have seen us and might wonder where we'd gone, but I hoped their confusion over why they were here in the first place would smooth out their memories and take us out of them.

"Are you all right?" Emrick asked, his low voice rumbling through me, setting my limbs trembling.

"No. So let's get this over with so we can put the world to rights, okay?"

He pulled off his gloves and wrapped his arms around me, pressing his lips against the top of my head. I relaxed into his embrace as the temperature in the bathroom dropped, and we stepped through the mists.

40

Katerina

I STOOD ON the edge of the summoning circle in the burned-out warehouse and stared at the amulet. Emrick stood across the circle from me, his hands in his pockets. I couldn't bring myself to look at him. I didn't trust myself not to cry if I glimpsed a hint of sympathy or concern peering back at me. But I was glad he was here.

"Was Shogaur telling the truth?" I asked. "Were you the one who sent him back last time?"

"Does it matter?"

In the grand scheme, it didn't. To me… "Why didn't you tell me?"

All these years, I'd been so proud of myself that I'd stopped the demon before Death had taken me. Emrick had saved me before I died, but he'd also saved the entire world from the fear demon.

How many fragments of his soul had that cost him?

How many had he lost today by dropping that talisman over my head? By helping Rhys?

"I guess I wanted to protect you in that sense as well."

Despite the mixed feelings flowing through me, I smiled. "You never stop watching out for me."

"Never. Even if I don't always go about it the best way."

I shrugged. "I guess there's always more for us immortals to learn."

The explanation helped, but my next actions would help more. I pulled the amulet out of my pocket and tossed it into the centre of the circle, sphere facing up.

As I did, I caught sight of my bloodstained hands and froze.

This wasn't the time to be distracted, but I couldn't help but think of Rhys, wondering if he was already in surgery, if Maera was on her way.

I'd called her as soon as we'd arrived at the warehouse, unwilling to leave her in suspense any longer than necessary. She'd broken down on the phone and started thanking me as she packed her bag. I don't think she'd registered the part about me stabbing him——she was too grateful that his mind was his own again and that he was alive.

Tears pricked my eyes, and I brushed my stained hands on

my leggings as though that would clean them off.

I was just about to begin the ritual when Murisa's phone rang. Cursing the interruption, I grabbed the phone to find Poppy calling me.

"I'm kind of in the middle of something right now," I said.

"We know, we know," Murisa's bubbly voice replied, "but we thought you should know about the summoner. She's blocked herself off. We can't find her anywhere."

I cursed. Abigail was still out there, her second plan thwarted. How long would it be before she came up with a third?

"We're still working on it. We haven't given up." By the steel in her voice, I doubted Murisa understood the concept of giving up.

"Thank you."

I made to end the call, wanting to finish here and sleep for a year when she spoke again. "Can we stay on the line to hear how it plays out? I really want to know how well the amulet works. Pretty please?"

I barely knew the woman, but I didn't have the heart to disappoint her. "Fine, but keep the noise down. I haven't said these words in eight hundred years—it'll take me a minute to remember them."

The last time I'd done this, I'd been on the edge of unconsciousness, caught in the agony of my flesh burning away. This time, the only discomfort was my impatience to be elsewhere. I couldn't help but feel this time was worse.

Closing my eyes, I recalled the banishing spell Emrick had taught me so long ago and let the words roll off my tongue.

On my second time through them, the air began to hum with a low vibration, and the spell grew heavy under the layers of power. Spellcraft wasn't the type of magic I was used to dealing with, and the unfamiliar buzz sat uncomfortably on my lips, but I pushed through and repeated the words a third time.

Shogaur's power resisted me, so much stronger now than it had been so many centuries ago. I pushed more magic into my intention, visualizing the gateway to the infernal realms opening in the middle of the circle and dragging the demon back where he belonged. Shogaur's energy thrashed against mine, and I squeezed my eyes shut tighter.

I hadn't heard Emrick move, but his strong hands rested on my shoulders, bracing me, empowering me to keep going.

I opened my eyes and grounded myself in his presence, in what I was doing, in the satisfaction that this time I'd ended this monster before millions died.

In the centre of the circle, the amulet took on a red glow, as though the sphere were heating up. The glow grew brighter… brighter… until the sphere exploded in a spray of glass.

Shogaur's smoky form spilled across the floor of the circle, and I prepared for him to attack. But before he got close, he hit an invisible wall created by the banishment spell. Slowly, he pieced himself together, his form more hideous and terrifying than I'd ever seen it, with his red eyes flickering with flame, the interior of his mouth charcoal black and oozing with molten rock. Slick, mottled green-brown flesh stretched across his skeleton, rising into a rack of moss-covered antlers. Bugs spilled from his nose to skitter across and out of the circle.

I ignored him, focused only on the spell, refusing to let fear interrupt me. I wasn't about to let him indulge in a last meal at my expense.

The chalk lines on the floor took on the same glow as the amulet, the space between runes folding downwards as though a trap door had formed, and Shogaur dug his dripping talons into the concrete as the pull of hell tugged on his legs.

I met his stare as I finished the ritual, wishing him a fond fuck-you as he fought against it. Try as he might, he was unable to hold himself back from sliding into the pit of fire. A last cry filled the warehouse, rattling in my ears as he disappeared. The doorway snapped shut, the circle settled, and the power of my chant evaporated so quickly I staggered with dizziness.

Emrick's arms slipped around my waist as he pulled me to his chest. His heart beat under my ear, the sound slow and steady until it wasn't. I tilted my head back to look up at him. His pupils were dilated, his breath quick, and my body awoke in response to his closeness. He brushed my hair out of my face, and I closed my eyes at the current of energy that ran under my skin at his touch.

"What's going on over there?" Poppy asked. "We heard a big bang, so I'm guessing the amulet worked? Is he gone? Don't leave us hanging."

"He's gone," Emrick said, looking into my eyes as though he were trying to look into my soul. I couldn't help but feel he'd said it as much to reassure me as to update the witches.

"Yes!" Murisa cried, and I pictured her throwing her hands in the air and doing a happy dance that her spells had worked. Fair. I owed the witch a cheesecake for that little miracle.

"We're not done yet, though," she went on to say, and I sagged against Emrick, immediately reconsidering the cheesecake. He chuckled into my ear and bundled me against him. "I'm guessing you want to make sure he stays gone, right?"

"Ideally," I said.

"Then add this spell to the list. It shouldn't take too much out of you, but it'll prevent him from responding to anyone else's summons. Not forever, but considering your power, the spell should hold at least a millennium."

A thousand years without another Shogaur sighting? I supposed that was worth a few extra minutes of effort.

With no end of reluctance, I pulled myself free of Emrick's grasp and took my place beside the circle. Then, with Poppy and Murisa's help, I crossed a line through this dark day.

Nightmares, rest in hell.

41

Emrick

ICOULD HAVE taken Kat home right away, but I knew she'd want to stay close to the hospital so she could visit Rhys when he woke up. I also knew she needed space to come down after what had happened, to process her guilt over what she'd done and soak in her victory without judgement or witnesses for either.

So as soon as she'd spoken the final words to bind Shogaur to his dark prison, I took her back to her room at Adrian's Toronto house.

The peace and quiet pressed in on us like a pulse—a relief after the noise and magic bouncing around since we'd arrived at the apartment building. Kat closed her eyes and drew in a deep breath… then stepped away from me towards the window.

My arms and heart yearned for her to return, but I remained where I was, giving her whatever time she needed.

"There's going to be a lot of fallout over this," she said without turning around. "The damage done to the shops, the shift against any new age thinking. We know it won't disappear right away."

"You can't fix the whole world. You removed the gas fueling the fires. It won't take long for their drive to fizzle out."

"The feelings will still be there."

I shrugged. "They always have been. Shogaur's influence wouldn't have worked if they didn't exist. You know that."

Before we'd ended the call with the witches, Murisa had assured us Rhys's videos had been removed from every social media site. The witch hunters had gone so far as to scrub Rhys's face from all possible footage, both social and official. None of it would come back to him, and in a few months, no one would remember his fifteen minutes of fame.

Kat rubbed her hands over her arms as though she were fighting off a chill, but still I kept my place. She was spinning, and my closeness would only make her feel claustrophobic.

"You can't beat yourself up over what you did," I said, hoping to interrupt her silent turmoil.

"I stabbed him, Emrick. You can't expect me to forgive myself so quickly."

"You did what you had to do. Rhys knew it. You could have

dealt with Shogaur without making the effort to save him, but you didn't. Yes, you stabbed him—yes, he'll be in pain for a few weeks, but he's alive. His mind is his own again."

We wouldn't know the extent of any lingering mental effects of his possession until we'd spoken with him, but the smile he'd given Kat, the attempt to lighten the mood even as he lay bleeding on the floor, gave me hope he would recover quickly. Kids were resilient.

Kat didn't respond, but the tension in the room seemed to shift, lighten. Her hold on her arms relaxed, and some of the stiffness seeped out of her shoulders. I knew she was far from finished punishing herself, but for the moment, hopefully, I'd helped ease her guilt.

Now that the rush had slowed, I took in the blood all over her sweater, her hands, smeared across her neck. Before she rested, she needed to wash the day off.

"Do you want me to run you a bath?" I asked, and turned to the ensuite with a frown. "This is the house with the jacuzzi tub, right?"

She laughed. "No, that's the Ancaster house."

I shook my head. "I can't keep all his properties straight. What does a man need with so many?"

"He could have collected shoes."

"I guess his loafer might have been a bit cramped for the two of us."

She looked at me over her shoulder with a spirited glint in her eye, and I smiled back at her. I'd missed this. The back and forth without animosity. The natural banter between two people who knew each other inside and out.

My thoughts jerked back to our last visit in this house only a day ago. The step towards reconciliation. The question of whether she would keep walking forward or retreat.

I swallowed around the lump in my throat and shoved my hands in my pockets. Everything that came next had to be up to her. She knew where I stood, what I wanted—how badly I wanted it.

Her expression softened, and she turned to lean back against the wall next to the window. The room stretched between us, an insurmountable gorge, and the silence that a moment ago had been calm now buzzed in my ears. I was aware of my heartbeat upping its tempo in my ribcage, my blood rushing through my veins, every shaking, impatient breath.

Light shone through the window, bathing the floor and the tips of my toes in its softness, but that was the only indication that anything outside this world existed.

"You stepped in," she said. "With the amulet."

"I couldn't stand by and watch him take you." My voice was rough with restrained emotion.

"It could have taken you instead."

I caught her eye and dared to take a step forward. "But it

didn't. Not today."

She nodded slowly and averted her gaze as she took a step of her own. "What do we do when we run out of chances?"

My heart pounded as I closed the distance another step. "Is that really the question, Kat? After what happened in that hotel room, does it really come down to what-ifs about the future?"

There were only three more steps between us, and I longed to cross them, but it was her turn to decide.

She did. A small, hesitant step, but she was a few inches closer than she had been. Close enough that if I held out my arms, I could touch her. I kept my hands in my pockets.

"I've never been great about living in the present, Emrick. You know that."

I found myself unable to take another step. The uncertainty of her wishes was still too great, and that wall held me bound.

"What else do we have but right now?" I asked. "Immortal or not, we're governed by the whims of Death. If we ever deigned to forget it, we've had a stark reminder."

A shudder ran through me, and I glowered at the floor. "When you died in that hotel room, you were more than gone from the world, you were gone from *me*. Our bond was ripped from my chest as though someone had torn out my heart. I searched the afterlife for you, and you weren't there. I nearly fed myself to the void trying to find you."

I closed my eyes as I fought back the torment threatening to take over. After I wrangled my feelings back in place, I raised my head to look at her, and whatever she saw on my face made her suck in a sharp breath.

"I don't care about the future, Kat. I don't care what might happen tomorrow. All I know is that I want to be with you today. And for all the todays we have left. If it means staying hands off when you run into trouble, fine, I'll try—but I won't make any more promises. Not if Death is waiting to pull you in. I won't do that to myself. I *cannot* do that to myself. Not again."

She took the next step. And the next. And then her arms were around me, her fingers buried in my hair, and her lips were on mine. The hair on my arms danced with the electrical current that sparked when our skin made contact.

A moan escaped the back of my throat as I deepened the kiss, desperate for more of her. I snaked one hand around her waist, pinning her against me, and twisted the other into her hair. Giving her flowing locks a gentle tug to tilt her head back, I trailed my lips across her cheek, along her jaw, and burrowed my face in the crook of her neck. Beneath the smell of blood and sweat, hints of aloe and wisteria teased every cell in my body.

She clung to me, her pulse hummingbird-quick, and pressed herself closer, as though she needed to remove every last gap as much as I did.

"During those few minutes, when you were so far gone, I was nothing," I whispered. "Without you, I may as well be nothing. You, Katerina, are my everything. My beautiful Kat. *Mîn êcnes.*" My eternity.

Her hold on me tightened, and I waited for her to speak, to break the final wall between us and put me out of my misery.

But when she remained silent, I accepted that I couldn't wait any longer. I'd allowed her to lead this dance for seventy-five years, but our separation had become a torture I could no longer endure.

I straightened so I could look at her. Tears glistened in her eyes, and a single drop rolled down her cheek. I wiped it away with the pad of my thumb. "Please, Kat. *Mîn hiertan, mîn brêost-loca.*" My heart. My soul. "Please don't send me away."

A whimper escaped her, and any conflicted feeling in her gaze disappeared as she cupped my face in her hands and pulled me down to her lips. I tasted salt and thought at first I'd missed a tear until I realized my cheeks were damp. Without Kat, I'd been broken, but with her kiss, something inside me revived.

"I love you," she murmured against my mouth. "Please don't let me regret this."

Then all thought of words was gone as the heat between us rose into an inferno of need and want. Without breaking our kiss, I guided us backwards to the bathroom. She hit the light switch without looking and kicked the door closed.

I pushed her sweater over her shoulders and flung it to the floor, then teased my fingers under her T-shirt, skating over the skin of her stomach until she gasped and goosebumps spread over her skin.

Her fingers fumbled over the button of my jeans, and her hand slid down my pants with a familiar dexterity that made me groan against her lips as I thrust into her palm. Seventy-five years of waiting, and it was everything I remembered.

I tugged her T-shirt over her head and threw it into the corner as I kissed my way down her neck, her chest. She dropped onto the edge of the tub to turn on the water, and I took advantage of her exposed position to run my tongue over one nipple then the other. She sucked in a breath through her teeth and wrapped her arms around my head to keep me in place.

I chuckled and sucked one nipple between my lips, teasing her as I worked on pushing her pants down.

Steam filled the room and danced around our entwined bodies, clouding the mirror. The heat from the shower only increased what was building between us. After Kat kicked off her pants, she set to work undressing me. My coat and T-shirt wound up on the floor with hers, and she slid my jeans down my legs, trailing her fingernails up my thighs, driving me to the brink of madness. Eventually, I had no choice but to pull her to me and carry her into the shower.

Desire rose with every beat of my heart, but I forced myself to stay on task as we stood under the spray. I washed her hair while she soaped my body, both of us exploring, savouring, relishing the familiar as though it were new.

We worked together to scrub the day off us both until the water ran cold and all trace of Shogaur's contamination had disappeared down the drain.

As Kat turned off the shower, I leaned out of the tub to grab a towel, then patted her dry, gentle with my touch, kissing every bare inch of skin within reach.

When I finished, I wrapped the towel around her back and used it to pull her against me. Our naked bodies pressed together, my arousal angled against her stomach, her fingers digging into my shoulders.

"Don't tease," she said.

I bent my head to kiss her, ravenous for another taste. She'd filled my senses until I drowned in her, and I never wanted to come up for air.

"Never," I said, my voice rougher now. "I'm yours, my sorceress. Whatever you need."

"Take me to bed."

I was in no place to make her beg. I swept her into my arms and carried her into the bedroom, stripping away the towel before laying her down on the comforter. Her hands were tight around my neck as I settled myself between her legs. I braced my weight on my forearm and used my free hand to brush her damp hair out of her face before I trailed my fingers down her body in gentle strokes and swirls. I focused my touch on the dragon tattooed on her right thigh, the symbol of Palonia, a symbol of everything this woman had come from.

She arched against me and shifted her hips to position me where she needed me.

Her blue eyes, so dark they threatened to pull me into their current, shone with a vulnerability that nearly shattered me.

"Tell me we'll figure this out," she whispered.

I dipped my head to catch her lips. "Of course we will. It's you and me, Kate. It's always been you and me."

She dug her nails into my shoulder and kissed me back harder, as starved as I was, as eager to seal our bodies together and keep the rest of the world out. The scent of her, the feel of her, everything about her overwhelmed me, and when I finally entered her with a roll of my hips, it was like coming home after nearly a century adrift.

42

Katerina

THE NEXT FEW days were a blur of lovemaking and sleep, and I didn't know which restored me most. Reconnecting with Emrick felt like putting my lost pieces back together, and although part of me feared what might happen in the future, Emrick was right. If Death took me tomorrow, my only regret would be wasting time not being with the man I loved.

The whispered words and the exploration of our bodies transported me back to our earliest days… though with more comfortable bedding and the joys of indoor plumbing.

Between the ebbs and flows of pleasure, we caught up with the others. Adrian and Barrett had opted to remain on the island with Gavin. The mob had snapped out of their overriding fear as soon as I'd banished Shogaur, but Adrian wanted to be sure there were no rationally-decided follow-up attempts now that the dam had burst.

Poppy and Murisa returned to Toronto—Poppy to figure out what to do with her business, Murisa to return to her studies. Though I suspected said studies would take a back seat to getting to know a certain necromancer. And figuring out how to keep said necromancer's undead cat in stasis. There was still no sign of Abigail, but none of us let our guard down.

On the third day, I received a call from Maera.

"Rhys is awake," she said. "He wants to see you."

She'd texted me almost every hour since arriving at the hospital, so I knew the surgery had gone well and Rhys was stable and recovering, but that didn't make me any less excited to hear he'd opened his eyes.

I left the warmth and comfort of my bed and rushed to get dressed, pulling on a pair of black leggings and a dark blue sweater, leaving my gloves in their wooden case next to the bed. For a precious change, I wasn't heading into a fight.

Emrick swept me into his arms with a kiss and brought me to the hospital, but he remained in the afterlife, letting me go in alone. My knees trembled at the thought of facing the young man I'd stabbed, and I had to summon my courage before knocking and stepping into the private room.

I was braced for accusations and anger from both patient and parent, but the first thing Maera did when she saw me was throw her arms around my neck. "Thank you. Rhys told me what he had to do to get that thing out of him, and I'm so glad you were there to help him."

I glared at Rhys over his mother's shoulder, and he offered a wan smile in return. He was such a liar.

I smiled and squeezed Maera back. "Next time, I promise to help before any stabbing is necessary." She pulled back abruptly, and I held up my hands. "Not that there'll be a next time. No more possessions. That was a one and done deal. We have the talismans now to hold off that threat at least."

"I very much hope that's true." She looked back at Rhys, and her green eyes crinkled with worry. "But that doesn't mean our problems are over."

My heart did a double beat, and the prickle of apprehension squeezed my lungs. "Here I thought you asked me to come because you missed my pretty face."

"I did," Rhys rasped, and he patted the bed beside him.

I looked at Maera and sat down, navigating around the various tubes sticking out of Rhys's arms. My poor boy. Up close, he looked rough. His hair was a shock of red against his pale-as-milk skin. Dark circles ringed his eyes, which lacked their usual emerald sparkle. When he shifted on the bed to make room for me, his body tensed and a groan of discomfort slipped out of him. I rested my hand over his where it lay on the blanket.

"How are you feeling?"

"Better than when I first woke up, but whatever pain is there, I'm enjoying it."

I raised an eyebrow. "Oh?"

He shrugged, then winced. "Physical pain is nothing once you realize how much worse it is not to be able to feel it."

I curled my fingers around his and held tightly. "I'm sorry, Rhys. I'm so sorry any of this happened." I didn't want to say too much, not knowing what he'd told his mother. Once he was out of hospital, he and I would sit down and have a good long chat about what he'd Seen before he'd run out of the house.

"My fault. Being cocky. I can't believe I started a video channel. I can never show my face online again."

He grimaced, then coughed, and Maera handed him a glass of water as she sat on his other side.

"The police have already been here asking questions," she said as she helped him drink. "Their working theory is one of the so-called witches tracked him down and tried to murder him."

"How ironic if it were true," I said, doing my best to smile through the guilt. "Are they going after you for the videos?"

Rhys shook his head. "The demon was clever. Never gave orders. Ideas, fears, never specifics. Responsibility is on the people who acted. They did strongly suggest I talk to a thera-pist."

"Actually not a horrible idea, though tricky given the whole demonic possession element." I patted Rhys's hand and forced myself to calm down. Shogaur was gone, trapped in hell, and we were here. "Have the doctors said when you can go home?" He and Maera exchanged a look, and I frowned. "What?"

"A few more days, probably," Maera said. She fluffed Rhys's pillows and helped him get comfortable. "They're impressed by his rate of healing. Shocked, even. We didn't mention Poppy's emergency salve."

Probably for the best.

"Okay, three days isn't bad at all. So what's wrong?"

Rhys sighed, and with the exhale, he deflated, his energy seeping out of him. "I don't think we should go back to the island, Kat. Not yet."

"What do you mean?"

Maera settled in the chair beside the bed. "Rhys had another vision."

"While I was in surgery," he said, wrinkling his nose. "It pulled me awake when the doc was cutting into my guts."

Nausea bubbled inside me, and I held his hand tighter. What could I say to that? To wake up from anaesthesia to find someone wrist-deep in your innards when your brain has just tormented you with a vision? How was this boy still sane? How much more could he handle?

"I'm fine." A hint of his familiar smile glinted in his eyes. "The nurses' reactions when I woke up made the shock worth it, and I was too out of it to feel anything." His smile faded. "Unfortunately, that means I'm missing a lot of details."

"That doesn't matter, Rhys. Whatever you remember—"

"No, it does matter." His lips curled, the pulse in his neck quickened, and he tightened his grip on me. "You're under attack."

I stiffened. "How?"

He released me to tear his fingers through his hair, and Maera rested a reassuring hand on his back. She opened her mouth as though to speak for him, but Rhys cut in first. "I Saw lightning. Great purple bolts that filled the sky over the house. You screaming. Crying. A house burning." He opened his eyes to lock gazes with me. "I Saw pain and suffering, and it's all focused around you. Everything we've seen lately—none of it compares to what's coming. And there was something else, but it's just out of reach. A sense of… finality. Like when it's over, however it ends, that will be The End."

I swallowed around my dry tongue.

Purple lightning like the spell circle in the hotel that had stopped my heart?

Had Rhys Seen my death?

I forced a smile as I rubbed his leg through the blanket. "Thanks to you, we have forewarning. Our secret weapon." I stood up and kissed his forehead. "Get some sleep now, both of you. You're right that you should stay off the island. I'll make sure the Toronto house is supplied with your things, and you can stay here."

"You're not staying with us?" Maera asked.

"If the end is coming for me, it's coming no matter where I am. At least if I'm away from you, you'll be safe."

I squeezed Maera's shoulder, reassuring her as she had Rhys. Then I walked out of the room, my feet leaden, my insides quaking.

When I stepped outside, Emrick was waiting for me, and I stepped into his arms without a thought.

"Is everything okay?" he asked, wrapping himself around me, his words laced with concern. "Is Rhys all right?"

"He'll be fine. He's a tough kid." I breathed Emrick in and considered telling him about the vision. But what was the point? Whatever was coming would come. Whatever end Rhys had foretold would happen. Why make Emrick worry about something we couldn't change? I leaned back and looked into his moonlight eyes filled with so much love and desire, and I immediately knew how I wanted to spend my remaining time. "Take me home?"

He bent his head to kiss me, and a moment later, we were back in bed, ready to pick up where we'd left off. I lost myself in every kiss, every touch, every climax, not sure which one would be my last.

Thank You for Reading

Thank you so much for taking a chance on an independent author. We're living in a wonderful age where it's easy to upload a book to the internet, but that doesn't reflect the blood, sweat, and tears that go into making a book the best version it can be. It takes time, patience, perseverance, and to have the final result end up in a new reader's hands is the best reward. You are the reason we keep writing, so thank you.

If you enjoyed the read, please help support the author by leaving a review at the retailer where you purchased the book. Reviews make a world of difference for an author, helping us reach new audiences and bringing more people into the worlds you've spent time in.

For exclusive character content, announcements, promotions, and special offers, sign up for Krista's mailing list at https://www.kristawalshauthor.com/pages/about-the-author

Acknowledgements

So many people deserve a tip of the hat for making this book (this series, my career, my sanity) possible.

Kate Sparkes, who always gets first mention because of how much she puts up with from first draft to final. You are my star!

The FAKAs for all of your support, advice, cheerleading, guidance, laughs, rages—everything on a daily.

Christopher Barnes for cleaning up the prose and making the words sparkle.

My ARC readers and Street Team—you've given me heart and strengthened my belief that this series deserves to be read.

My Patrons, you are my bedrock. Thank you for showing up every month and giving me the shove I need to keep going.

Traci, Mardie, Becca, Jillian—your commentary during your beta reads made me laugh, cry, and be filled with warm fuzzies. Thank you!

Chris Reddie, thank you for being your supportive, wonderful, creative, wild self and for helping me raise our supportive, wonderful, creative, wild daughter.

And my readers. That you're here is a constant source of gratitude for me. When I took my first steps into publishing, I never imagined I would get the emails and notes and interaction from so many wonderful people. Every day you make dreams come true for me.

I'll see you at the next book!

About the Author

Known for witty, vivid characters, Krista Walsh never has more fun than getting them into trouble and taking her time getting them out.

When not writing, she can be found reading, gaming, or watching a film – anything to get lost in a good story.

She currently lives in Ottawa, Ontario with her husband, toddler, and epileptic blue heeler.

You can find her at www.kristawalshauthor.com or at the local Second Cup coffee shop... but only if you come bearing a Vanilla Bean Latte, half-sweet.

Other Works by Krista Walsh

Epic Fantasy

The Meratis Trilogy
The Cadis Trilogy
The Nayis Trilogy

Urban Fantasy

The Dark Descendants
The Ghostmaker Trilogy
The Immortal Sorceress Series